LIGHT BETWEEN TWO DARK PLACES

LIGHT BETWEEN TWO DARK PLACES

When Souls Collide
book two

by

GINNA MORAN

For Eric, the one who loves even my darkest sides.

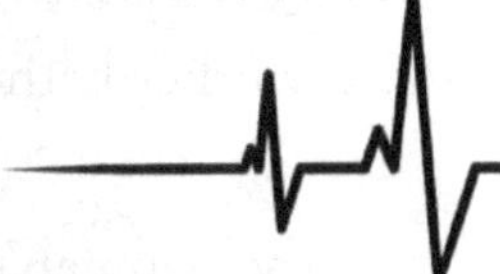

PROLOGUE

LIFE BEFORE

"COME OFF ALREADY," I say, pressing the button for the soap dispenser again.

Blood stains the sink water pink as it swirls down the drain. No matter how hard I scrub my hands, I can't get the blood off completely. Lines of it stick under my too long nails, giving me a gross manicure. The stained sleeves of my jacket don't help much either, dripping the now thawing blood down the tops of my hands the longer I stand and stare at my reflection in the gas station bathroom's mirror.

A knock on the door startles me, nearly sending my soul from my skin. Closing my eyes, I listen with my mind. *"God, I really have to go. Maybe I should use the men's room."*

"Occupied," I call, pushing the annoying thought from my head. "I don't think anyone will care if you use the other bathroom. It's late."

A voice grumbles through the door, but the woman's thoughts turn away from me to the condition of the men's bathroom. She'd be glad she used it if she saw the mess I've made. Blood coats both knobs and the metal faucet of the sink, as well as the roll of paper towels just left sitting on top of the toilet. If it wasn't for my black jacket, people could see Luka's blood covering me, from my hands and sleeves to my shirt and jeans, now damp from this freezing winter night.

"Luka," I whisper to my reflection in the mirror. *"Luka, please. Please don't leave me."* I send the silent thought into the universe, wishing with everything inside me that he'll respond, that he'll tell me he's okay. But he can't. Not now. Because I blocked him from entering my mind. If I even open up a crack for him, it'll give others the chance to try to sneak their way into my head. I've grown careless, always keeping the telepathic channel to Luka open. I never got the chance to train him enough, to block his mind completely. I let my love get in the way. And because of that, he's lost to me. For how long? Could be forever.

Tears blur my eyes, dripping to my cheek. Reaching up, I smear them away and leave a streak of blood under my eye. My stomach heaves, my insides wishing they could escape. I wish I could escape me. Escape this moment. This dark spot in time. Because none of this was supposed to happen. I should've had another day at least.

But I was too confident.

Too naïve.

Of course Nikolai Knezha would track us down the second I blocked off his telepathic channel. It just got too hard keeping it open without slipping up. And I did mess up. Big time. He discovered what I was planning. He knew I decided to forge my own path in life away from him and the Knezha Family. He knew I was having doubts. The only thing protecting me now is that his beliefs in what the reasons for my doubts were are wrong. That's where he underestimates me. He blames Luka. He blames the boy whose soul collided with mine. But he has no idea.

I'll die a thousand deaths, give up a thousand last breaths, and take on the pain over and over again before I ever let him pull the truth from me. Luka isn't the only one counting on me, and I can't fail the others—my real family.

My cell phone rings, cutting over my heaving breath, forcing me to turn away from my horrifying expression. I flick water off my hands, pulling a few seat covers from the dispenser, since the bloody paper towels are now of no use to me, and dry my hands.

My fingers lock around my phone, brushing against the cool metal of my pocket knife, the only weapon I have left. I swallow, sucking in a shuddering breath through my nose.

"Luka's dead," I say into the receiver without a greeting. "I had to leave his body. You need to get out of there. Tonight. Now. You have ten minutes."

"Where are you?" Avery asks.

Her question sets me off, and I groan into the phone, staring at my face in the mirror—the blood smeared on my cheek, my red-rimmed eyes, my snow dampened hair. I look like the murderer I've become, the one Nikolai turned me into. If only it were his blood on my hands tonight.

"Skye? You there? Where are you?" Avery huffs into the phone.

"Just get out, okay? I'll find you."

"And Luka?"

"I don't know. Nik will—" I snap my mouth shut. I can't even think about all the possible things Nikolai could do to Luka to break him, to guarantee that I can't have him unless I return to the false prophet's side. "He's strong. He'll hang on until I can figure things out."

Except I have no idea what to do. As much as I love Luka, how much it kills me that I've failed him, I can't drop everything to save him. Not in the condition I'm in. I have too many people to protect. Too many people Nikolai would love to break and mold to join the Knezha Family. I am the bridge from the acquired—I mean, awakened—ones to the Knezha Family, and I need to burn it down. I can't risk him getting into my mind. I have too much to lose even if all feels lost without Luka.

I clear my throat. "I just need you to get out of there. Leave everything behind, even your phone. You can't look like you've left because I need you to go back. Meet up with Gemma. I'll arrange a pickup," I say, pressing the phone to my ear to silence the pounding in my head. "Don't worry about where. Like I said, I'll find you."

"Skye," Avery says. "Don't do anything crazy, okay? Remember, this isn't the end."

I nod at myself, even though she can't see me. "No promises."

"Skye..."

"Just get out."

Without waiting for her to respond, I end the call and toss my cell phone in the trash can. I can't risk carrying it anymore. I can't risk Nikolai finding me again until I'm ready for him. Because he won't stop trying. He'll tear the whole universe down with everyone in it to get to me, to gain access to the knowledge I keep locked away from him and his precious Knezha Family.

But I won't go down without a fight.

Nikolai can't control the world.

He can't control me.

Not in this life or the next.

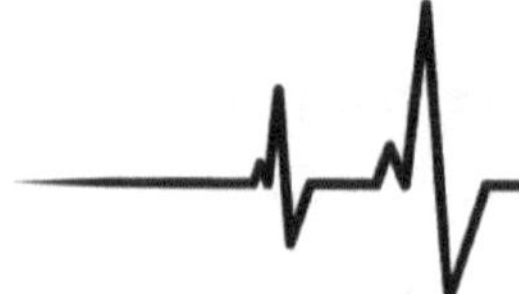

Chapter 1

CAN'T BREAK THE BROKEN

"**M**Y NAME IS Skye Stone. I'm seventeen years old and from Los Angeles, California. I have blond hair and gray eyes. My birthday is January first, and I'm an orphan." Licking my lips, I stare at my reflection in my vanity mirror. "Nikolai Knezha is the leader of the Knezha Family, and I'm a prisoner in his household. I'm not part of Nikolai's family. This is not my family."

I straighten my shoulders, repeating the words over and over again in my head. I'm afraid I'll forget them if I don't, and I can't afford that. If I do, I'll lose myself all over again. Lose the person I'm okay living in. The person who knows what's real and what isn't. This life, living as a girl with something to fear, cowering within the walls of a mansion, is nothing but an illusion hiding the secrets of a man who has broken many to serve a purpose he created for this life.

And the rules are simple: Always protect our family. Always put others before myself. Always be the perfect girl and do as Nikolai says. But I have my own set of rules to live by. One, don't draw attention. Two, never let them in. Three, don't lose the part of me I just got back.

Because that's what Nikolai wants.

Every little memory that shifts back into place is another memory for Nikolai to take and mold into something he can use against me. And he will try everything in his power to finally gain control over my mind, stealing my freewill, turning me into the perfect adopted daughter who obeys all the rules—who guarantees others follow as well.

As much as I want to give in and give up, something holds me back. A nagging feeling deep in my soul pinches my essence every time I think about how easy it would be to fall into place because Nikolai already got to Luka. Controlling my soul mate controls me. Because I'll never leave without him, and right now, Luka won't leave Nikolai. He doesn't remember the real life we had in the outside world or everything we lost to the Knezha Family.

I blink the tears from my eyes, continuing to stare at my reflection. It's strange to peer at myself after forgetting what I had looked like. The flecks of blue in my gray eyes. The splattering of freckles across my nose. The line constantly puckering between my brows every time I'm alone because faking a smile every time I leave my room annoys me when all I want to do is pout.

"My name is Skye Stone. I'm seventeen. I've died too many times to count. I'm missing memories of my life. Sometimes, I don't know what's real. But I know Nikolai Knezha tries to get into my head. He tries to pretend he didn't lock me in a basement to break into my mind through death. But I remember. I know. Even if no one else does. Even if they tell me otherwise. Nikolai's a master at mind games. This is a game."

It's also my life.

A knock sounds on my door, drawing my attention from my reflection. Luka cracks it open without waiting for me to respond. Closing the door behind him, he leans his back on it, smiling in my direction, though I don't turn to look at him. He flicks the lock, and our eyes meet in the mirror.

The way he looks at me, a grin lighting his face, stirs memories of the boy I remember before the basement through my mind. I love and hate him like this. It kills and revives me over and over again, my heart racing and stopping, yearning to let him in. I never thought it'd be possible to miss the brooding boy, who wore a scowl on his face nearly all the time. The boy I know in this version of myself. I've already created new memories of Luka separate from the girl I was before I died in the forest and ended up back in Nikolai's hands.

It feels like Luka and I will never be on the same page, aligned together as we should be ever again. We're two different people, broken and molded back together enough to be familiar but different enough to notice.

Luka's too lost to see it, but he can feel it. He can feel that only parts of our souls connect and pieces are missing, scattered about through the universe. If only he were strong enough to remember. To fight the sharp anchors Nikolai put on his mind all because I let him get to Luka.

"Hey," Luka says, his voice smooth yet weighted with the same mischievousness in his eyes.

I don't get up or say anything. I can't help it. I can only smile at him in the mirror because facing him doesn't get any easier. Resisting him is the hardest thing I can remember experiencing just short of losing him completely.

Crossing the room, Luka comes up and stands behind me, sliding his arms around my shoulders. He brushes his lips along my jawline, waiting for me to give in to his affection. And I want to. I want to so badly because it hurts me that I don't. My soul craves to feel him, to explore every inch of him, to compare him to the boy from my memories.

But Luka isn't the boy I know he should be. He looks like Luka, sounds like him, feels like him, but a piece of him I need most is gone. Nikolai stole it and left him with a gaping hole that he doesn't even notice. But I can't tell him. I can't tell anyone. The only way I'm going to survive this with my mind unbroken is if I pretend the hole isn't there. Pretend that I don't remember any differently. Fitting in is the key. Obeying the rules will keep Nikolai from attempting to manipulate my head again. He almost won. I can't risk it. Not again. Not if I ever want to leave and take Luka with me.

If only I wasn't alone. Me against the entire Knezha Family won't end well, especially because I'm here on the compound, being watched every second. Even Luka watches me.

"You okay?" Luka whispers, spinning me in my chair to face him.

The moment our eyes meet, I feel a piece of my soul crack, and the crack turns into a fissure. I let Luka in for a second, let him fill me up. Then I close him off, building a fortress around my mind.

It doesn't stop me from kissing him, though.

Tugging him down, I scoot my chair closer, resting my knees on his stomach to keep a little space between us. I brush my lips against his in a sweet kiss, light enough to make me crave more but also stop me from sinking into him.

He pulls away, tucking my blond hair behind my ear. "You didn't answer my question."

I take a deep breath and groan. "I'm fine."

"I know when you're lying."

"You should also know better than to call me out." I close the space between us, hooking my arms around his neck to rest my cheek on his shoulder. My knees rest against his sides instead of his stomach, and he pulls me closer, so I'm wrapped around him completely.

"And you should know better than to brush me off and try to distract me with—"

I kiss him.

He laughs against my mouth. "Damn, but I do love those distractions."

It's my turn to laugh.

"How much?"

Before I can kiss him again, he brings his hand to his mouth, blocking me. "Nu-uh. Not working."

I kiss the back of his hand. "You sure?"

He chuckles, dropping his hand. "What were we talking about?"

My smile falters at his joke. The blip of happiness washing through me drains away. "I miss this," I say, flicking my gaze toward the sunlight shimmering behind my sheer curtains.

The sparkle in his eyes dims with my admission. "What do you mean?"

Rolling back, I shift sideways, blocking the imaginary blade Luka thrusts at me to cut me open to get me to spill my heart out to him.

"It's nothing—just—" I sigh. "I'm getting restless. Nik's become overbearing since the accident." An accident that never happened. Keeping my thoughts straight, my memories straight, takes nearly all my energy. I have to remind myself I didn't fall and hit my head trying to bring a new person into the Knezha Family. It took me sitting in front of Nikolai, staring into his eyes, to realize he would do anything to see to it that I return here. So, I go along with his fake memories of my head trauma, instead of letting him in on the secret I carry. That after forgetting everything I've ever known, I wouldn't lose any more of myself. Not to Nikolai. Not to anyone.

"Can you blame him? You suffered head trauma and hallucinated about being imprisoned in a basement by Sienna," Luka says, drawing me back to the present, though I find myself getting lost in my memories more often than not.

He gives me a once over, nearly breaking through the fortress protecting my mind. If I invite him in, he could discover the truth. But, if I allow him in, others can follow.

I stiffen, pushing the memories of fighting for my sanity away and how Nikolai used the people I know to break into my mind long enough to drag me back here. Luka broke through first, and he tried his best to undo the damage caused to me, but Nikolai was faster. He was trying to rebuild after the damage. Gemma and Avery warned me he'd break me. Luka warned me. But I didn't know the extent of the damage at the time. I still don't. Because Gemma's still missing. Nikolai tried to make me believe she ran away, but I know the truth. No one talks about Avery, but I know she's dead. And Luka? Luka's here. Now I have to pretend all is well. Pretend to have some memories that never existed.

"But I know it wasn't real. I know I was hallucinating."

"And things will return to normal once Nikolai is certain you're okay."

"I *am* okay," I snap.

I hate how he treats me like I'm the one in need of looking out for. I had really thought I was going crazy. My memories sound crazy. Because who can believe that I was imprisoned in a basement and killed over and over again by a murderous psycho who deemed herself my caretaker—the same person who now lives in the wing on the other side of the Knezha Estate like she was destined to be here. Or that Luka was in a cage next to me, and how he helped bring back the memories I had lost and helped me rediscover I can manipulate death, beat it even, by accessing a door that leads to a spiritual world that allows souls to collide and come together as one. A family. But a family I want nothing to do with.

Getting to my feet, I stroll away from Luka and to the window overlooking the sprawling grounds of the Knezha Estate. From this spot, I can't see the compound walls imprisoning me and can almost imagine that if I kept walking toward the eucalyptus trees in the distance, I'd be free.

"Then why do you always look at me like I've done something wrong? Why have you missed so many morning vows lately? The newcomers barely even see you."

I wring my hands together in front of me. "You're reading too much into things."

"What else am I supposed to do? Something about the accident changed you. You're keeping me out."

I swivel to face him. "I keep everyone out."

"Not me."

Fear trickles into my heart, and I can't help wondering if I'm losing Nikolai's game without even realizing it.

"Luka, I—" I send the thought to him. *"I'm worried you're distracting me."*

The words stab me, cutting around my heart to slice it free from my chest. Luka stiffens next to me, his concern shifting to something darker. He glares at the window instead of me, and I know he probably feels like the imaginary knife cutting my own heart out is double bladed, cutting his out all the same.

"Distracting you?" he thinks back.

I close my mind off. "I'm sorry. I didn't mean it as a bad thing. I just—I need a clear head right now. I'm afraid I'll mess up again. What if Nikolai..." I don't finish my words.

"That monster can't touch us." Luka's voice comes from in front of me instead of next to me, a memory of us together breaking free from my mind. It's been weeks since I've had a memory of Luka that wasn't messed with.

Without him having to say his name, I know Luka in the memory is talking about Nikolai.

"But he'll try. I don't want to test him. Not now," I say, running my hand over Luka's shoulder. Wearing jeans and a T-shirt, he appears like the boy from my memories before the basement. His worn tennis shoes kick the toes of my boots like he can't stand the space I keep between us.

"Then when?" he asks.

"I'll tell you soon, I promise. This is bigger than us, okay?"

He nods without questioning me, though I wish he did. The memory does nothing but leave me with more questions. What's bigger than us? Why won't I tell him now?

"I just need a few more days alone with you. We can't leave until I put the block in place," I say.

The block? The conversation stirs something within me, reminding me of Gemma and Avery. Back in the basement, when I was forced to fight to the death against them, I remember them mentioning a block. How Nikolai broke in. It prevented them from remembering me until Nikolai broke their minds. But Luka? He knew me.

I wonder if I...

"You said he couldn't get to me," Luka says.

His dark eyes hold me in their intensity, and I wish I could lose myself in this memory forever, lose myself to a spot in time where all wasn't lost. I wish I could change the outcome. But it's just a memory. I can't change anything. All I can do is relive it like I'm watching things through my eyes without any control.

"He can't, but you're not the only one I worry about," I say.

"Skye, stop worrying about Nikolai," Luka thinks to me, pulling me from my thoughts.

I blink the memory from my mind, a tiny burst of fear erupting in my heart. Subconsciously, the memory let my guard down and let Luka into my mind. I should've never let him in a minute ago. Now, I'm afraid I can't stop.

I shrug my shoulders. "I worry he'll do something to me if I..."

"He would never."

The problem with his words? Nikolai already has. He's trying to fill in my lost memories to suit his needs, taking advantage of my amnesia. I'm missing a year of memories—almost all from the days after I shot Luka in the forest to waking up in the basement as subject four. But no matter how hard I try, I just can't unlock them. It's like they're not there anymore. I think Nikolai is the reason I can't. We're the same in a way, both people who gained special abilities through dying and coming back to life—the acquired—as I know us as, but Nikolai is different. He's powerful. Manipulative. He's using me like he always has.

"You're right," I say. If I let this conversation continue anymore, it'll head in a direction I can't face. Luka might be worse than Nikolai in a way, because I want him in my mind. I want to ignite our connection, to feel him as my soul mate and not like he could possibly be my enemy. "I'm letting the pressure get to me. Being in Nikolai's shadow is hard."

Luka pulls me into his arms, hugging me. "Don't think about it like that. You're not in his shadow. No shadow could touch you through all that beautiful light you carry."

I squeeze him tighter so he can't see my frown. He sounds like one of the Knezha Family pamphlets the newcomers are given—the Knezha Family summed up in a few paragraphs to lure outsiders to our door. To convince them to stay. To steal away everything they are and turn them into just another star shining over the journey to everlasting life as a family Nikolai promotes.

If only everyone knew the cost. Knew what it meant to be a Knezha.

Clearing my throat, I pull away from Luka. "Think Nik will let me out for a bit? I'm going crazy staying in here."

A smile crosses Luka's face. "You sure you want to leave? Nik went into town, which means..."

I lightly slap his shoulder. "And I thought you snuck into my room to just hang—"

He cuts off my words with a kiss, linking our fingers together and pulling me away from the window. Luka moans against my lips. His hands release mine, sliding around my waist to tug me closer to him.

I kiss him deeper, moving my hands to his chest to feel the thrum of his heartbeat against my fingers. My whole body tingles with a dozen memories from different points in time of him touching my skin, kissing my neck, hooking his fingers to my hips. All the memories flash in a loop before fading to this single moment, leaving me wanting to drown in our history, the same history that threatens to ruin me.

Luka's breath shudders into my neck. He stops a second before my soul and heart get pulled apart by my desire for him and my need to protect myself from who Nikolai turned him into. If I could glimpse the boy from my true memories of him for a second, it would help ease the conflicting emotions rampaging within me.

"If you're sure you want to leave, we gotta move now," Luka says, his voice low, breathless.

I nod, resisting closing the space between us for another kiss. "You can sneak into my room anytime, you know."

He chuckles. "But sneaking you out..."

"You're going to sneak me out?" I ask. "What a rule breaker."

"For you, anything," he says with a smile. "Plus, I've been promoted to guardian, which makes things easier."

I frown. "Guardian?"

He nods. "You'd know if you had shown up to morning vows."

I blink, trying to suppress the deep-seated need to knock

Luka out to drag him away from here. If he's been promoted to guardian, I'm one step closer to losing him completely. Becoming a guardian means our connection will no longer matter. The Knezha Family will come first. Nikolai will come first.

Luka grimaces, his brows lowering on his head.

I remember to smile because being promoted to a guardian is a big deal. It's something to celebrate and not cry over. Reaching up, I touch his cheeks. "Oh, Luka, congratulations."

"You're sad," he says, calling me out.

A tear splashes my cheek. "No—I just. I missed your ceremony. Nik didn't even tell me. I always thought—"

He releases a deep breath, his eyebrows shooting up on his forehead. His fingers touch my face, brushing away the tear. "Everything's good, Skye. Don't cry. Nikolai pushed the ceremony to give you some time. He wants to make sure you're well enough to help perform it."

I compose myself, a million thoughts rushing through my mind, though I keep them sealed off from Luka. If there wasn't a ceremony, I might still have time.

Beaming a smile, I blink away the remaining tears from my eyes. "Thank the stars. Now we definitely have to get out of here and celebrate."

He kisses me softly. "I'm the luckiest guy in the universe, you know. Promoted to guardian of you."

"Me?"

"We *are* soul mates."

Linking my fingers through his, I stroll toward the door, so he can't see the shift in my emotions. I can't risk Nikolai breaking Luka even more. If he breaks Luka, he'll surely break me. I wish I could break...

I know what I have to do.

Because Nikolai can't break what's already broken.

If only it didn't jeopardize everything.

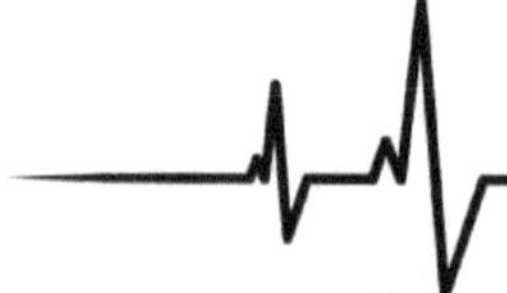

Chapter 2

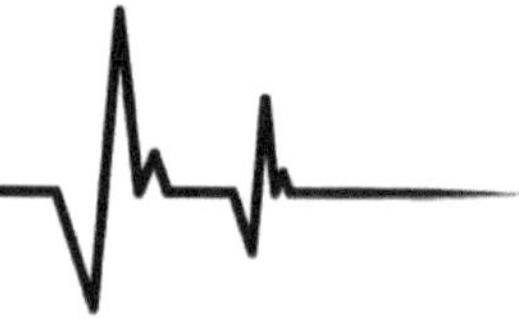

REMEMBER

"WE SHOULD CLIMB the wall," I say, strolling hand-in-hand with Luka as he leads us to the guard house two miles down a paved road away from the main estate. "If we get there, and they deny me a day pass, I'll kick your ass."

Luka laughs, shaking his head back and forth.

Cool winter air drifts around us, sneaking in through my fleece-lined coat, which does nothing to warm my legs under my long skirt. I knew I should've worn the tights, but I hate them just as much as the heels that sit in neat rows in my enormous wardrobe. And unfortunately, I'm wearing a pair. I wanted to wear my tennis shoes and athletic pants, but appearances are everything to Nikolai. Unless I'm lounging in my room or working out, I must wear my dress clothes.

"Deal," Luka says, draping his arm over my shoulders. "I'll even carry you back."

I bump him with my hip. "I'll kick your ass if you even try."

Laughing, he hugs me close to him, sliding his hand from my shoulder to my waist. Up ahead, the guardhouse comes into view. We're so close to freedom that excitement sends my heart racing. I haven't been into the real world since—I don't even know—before the basement, maybe. I'm not even sure what it's like. The few memories I cling onto only show the cabin in the mountains, a park near a beach by Luka's old house, a diner, and the Knezha Estate. Beyond those things, I have no idea what to expect from the outside world. Nikolai says it's of no concern to me.

A woman in her late forties, with copper hair twisted neatly in a braid, waves at us from the window of the guardhouse. I rack my brain for her name, thinking of all sixty-three family members within the estate, not counting those who live else-where, where Nikolai sends them.

"Good afternoon, Jillian," Luka says, reminding me of her name. "I hope your morning has been pleasant so far."

Jillian nods, her mouth cracking into a gigantic smile that takes up the whole bottom half of her face. "Afternoon, you two. Skye, it's lovely to see you out and about. The stars look like they've been treating you well."

"Thank you. They've blessed me so, especially giving me such a guardian to watch over me," I say, eyeing Luka in my peripheral vision. Hatred sneaks through me. I can't stand the sweet sound of my voice, how I have to remain on guard and remember to be someone I'm not. Skye Knezha would tell the world about Luka's promotion. She'd thank the universe for Nikolai deciding to give Luka such a position. But Skye Stone? I want to puke a little. "I just wish I had been well enough to hear the announcement myself."

Jillian tilts her head slightly, pouting her bottom lip, genuinely sympathetic to the fake sadness lining my words.

"And that's why we're going to celebrate with a walk on the beach," Luka says, hugging me close.

Jillian raises an eyebrow, tightening her lips. "Nikolai didn't mention—"

Luka rests his hand on the partition separating us from Jillian. "It's kind of spur of the moment, but he wouldn't mind. You can call him if you want."

I knew this wouldn't work. I knew she'd question Luka, and we'd have walked all this way for nothing. Now, I'm going to have to walk back barefoot because these damn heels already kill my feet, and there's no way I'm getting carried around, no matter how much Luka likes annoying me in a sappy way.

"Please, let us out. Please, let us out," I think silently, shifting on my feet.

Jillian darts her eyes from Luka to me and then bobs her head. "You're right. Nikolai would be fine with letting you two stroll the beach. Just be back before dinner, okay?" She bends down, reaching under the counter. "And take these, will you?"

I hold my face expressionless even though I want nothing more than to burn the stack of pamphlets to ash with my eyes.

Before I can attempt such a gesture, Luka scoops them up and tucks them into the deep pocket of his trench coat. It's taken getting used to seeing him all dressed up, because he's always in jeans and a T-shirt or a hospital gown in my memories, that his clothing alone reminds me of who Nikolai turned him into.

"See you at dinner, Jillian," Luka says, linking his fingers through mine to pull me away.

"Protect Skye with your life, Luka," Jillian says. "May the stars bless the rest of your day."

"And yours also," Luka and I say in unison.

I cringe at how automatic the response came like I've said the words a million times before. They've been ingrained in me from my life before, even without the memories, my tongue knows. Like breathing, like swallowing, my heart beating. Muscle memory. But my soul isn't into it. The words have no meaning and are as empty as the morning vows—the Knezha Family promises.

The scent of the sea wafts through the air. I can't see the ocean yet, but I know it resides nearby. This whole town practically belongs to the Knezha Family, including the long stretch of beach walking distance away. It's information I know, but I can't remember the feeling of the sand, how blue or green the water is—anything. I don't think I made a habit to go to the beach, not with the indoor pool. Not with everything I needed within the Knezha Estate walls.

But what I do remember is that Luka loves the beach. He grew up in a small house near the ocean. Going to the cabin in the mountains, seeing the first snowfall—I can envision his face. How he tilted his head toward the sky, letting the tiny flurries melt on his cheeks. I remember shivering and him pulling me into his arms...

Luka squeezes my hand. *"Skye?"*

The sound of Luka's voice in my head draws my attention from my memory. Looking up, I meet his gaze, bright sunshine lighting his face, illuminating the gold dust in his eyes. "Hmm?" I ask. "Sorry, I was just thinking."

"About?"

"You, of course."

"Like how you might actually give me the chance to keep you safe? You heard Jillian, right?" he asks, chuckling.

I roll my eyes. "And who would you have to keep me safe from? You know I can throw a better punch than you."

He laughs again. "Ouch. Being your guardian's gonna be hell on my ego, huh?"

"You should be used to it."

His nose crinkles. "And you should get used to me protecting you."

"Never. It's me who keeps you safe." As the words come from my mouth, doubt snakes through my chest, tightening around my heart. I blink, trying to summon some sort of confidence in my voice. "Got it?"

Since the moment I had met Luka in the galaxy world where our souls collided, I've wanted nothing more than to keep him safe, keep him away from Nikolai and the Knezha Family. But I failed him. I failed us. Because it has been weeks since returning to the confines of the Knezha Estate, and we're locked away from the world, despite now stepping from the premises. Instead of stuck within chain-link barriers like the basement, we're trapped in a world of luxury, like royalty imprisoned in a fortress for safekeeping, only brought out under guard. The outside world is supposed to be the dangerous place according to Nikolai. I'm supposed to feel safe by Luka's side and under Nikolai's guidance, with the entire Knezha Family. But I don't feel safe at all. It feels like at any second, my world will come crashing down around me, and I'm too weak to fight back.

If only I knew what I was doing. I might not like remembering the old me, the version of myself tailored by Nikolai, but she had a plan. I bet she'd have already burned the whole Knezha Estate down and threw Nikolai to the stars.

"Got it." Luka smiles, though something dark suddenly lines his eyes. He knows me better, even without knowing this version of myself, to know that something's wrong. It doesn't help that my acting sucks. He can see through me. But what am I supposed to say? He's not the boy from the basement or the boy from the cabin. He's not Luka Landon. He's Luka Knezha. Nikolai is in his head. Telling Luka what's going on here, asking him to help, would risk him telling Nikolai. For now, I have to play along until the right moment.

"Good, glad we could clear that up," I say.

He chuckles.

"Guardian or not, I'm not going to let you turn into my babysitter every time we go out."

His dark eyes soften. "Now that's the Skye I know."

With a brilliant smile, one almost shining with the light of the galaxy world I miss as much as the version of Luka from the basement, he brings my hand to his lips to kiss. We stop right in the middle of the sidewalk, a few cars passing us by, and face each other. His lips meet mine. With our hands still twined together, he pulls me closer to him.

If I close my eyes and just listen to our breathing, I can almost pretend we're not here, that we're alone in the world even though I'm sure someone watches us even now. Sinking against him, I concentrate on his hands on my hips. His fingers travel up my jacket, brushing the skin between my blouse and skirt. Tingles blossom in the spots his gentle graze touches, and it takes everything in me not to lose myself and let him into my mind, where I can feel him prodding, trying to glimpse what's going on in my head in this second.

He nips my bottom lip, releasing a warm breath with a hint of a moan. Pulling back, he captures me in his gaze, a look of desire squinting his eyes. "You sure you want to go to the beach?"

I giggle against his lips, the sound more breathless than anything. I don't even know what I truly want anymore. Shouldn't I just be happy to be alive, away from the basement, and with my soul mate? While the blips of memories of Nikolai frighten me still, so many more make it easy to forgive him. He hasn't proven himself a horrible man at all over the last few weeks. It's what makes me wait things out. Play along.

But the basement.

Avery and Gemma.

I can't pretend that never happened.

"You do make it hard to decide," I say, smiling at Luka.

He kisses me again, trailing his hands lower, past the small of my back. "Here, let me persuade you."

"Luka," I whisper. I can't help it. Blush heats my neck as I pull away. Luka might be my soul mate, but I'm still figuring things out. Figuring me out. He still feels so new to me despite the memories I have of us together from our past. He obviously has some, too. I just wish I didn't feel like my whole being was at war.

Luka makes a great distraction, but he is also a reminder. Reliving memories isn't the same as being in the exact moment. And I need time, a sign, something that tells me it'll be okay. That opening up to Luka in such an intimate way wouldn't leave me vulnerable. Right now, it very well might. I can't stop the worry constantly clutching my chest, knowing that Nikolai is using Luka to get to me, to break me. Nikolai might be tolerable now, but things change. People do. It's the only constant in the universe.

"You know what? We should go to the snow instead. I miss the mountains," I think to Luka, pushing my thoughts into his head. The only reason I'm communicating telepathically is to hopefully remind him of the pieces of our lives now shifted and unable to be pieced together. Maybe he'll feel the need to truly escape deep in my soul that he won't be able to ignore it or re-

sist me.

He tilts his head to the side. *"We have to be back by sunset."*

I pout. *"So."*

"How about the beach today and the mountains tomorrow? I'll be able to arrange transport for you then."

Transport. Like I'm some sort of possession. I try not to let the words get to me. I should be used to them by now. Luka's the perfect Knezha Family member, promoted to my guardian. And this is why I need to remind him. Break through the false memories created for him by Nikolai. The mountains, the cabin would be an ideal place. Like how Luka pulls my missing memories from me, maybe the cabin can shift his, override what Nikolai has done.

"It'd be safer. You know the dangers of leaving the area without a plan. People don't understand us. They don't understand our journey."

Hearing Luka's thoughts in my mind about the outside world, about the people who would stand against the Knezha Family, forces me to raise my shield up, blocking him out. I grimace. "I can handle myself, you know. And protect you."

His eyes shift behind me, looking down the sidewalk. Someone honks their horn, startling me, but a familiar man—a guardian, patrolling the streets around the compound—waves.

I cringe inwardly, feeling Luka's gaze on me. He saw me jump.

"I know," he says with a lightness in his voice, teasing almost. "And you can prove it on the rest of the way to the beach."

Stupid car and guardian. Now I doubt my own words.

I sigh, letting him drag me toward the walking path leading between two apartment buildings owned by the Knezha Family.

I kick off my shoes when the cement turns into soft sand, too awkward to walk on in heels. The private beach stretches out before us, the grainy sand turning powdery the closer we stroll toward the greenish-blue waves cascading in frothy curls toward the sand.

A young couple snaps pictures of the water from a giant beach blanket. The locals use the beach even though they shouldn't. Nikolai would never send visitors away from our compound or outside properties unless they posed a threat to our existence. He encourages people if anything, embracing anyone with even a small sliver of interest.

The couple peers in our direction, neither of them smiling when I offer a small wave. The girl, who looks to be around my age with her chin-length brown hair clipped from her face, shifts on the blanket, blatantly staring at me. I realize her gaze locks onto the platinum brooch with the letters K and F encrusted with diamonds pinned over my heart on my jacket.

Luka wears a much smaller KF crest on his collar. I wish I had something so small to declare who I am, but every crest I have is a glaring beacon for the world to identify. It highlights my rank in the Knezha Family as well.

I fiddle with the brooch, wishing I didn't have to wear it. I wonder if Luka would say anything if I took it off. He probably would. Turning my gaze away from the girl, I glance at the ocean. I hadn't realized until this second how people from the outside really treat us. I'm sure it's out of curiosity, but it doesn't make it any less uncomfortable.

Brushing my blond hair onto my shoulder, I cover up the brooch. I know it's not the first time people gawked at me for my relationship with the Knezha Family, but it is since I returned. People whisper that Nikolai is a cult leader. I could never forget the man who tried to stop my induction to the Knezha Family for that very reason. And they might all be right. But it doesn't change anything. I'm still Skye Stone, seventeen, from Los Angeles, California pretending to be a Knezha. I'm still me even if I'm slowly figuring out who exactly that is.

"If you use our beach you should at least say hello and not look at us like we're freaks," Luka says, confronting the couple.

I cringe, wishing he wouldn't.

"Not freaks, just freaky." The girl's thoughts drift to me, and I turn my gaze to hers.

"You're damn right about that."

The guy doesn't look at me but at the side of the girl's face. I stiffen, blinking my eyes, trying to determine if he heard her thoughts and was responding or if I missed something he thought to himself.

"You knew not to expect anything less from Knezha," the girl thinks, the corner of her lips pulling up to the side like she's daring me to say something out loud.

I don't get the chance, and I'm not even sure I'd take it if I did. Luka reaches into his pocket and pulls out one of the pamphlets Jillian gave to us to pass out. "Why don't you stop by our estate for dinner on Friday night and see things for yourself?

Nikolai would love to meet you."

"Oh, I bet he would," the guy thinks, now peering at me as well, his green eyes sparkling. Neither of them even gives Luka a second glance.

"Yeah, no thanks," the girl says, staring at the pamphlet instead of taking it from Luka's outstretched hand. "We've made plans."

"And your plan sucks." The voice sounds like the girl, but it doesn't come from her. It comes from behind me.

A memory breaks free in my mind and pulls my attention away from Luka and the couple. Spinning around, I meet the gaze of the girl, now standing a few feet away from me down the beach, her hands on her hips. Her dark eyes, nearly black, flick from the ocean to the path leading back to the street behind her.

"Well, do you have a better idea? I can't leave them," I say.

"So you're leaving me?" she asks.

My gaze shifts to the cloudy sky above. "I'd do the same for you."

"I'd never want you to, Skye."

"Well, that's too damn bad."

She groans. "I'm not helping you, you know."

"Whatever."

Luka's fingers tighten around mine, yanking me right from a weird memory about the girl who still half smiles and half glares at me from the beach blanket.

"If you change your mind, I'm sure you know where to find the place. Tell them Skye and Luka Knezha invited you."

"Ugh, I can't deal," the girl thinks. Without responding to Luka, she gets to her feet and stomps away from us without another word, leaving her boyfriend now glaring at me in the sand.

Leaning forward, he snatches the pamphlet from Luka, flicking his gaze over it. His long hair spills over his shoulders and hangs over his cheeks. *"Damn signs. Damn universe."* The guy glares at me once more and turns back to the ocean and rests back on his elbows. "See you around," he says out loud, tipping his head back to look at me.

"We hope so," Luka says.

"May the blessed stars light your journey." The words automatically come from my mouth.

"Let them do something," he responds.

Tugging me away, Luka drags me down the beach. I crane my neck to glance behind me at the couple and catch sight of them arguing, the girl pointing her finger at the guy's chest. She draws her attention to me like she knows I'm watching her, causing me to jerk back to the beach in front of us.

I shake the eerie sensation crawling over my skin, pushing away how strange their thoughts were coming into my mind, especially because I'm pretty sure I was closing myself off from the world. But maybe not. Luka's presence unintentionally messes with my head—the memory I had of the girl, too. Yet why didn't she confront me? Who was she?

Clearing my throat, I say, "I think I knew them."

Luka glances at me in his peripheral vision. "Yeah, they're locals."

"You sure?"

"Definitely. I could tell we're not the first Knezhas to have ever approached them."

"About that—"

He chuckles. "You're mad I tried to recruit them."

"You really do know me, don't you?" A smile plays on my lips. I can't help it. It's like Luka's read my mind without even having access to it in this moment. He just knows. And knowing me, probably better than I know myself, elicits the warm, loving emotions I crave. The ones where Luka and I feel like it's us against the world—against the universe.

Reaching out, he brushes his fingers to my cheek, making me look at him. "Just a bit." He grins. "Sorry I couldn't keep my mouth shut. I know this was supposed to be about you and me. It's just—I hate when people stare at us like that."

"That's why I didn't want you to try," I say, which is technically true. But I'd hate it if he did it regardless. "Wasted time and energy."

"Maybe not. He took the brochure. I think you charmed him," he says, grinning at me.

I roll my eyes. "You mean scared them."

"Don't doubt yourself. You have this unforgettable presence. People love you."

I shift my head, hiding my smile, hating that a laugh is trying to sneak out of me. "Me?"

Smirking, he wraps his arms around me and lifts me off my feet. "I can't get enough of you."

"Is that so?" I ask, leaning forward to kiss him.

"Let me prove it."

I groan, pushing from him, making him set me back on the sand. The salty sea breeze plays with strands of my hair, blowing it out of my face. Luka shifts to stand in front of me, blocking my view of the sun hanging over the water. Without even having to say anything, I can tell he feels the same awkwardness I've suddenly created. It's hard hiding anything from him.

He puffs a breath, sending a small stream of fog into the air. "Skye, what's wrong? I thought getting you out of your room would help, but I can tell something still bothers you. Have I done something? You can talk to me about anything, you know."

"I'm fine," I say, cutting him off. Because he's wrong. I can't.

"Skye."

I close my eyes. "What? Are we really doing this?"

Anger sweeps across his face. "Yeah, we are. You're so damn stubborn sometimes, but I'm tired of acting like everything is okay. You pull me to you and then push me away. You've been blocking me for weeks. I just—what can I do? You're my soul mate, but it feels like you're trying to rip away, like you wish you weren't."

I swallow the knot in my throat, trying to stop me from spilling my heart out across the beach. "I—I'm sorry. I don't mean to, but—" It takes everything in me to spit the words out. I was planning this moment. I wanted to try something to get to Luka, but fear grips my throat, strangling my words before I can put them into the universe.

"Skye, you can trust me. I'm trying to be here for you. Please, let me," he says, pleading with his dark eyes. "I don't like feeling like you're forcing things."

My bottom lip quivers. I guess I'm worse at acting than I thought. Who knew a single gesture could set him off like this? I didn't think he noticed the hesitation all that much. But obviously he has. "It's hard because I don't know if I see the point in it. Everything's so messed up. Haven't you ever felt that something might not be right?"

His brows furrow. "Between us? I don't understand. What's this about?"

I shrug. "It's about everything. About Nik."

"Nik? This isn't about us?"

"It's what he's doing to us. You don't feel it?"

He shakes his head, his eyes widening, turning wild. Something strange crosses his face, and I don't recognize him. "No, I don't. What exactly do you feel?"

I tense. I don't think the questions come from Luka. This is something Nikolai would want to know. I shouldn't have let my guard down with Luka. Now things might be worse off. If Nikolai knows I'm pretending, I'm screwed.

"Nothing. Never mind."

"You know he's given us a place to live. A family. He made me your guardian. If—"

"Stop!" I squeeze my eyes shut, spinning away from him. Anger floods my being, hearing him defend the man who tries to break my world apart to put it back together the way he wants it to be.

The memories of being locked away in a basement flood through my mind. Fear sends a shiver down my spine, remembering the pitch blackness of the dark freezer, how much the poison Caretaker Sienna used burned when she sprayed it in my face, how empty everyone's eyes looked after they died. But that's not all I remember. I remember Luka's broad back through the thin cotton of his hospital gown. How he would always meet me in the galaxy world because he was afraid I'd give up. I remember the door that took me from him but also reunited me with him in a moment where nothing made sense. It still doesn't.

Warm hands touch my face, and I force my eyes to open. Luka stands in front of me again, cupping my cheeks between the palms of his hands. His dark eyes bore into mine, trapping me in their intensity. I can't stop my gaze from trailing to his thin lips pressed together in a frown. Even now, staring at me like my very essence pains him, I want to kiss him and forget everything all over again. Things were simple without a past. Now, I'm not so sure I'll even have a future because of it.

"I think you should talk to Nik, Skye. You're scaring me."

I ignore his remark, because the second I shift my gaze from his, I see it. A red door. Waves crash around it as it stands in the surf. I've only seen it once since leaving the basement, and I only got close enough to glimpse the galaxy world. It confirmed I wasn't losing my mind, that everything I had been through was utterly and tragically real.

Without thinking, I push Luka back as hard as I can. I don't care if I have to drag him by the hair. There's no way I'm leaving him behind on this beach when I can get us through the door. This was exactly what I needed. Fate. A little push from the stars. Because I know if I can get him through the door, I can fix things. I can fix him. Us. We can escape.

We fall into the waves, me on top of him, and his eyes widen upon seeing the door.

"Skye!" he yells, his voice ripping through the air. "Sto—" Sea water crashes over us and cuts off his words.

I scramble to my feet, dragging him by the collar of his shirt through the surf. I'm far too afraid to tell him what's going on because he's too connected to Nikolai. He could accidentally reveal what I'm doing through his thoughts. Nikolai's never far away. He might already be nearby if he knew we left the estate.

"Close off your mind," I think to Luka. *"Do it now. Don't let anyone in."*

"Skye, tell me what you're doing," he thinks back to me.

"You trust me, right?" I ask.

He turns his head and spits the saltwater from his mouth. "I trust you."

"Release your breath and follow me."

Another wave collides into us, and I cling onto Luka as the foamy ocean drags us out to sea and straight toward the door. Through my blurry vision, I watch it swing open, the splatter of glittering stars shining brightly through it despite the haze of the sun from above.

Five.

My head spins as I lose myself in the rough current.

Four.

My lungs burn to breathe.

Three.

Luka thinks my name.

Two.

I hug him tighter.

One.

We enter the stars.

Floating on my back, I stare at the galaxy world around us, letting peace wash over me. Here, I feel safe. Here, I feel alive and free from everything. I flip around, turning to face Luka. He floats next to me, his arms dangling at his sides, wisps of blond hair hanging on his forehead. His dark eyes stare above us, shifting back and forth as something crosses his mind.

"Luka?" I ask. "Can you hear me?"

He gasps, sucking in a deep, unnecessary breath. "Help me." The low tone of his voice buries in my soul, sending panic racing through me. "Stop. You can't do this to her."

It takes me a second to realize he's not talking to me. A memory. He's lost in a memory. I'd recognize what he's experiencing anywhere. Whatever happened to us allows our minds to recreate specific moments in time, forcing us to live out the memory again but trapped like a viewer without control. Because the past can't be changed no matter what Nikolai thinks. He's behind this. I know it.

I reach out and grab his hand, lacing our fingers together. "Luka, it's okay. It's not real. Come back to me."

Blinking his eyes, he shifts his gaze from nothing to me. A tear slides down his temple and disappears into his hair. I pull him closer and brush my lips against the glittering trail. I'm almost afraid of what he remembers. What if it's something bad? Something about me, and he can no longer forgive me like he used to. What if it changes everything between us? My eyes water, and it's Luka's turn to wipe away unwanted tears.

"I remember," he whispers. "God, Skye. He's in my head. I wasn't strong enough. I couldn't help you fast enough, and now Nik's—"

"But how did you even end up with Nikolai? I left you dead in the basement," I say. "I locked everyone out until Sienna pushed me through a door."

"No, Skye. You didn't. I remember. You opened your mind. That door you saw wasn't real. It wasn't our door. And Gemma and Avery, they're—"

Panic snuffs out all the good feelings swirling through my soul. "What? I don't understand. Avery's dead. And Gemma, she's—" I snap my mouth closed. I don't know where she is.

Reaching out, he grabs my hand and pulls me to him. "She's still in the basement, Skye. Nikolai broke into her head, but you did something to her, and it messed up what Nikolai was trying to do. She's a fighter. He can't risk you two together."

"So, we can find her?"

"Yeah, I'll show you. I remember where he was keeping us now."

Relief rushes over me, and I press into him, nearly turning our souls into one entity. "He's a dead man, Luka. I'm going to murder him for doing this to us. I'm just so relieved I could get through to you. I'm so relieved I'm not going crazy."

"You're definitely not crazy. He broke into your head, Skye, forcing his way in. He tried bringing back only the part of you he created and didn't expect that Skye Knezha was the smallest facet of who you were."

"No, he didn't break into my mind. I let him in," I say, knowing it's the truth. He got to me through violence and my love until I gave in, but it worked to my benefit. It saved me. "I think it's how I managed to hold onto some memories. He was going to break me, but I opened up. And my memories...they're still returning."

"More of me?"

I nod. "Are you doing it?"

"I—I'm not sure. You lock me out."

"I'm sorry for that."

"You do what you have to."

"I remember others as well. The girl on the beach..." I let my voice trail off. Something stops me from saying any more—dread, fear—something deep within me doesn't want Luka to know. Why? I'm not sure. "It keeps Nikolai out of my head. He can't manipulate memories he doesn't know about."

"You're right. I think that's why you remember. I can do the same. I won't let him get to me again."

Hope blooms through me, lighting my skin like the stars seeped into my soul to warm me from the inside out. "I won't let him, either. We're going to run. Be smarter, more prepared this time."

Luka scowls. "But we can't just let him get away with this.

He stole my memories. *Your* memories. You were a shell of a person when you showed up at the mercy of Monster Sienna. Because of him. I'm willing to risk staying and fighting."

"You want to fight?"

He nods. "I want to destroy him."

"If that's what you want—or we can stay here and never return. Never worry again."

He frowns. "We made a promise."

I smile, hearing the familiarity of his words, knowing for sure Luka's the same boy from the basement. "That's all that I needed to hear."

Peering past Luka, I look for the darkest part of the galaxy in search of the door back to the living. I grip Luka's hand, our souls mingling together. He feels like my heart and soul—my everything—living outside of my body in this world, and by taking care of him, I can take care of myself.

I push the panic of returning to a world that feels out of my control to the back of my mind.

Five.

My lungs burn.

Four.

Ice slides over my skin.

Three.

Light shines in front of my eyelids.

Two.

My heart beats.

One.

I spit out water, gasping. Wet sand clings to every inch of

me, and I pull myself from the ocean and back onto the beach. Luka lies face down, his wet hair slicked against his head. I roll him over and use the tide to rinse off his face.

I cup his cheeks. "Luka! Luka, wake up."

He groans before snapping his eyes open. "Skye? What the hell? Did you try to drown me?"

My chest clenches, but it doesn't stop me from getting to my feet. How am I supposed to respond to his accusation? I didn't try to drown him. I did drown him. It was the only way to fully enter the galaxy world. "Luka..."

"Come on, Skye. We have to go. You can tell me what happened on the way back. I don't want to miss curfew."

"Miss curfew? That shouldn't matter. We still need to make a plan."

"A plan to what?"

"I—" Oh, no. No. Please. "Luka, what do you remember?"

His brows pucker together, confirming he doesn't remember anything. Not his promise to fight or his promise to take me to the basement. Nothing. His eyes no longer hold the same brooding stare as the boy I spent days with, shivering and cold, scared and confused—the boy who told me nothing but still managed to make me remember that he was my soul mate. The boy who knows every version of me.

I heave a breath. "I don't think we should go back. I want you to come with me, okay?" If I have to open another door and drag him back in to get him to remember, I will. Because right now, my heart shatters, shooting agony through me. I can't stand the thought of returning to the Knezha Estate with him like this. If he's not my Luka, I don't want to go back at all.

When I reach for Luka's hand, he shifts so I can't grab him, sending a storm of grief and fear, of pure devastation through my soul.

He pushes to his feet. "What are you saying? We have to go back, Skye. It's almost sunset."

I blink the oncoming tears from my eyes. "Luka," I whisper. "Please, you have to remember."

"I think you should see Nik. You're acting really strange."

I shake my head, the hope I siphoned from the galaxy world now drifting out to sea. I search for the red door, but it's no longer there. Once again, I'm trapped. I don't want to stay. But I can't leave. I want to fight. But I can't without Luka. I won't stand against him. And Nikolai would make me. "No, I'm fine. I'm sorry. I just—I hate curfew. I want to stay out all night with you."

He stares me down, his intense eyes trying to see past the armor I've built around myself. Whatever moment we had in the galaxy world is now lost. Luka doesn't remember anymore. We're not fighting together. I don't even know if we'll ever be truly together. Not like before.

I wish I could force him to leave with me, but I don't have the energy to face that battle yet. Even if I did win, I might make things worse. I couldn't survive him hating me for ripping him away from the Knezha Family. Because right now, as he stares down at me, assessing what's going on in my head, I know he would. Nikolai's hold is far too strong. There's no breaking it. Not tonight. But I won't stop trying.

"We don't have to stay out all night to be together," he says, closing the distance. Bending down, he grabs my hands and helps me to my feet. I comply, defeat turning my movements automatic. He touches the torn fabric of my jacket, the diamond-encrusted brooch now lost to the ocean.

"Fine, yeah. You're right." Turning my gaze away from him, I search the empty beach. The couple from earlier is long gone. "Let's just go home, okay?"

"You know I'm trying to help you, right? You say some things you don't mean because you've been through a lot."

Yet, I know there's more to come.

I hope I'm strong enough.

I hope I can keep Nikolai locked out of my head.

"You can."

I push the foreign voice from my mind, resisting the urge to look around. *"Who are you?"*

"Remember."

"Skye?" Luka asks, drawing my attention away from the feminine voice sneaking into my mind. The voice of the girl from my memory—the same girl who was on the beach. "Yeah, I know," I say. "I've been through a lot." I'll repeat whatever anyone tells me, even him. I'll be the doll in Nikolai's dangerous game.

"So stop keeping me out. Let me help you. It's all I want."

I frown. No one can help me.

I don't even think I can help myself.

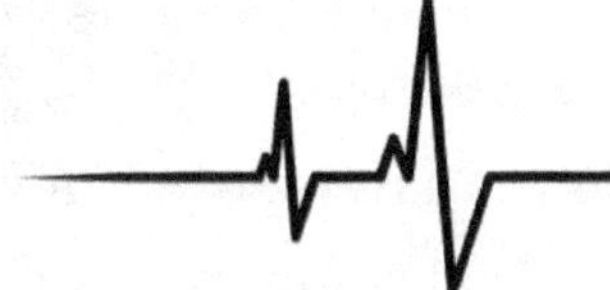

Chapter 3

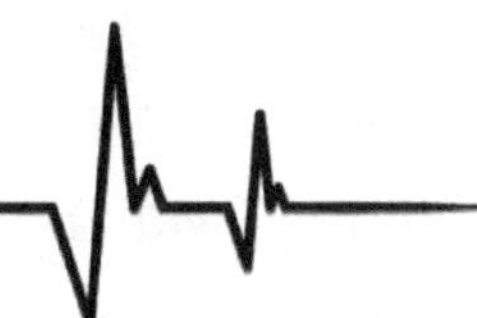

DEAD GIRL

TWO DOZEN PEOPLE stand in a circle in the middle of the lush lawn off to the side of the rose garden. Luka steps back to allow me into their formation where Nikolai stands in the dead center. The circle of people closes, locking me in with linked hands, and I force myself to greet each person by touching my hand to their hearts.

"Skye, what a pleasant surprise. Blessed the stars to have you join us for morning vows," Nikolai says, motioning me forward.

A few newcomers, who haven't been initiated into the Knezha Family yet, wear nametags. I want nothing more than to tell them to run away as fast as they can before Nikolai gets to them, but I don't think they'd listen even if I tried.

Nikolai holds open his arms to me and kisses each of my cheeks. His ice-blue eyes sparkle in the winter sun overhead, and pressure erupts in my skull. I know he's trying to break through the wall I built to protect myself from him.

He lifts an eyebrow in response and leans forward to whisper in my ear. "You know this is an open circle. How are we to connect if you've closed yourself off?"

Instead of snapping at him and telling him I didn't plan on connecting with anyone, especially him, I crack my guard enough to keep a line of telepathic communication open. *My apologies, Nik. I've been practicing my isolation techniques with the newcomers. You know if I don't practice I get sloppy. And after..."* I let my thought trail off while giving him a believable enough excuse that ties to the false creation of my head trauma memory.

Nodding once, he shifts back and turns toward the group. "How about you lead the morning vows, my girl? Everyone's missed you so."

I fake a smile. "Of course."

Nikolai touches his hand to my heart, where my KF brooch is obviously missing and doesn't go unnoticed before he moves to join the others in formation. Taking the hands of two newcomers, who stare at him with such adoration it makes me sick to my stomach, Nikolai offers me a small nod.

"Good morning, my family," I say, spinning slowly to greet everyone once more with just a smile.

"Good morning, Skye," they all respond in unison but not in a brainwashed, zombie way. Their words fill me up with a sudden wave of love only felt when spending time with the people you care about—with family.

"They are not your family," I think to myself. *"You are a prisoner here. This isn't the life you want to lead. Just keep remembering that."* But I'm afraid I'll forget. My actions and thoughts, especially around the others, come naturally. Automatic.

I straighten my shoulders, composing myself. "Seeing all of you here, feeling the love you share with me, makes me eternally grateful to be standing by your sides as part of your family. As you know, Nik welcomed me into the Knezha Family when no one else wanted me. I was trying to survive on my journey alone. He showed me it didn't have to be that way, because each of our journeys is connected, and we're supposed to travel our paths to eternity together, protecting and guiding each other as the stars intended." My mouth spits out the words before my brain even has time to catch up. I can hear hundreds of memories of myself saying the same thing, repeating the same story I always share with newcomers, though it's not true. I've tailored it for Nikolai. It was Angelica, the woman who brought me off the streets and introduced me to the Knezha Family, who ingrained the idea of an eternal family in my mind. Nikolai took over after her death.

In this moment, it doesn't feel like the universe blessed her with a new journey apart from this life as Nikolai would say. The universe robbed her.

"Blessed the stars for shining on our Skye," Nikolai says.

Everyone repeats after him.

"And blessed the stars for shining on my family," I say. "I vow to always protect you on our journey in this life."

"I vow to protect you on our journey in this life," the others say.

I close my eyes. "I vow to teach you and learn from you."

"I vow to teach you and learn from you."

"You promise it'll work?" The familiar thought drifts into my mind, yanking my attention away from the others.

"I promise," I say, my voice sounding through the small room. My breath catches as the memory unfolds in front of me. I have no choice but to lose myself in it.

Gemma and Avery sit on a black leather sectional, both facing me. Sitting cross-legged on the floor beside me is the girl from the beach. Something familiar in her black eyes tugs at my subconscious, but pain pinches the backs of my eyes the more I try to pull the information free.

"It's the only way to protect you," the girl says from next to me.

"You won't even know. I'll set the block trigger on command," I say.

"Maybe we shouldn't go back," Avery says. "I'm scared."

"Please, Avery. Nikolai took Luka. I need to know where, and I can't risk going myself. He thinks I'm acting out of stubbornness, and I have to keep it that way. He can't know about the others. I need him to keep waiting for me until I'm ready." The sudden realization about this moment taking place after I shot Luka, basically handing him to Nikolai, weighs heavy on me.

I'm not the only reason why Luka ended up in the basement, but I'm also the reason for Avery being there as well. She returned to the Knezha Estate for me, and Nikolai got to her, too. She was subject two after all. Luka has said she crashed into a lake with her boyfriend, and he didn't make it, though I know it wasn't her first death or the one that led her to the Knezha Family. The car crash did lead her back into Nikolai's clutches. I know that. I feel it deep in my bones. I also know I must be responsible for Gemma, too.

"Damn it, Luka," I think to myself, pulling away from the memory. I wish he'd remember so he could show me the basement.

"What's wrong, Skye?" Luka asks, sending his thought to me through the tiny crack I've allowed in my head for telepathic communication in the vow circle.

Dread seeps through me. Luka wasn't supposed to hear that thought. If he heard it, I'm afraid Nikolai has as well.

Opening my eyes to see the two of them and everyone around me for myself, I startle at the sight of a familiar girl with wild dark curls styled in two buns on her head like ears. She stands near the tree line, leaning on a tall eucalyptus trunk. Icy realization drips from the top of my head and down my face, surely taking the flush from my cheeks with it.

"Skye, my girl, are you okay?" Nikolai asks.

The vows I was automatically saying without thinking about them stopped coming from my mouth, and now silence hangs heavy over me, weighted by everyone's eyes on me.

"I—" I can't remember what I'm supposed to say next. My train of thought vanishes as I stare at the girl—at Avery—who died by my hands in the basement because Nikolai made Caretaker Sienna push me into it in an attempt to break into my locked memories.

"I vow to always stay on the path the universe laid in front of me," Nikolai says, picking up where I left off. "Because that path, my family, it leads to our magnificent eternity. We will be rewarded immensely. I have seen it. I've touched the stars. What you give you regain a million times more."

"Blessed the stars," one of the newcomers says. "I vow to never stray from my journey with my family. I want to see the stars."

"And you will," Nikolai says. "You just have to open up your mind. Let our family in."

"I'm ready," the man says. *"Come on, Joe. Show him how much you want this."*

In the side of my vision, I watch Nikolai move from his spot to touch the man's chest. "You must want it enough."

"Oh, I do. Blessed the stars, I do."

"Skye," Nikolai says. "Will you do the honors?"

I don't respond. I can't drag my attention away from Avery, who still hovers among the eucalyptus trees, watching us. I need to turn away from her. I need to concentrate. Our morning vows are fundamental for newcomers at the Knezha Estate. This moment cements most of their faiths in the Knezha Family because Nikolai doesn't ask them to follow us blindly. He shows them what's possible. He gives them just a taste to get

them to crave for more. To want to give everything they have—
material items, body, mind, and soul.

I blink my eyes, praying Avery disappears. Because I'd
manage if I'm hallucinating a person from my past, seeing a
fracture in my mind Nikolai tried to adjust. I could get through
it. Ghosts don't scare me. Ghosts are easy to separate from
what's real and what's not.

But Avery doesn't disappear, and now I'm questioning my
reality once more.

"*Focus, Skye,*" Nikolai thinks, speaking up in my mind.

Pressure erupts in my head, shadowing my vision.

I need to get out of here.

"I—I'm not feeling so good. I'm sorry, everyone." I rush
toward the people opposite of Nikolai and far enough away
from Luka that he can't stop me. They let me out of the circle
before I break through their linked hands.

"*Skye, what's the matter? Where are you going?*" Luka only
questions because I'm racing toward Avery instead of back to
the mansion and my room where I'd go if I really were sick.

Ignoring his questions, I push my legs to move faster. I'm
afraid if I don't hurry, Avery will suddenly disappear. I need to
talk to her, to touch her, to do something to assure myself I'm
not imagining her. This version of myself doesn't know her
well, but it doesn't make me feel any less responsible for her.

"*Avery!*" I call out telepathically. I'm still too close to the
vow circle that the others might hear me if I call her name out
loud. And the last thing I want is for them to realize I have to
do odd things to make sure I keep my memories straight. I

don't need them to think something's wrong with my head, especially if Avery turns out not to be real.

Avery slips behind the eucalyptus tree, sending my heart sinking into my stomach. I charge past the tree line and deeper into the forest. With my chest heaving, I clutch my knees to catch my breath and then raise my head to look around.

"Avery?" I whisper. "It's okay. It's me." I keep my voice soft for a reason. The last time I was with Avery, she was attempting to murder me, vowing loyalty to Nikolai. She was rightfully pissed that I messed up her journey by murdering her and bringing her into the Knezha Family early. But even though she was furious in that moment in the basement, I know now that it didn't change our friendship. We were loyal to each other after that. Because I saw her in my memory. It was Nikolai trying to break the bond we shared.

A branch snaps behind me, and I spin around and face Avery. Seeing her this close, smelling the faint scent of lavender shampoo in her hair as it catches on the breeze, leaves me both relieved and confused. She was dead. Not just hiding in the galaxy world, waiting for someone to revive her, but dead-dead. Her journey in this life had ended. Yet, here she is alive and standing in front of me. Unless...

No, the basement was real. I will not forget it.

But me killing Avery? Nikolai was playing mind games. I should've seen it then. Our deaths in that moment were different. We saw each other outside our bodies. It was nothing like all the other times Caretaker Sienna killed us and revived us.

But even if I might not have actually killed Avery, the fact that my mind led me to believe I did doesn't make it better. Murder runs deep in my soul, all because of Nikolai. He turned me into one in every version of myself.

"Avery?" I ask again. "Do you know who I am?"

Her brows crinkle together. I expect fury to pinch her face, for her to charge me, attack me with her telekinetic ability, to do something as she remembers what happened to us in the basement, but all she does is tilt her head and say, "Of course I do, Skye. What kind of silly question is that? We hung out a few days..."

I try not to react, but I can't stop the strangled groan erupting from my mouth. "A few days ago?"

She frowns. "I'm sorry. A few weeks ago. I'm still adjusting to my realignment."

"Your what?" My voice shakes, her words getting to me in both a good and bad way. This isn't the first time I've heard about an alignment. I remember Caretaker Sienna mentioning it in the basement, that being there and dying over and over again was part of some realignment.

"My realignment," she says again. "Come on, Skye. You don't have to pretend like you didn't know it happened for my benefit. We both know I needed to be readjusted for our journey."

I hear her, but I'm having a hard time wrapping my mind around what she's saying. "So, you remember everything that happened in the basement."

If she confirms she does, it'll mean Nikolai messed up. It'll give me enough hope to fight through this, to believe that I can save Luka. Give me enough hope to save Avery, to find Gemma. To destroy Nikolai.

Her serious expression melts into a smile, and she laughs. It's a strange sound coming from her, stirring up memories of a dozen laughs we've shared before. "Oh, Skye. Nik mentioned you weren't feeling well. I'm sorry I couldn't be here for you, but I'm okay now. We're both okay and back on the correct journey."

I frown. "What?"

"Skye, please don't make me say it. I know Nikolai says it's important to talk about it, and I shouldn't be ashamed, but I can't help it. I can't believe I was ever having doubts about our family."

My mouth drops open in surprise. I can't form the words to express to her what's on my mind.

"But I'm okay now. I'm here and more certain than ever of my journey with everyone. It took a bit of time to realize how much the Knezha Family means to me." Avery touches her hand to my heart. "I won't turn my back again. If Nikolai didn't help me, I'd be so lost. I'm just so grateful I still have a place here. I don't know what I'd do without you or Nikolai or everyone else."

"What do you mean Nikolai helped you?" I ask. "How? Where were you?"

She tilts her head. "Skye, really? You're going to make me say it?"

I press my lips together in thought. Apparently, these are things I should already know. Things I have experience in from being by Nikolai's side. "It's for your benefit."

"I still wish you could've been my guide through the isolation therapy. Nikolai said we were too close."

Dread sinks from my heart toward my feet. I have no idea what she's talking about. None of my memories show me anything that relates to the kind of realignment she claims to have gone through.

"I have to go, Avery," I say. I need to find out where Nikolai had taken her. I need to find the basement. I don't think it's on the estate. A part of me fully believes it might be near the cabin. It's the only place that makes sense. But why there? How did Nikolai even know?

"You can't leave me." The memory hits me hard and fast. A wave of nerves washes over me, reflecting the mood of my past self in this particular moment.

"I promise I'll be back for you, but I have to do this," I say.

Avery leans against a eucalyptus tree wearing a belted dress with a silver KF brooch pinned to the collar. She looks different with her hair flat-ironed straight and wide, innocent eyes. Eyes that haven't seen the horrors we faced in Caretaker Sienna's clutches, even if the girl I just found watching me during the morning vows might not remember any of it. Her soul does. That I'm certain of.

"Then I'm running away with Cooper."

I blow out a long breath. "He's been shunned. It's dangerous. Guardians keep tabs to make sure no one reaches out to him before..." My voice trails off.

"Before nothing. You don't have to do what Nikolai asks.

Just because he had doubts about our family and didn't want to go through with the ceremony doesn't mean he can't follow his own journey." Avery reaches out her hand and grabs my arm.

"Avery, I—"

"Please, Skye," she begs.

"It's a huge risk."

"You promised you would take care of us before things got out of hand. And now you're leaving, all for—"

I release a groan. "I know! I'm sorry. It's just—it's bigger than you and me. Bigger than Cooper and Luka. I had no idea until Nikolai granted me freedom, and I can't risk him finding out what I've been up to."

"Then my mind's set. I'm leaving with Cooper. I can't do this without him, and he can't return because he doesn't believe in an eternity that doesn't include his mom. Nikolai gave him an ultimatum."

"And you're willing to risk everything going with him?"

"I love him, Skye. You would do the same for Luka."

I shake my head. "I wouldn't."

"You're a liar."

"If you love Cooper, then you'd stay far away from him. I'll do what I can to help him, but if Nik finds out you want out of the Knezha Family's eternity because of a boy, he'll send you to—" I huff. "I can't lose you like that. Not after finally getting you back after..."

"*Skye? Can you hear me?*" Luka's voice pulls me from the memory, leaving the world spinning around me.

I blink my eyes, pushing the Avery from another time

away. Whatever happened between us, I failed to uphold my promise to get to her, to help her and Cooper, whoever he is. He's only a name in my memory. A dead boyfriend who drowned in a lake when Nikolai took Avery to the basement.

Blinking, I pull myself together in the present to face Avery. I have so many questions to ask her about Cooper, about what she remembers, to help me piece together our real history. But when I regain focus, Avery's gone.

I rub the heels of my hands into my eyes, smudging my makeup. Holding my breath, I listen for movement among the trees, but nothing changes. Silence greets me. I can't tell if seeing Avery right now actually happened. She was a dead girl to me after all. Anxiety rushes through me, making me wander deeper into the forest to lose myself. Maybe I can concentrate hard enough to find the door to the galaxy again and ask for a redo.

Because I can't stand feeling like this.

Like I'm crazy. Like I'm seeing a dead girl from a past that contains the answers to my future. I'm afraid my head has been messed with too much that even if the answers were before me, I wouldn't even know they were there.

Sucking in a deep breath, I clutch my knees. "My name is Skye Stone. I'm seventeen years old from Los Angeles. I'm a prisoner of the Knezha Family. My boyfriend, Luka Landon, has been brainwashed. We can both read minds. We are both acquireds. I will remember," I whisper to myself.

"Skye, I know you're here. Say something." Luka's voice trails into my mind again, pushing in when he shouldn't.

I pull myself together, building my guard again, wishing I never had to risk letting it down. "Over here, Luka."

Soft footsteps crunch against the forest ground, and Luka strolls from where I know the morning vows have just ended. He probably hadn't taken his eyes off me the entire time as I abandoned one of the more precious moments of our day as a family.

"What are you doing out here?" he asks, stopping short to study me.

I shrug. "Saw someone."

"Who?"

"You don't know her."

He cocks his head slightly, his brows pinching together in the center. "Was someone spying on us?"

"Her name was Avery."

His shoulders slump as he relaxes. "Avery? I know Avery, Skye. Why would you think I don't know Avery?"

"Because—" Because according to Nikolai, the basement never happened, and I know my Luka didn't know Avery outside the basement, though she knew about him. I refuse to tell him that, though. Not after what happened at the beach yesterday. I whip my head back and forth, letting my hair hit my cheeks. "I don't know. I'm a little confused. I don't feel so good."

He pulls me against him. "Come on. It's freezing out here. Let's go back inside."

All I can do is nod and let him pull me away. "Okay," I agree. "Will you take me to Avery's room? We weren't finished talking."

"I don't know, Skye. I think you should get checked out by Sienna. I'm worried about you."

My heart falters, beating erratically at hearing the caretaker's name.

"I'm fine," I snap.

His hold tightens on my hand. "You don't have to pretend with me."

I try to tug away, but he doesn't let me go. "Please, Luka. Not her."

"But she's a doctor."

"I can't face her."

He sighs. "It's okay. She's forgiven you."

But I haven't forgiven her.

"You'll feel much better if you do," he adds. "What if I take you to see Avery after?"

My lip quivers. Can I face Caretaker Sienna now after everything? "Okay," I whisper. Because I don't think I have a choice. If I have to face the monster from my past to see Avery again, I'll suck it up. Maybe it'll help me remember more.

Maybe facing my past is what I need to figure out how to move forward.

"Good girl," Luka says, his voice sounding weird. He sounds like Nikolai.

I stiffen but don't say anything.

I pretend none of this is happening instead.

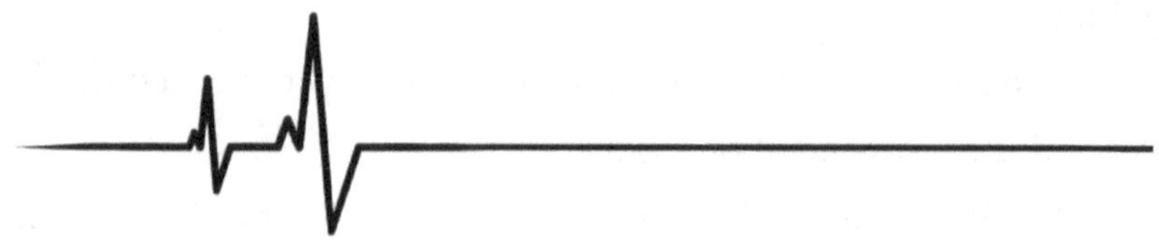

Chapter 4

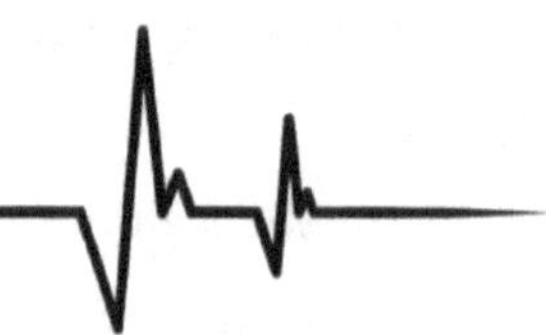

UNRAVELED

I SIT ON the edge of a cot in the infirmary on the backside of the estate. A heavy curtain blocks out the light from out-side, and as much as I want to open it to stare at the grounds, I remain stiff and on guard under the fluorescent light-ing.

Luka squeaks his chair closer, reaching up to link his fin-gers to mine. "She should be here any minute."

I sigh. "I'm tired of waiting. It's been ten already, and I'm feeling much better, really."

"You never had a lot of patience," Luka muses, bringing my hand to his mouth to kiss my knuckles.

Tugging my hand away, I slide off the cot and get to my feet. "So you should know that the only way I'm going to stay here is if you restrain—"

The door to the room swings open, and Caretaker Sienna hovers in the doorway in complete protective gear just like what she wore in the basement. I take an automatic step back, hitting the backs of my legs on the cot and fall back to it.

Caretaker Sienna reaches into her pocket, and I release a yelp scrambling back, expecting her to pull a black canister from her pocket to spray me in the face with poison. She freezes, her hand only holding her cell phone up with the screen glowing to display the time.

Yanking off her medical cap and then her mask, she steps forward with her hands raised like I'll attack her otherwise. Her wide eyes glance behind her to the door and then back to me. Luka gets to his feet, latching his hand to my wrist to pull me closer.

"Hey, Skye. Luka mentioned you weren't feeling so good," the careta—Sienna says, her hard voice much sweeter now that we're outside the basement, though her wardrobe makes me wonder if I was wrong about it being in the forest. I never knew where she went when we were left alone, and it very well might have been here.

"I'm fine," I snap. "I was just leaving."

"Mind sitting down for a minute?" She blocks my way to the door, not exactly giving me a choice. It doesn't help that Luka still clutches my hand.

"I do mind. Like I said, I'm fine."

"I can't help you if you don't tell me what's wrong. Luka voiced some concerns he had over your behavior. He mentioned you experienced some conf—"

I yank my hand away from Luka's, glaring at him. "He was mistaken."

Sliding around Sienna, I jog from the room so neither she nor Luka can stop me. Luka calls my name, forcing me to push my legs faster. I don't want him to try to drag me back. I glance over my shoulder, catching sight of Luka and Sienna watching me leave without coming after me. I slam into a solid body, winding myself, and fall toward the tile floor. I don't hit my back on it. Something—someone suspends me in the air on invisible lines for a moment before setting me gently on my back.

"Thank you, Sienna," Nikolai says from above me. Without giving me a chance to scramble away or react, he reaches down and takes both my hands in his, pulling me to my feet.

Conflicting emotions fight with each other—fear and love, rage and respect—when our gazes meet. Nikolai's ice blue eyes capture me in their probing depths, his scrutiny digging past my exterior as he tries to break into my mind.

"My beautiful girl, what do you think you're doing?" he asks, righting me on my feet without taking his hand off my arm. He grips me tightly enough to confirm if I tried to pull away, he'd probably hurt me. I don't test my theory though.

Huffing a breath, I say, "I was heading back to my room. I don't need a checkup or whatever. Luka's overreacting. I'm not sick."

More pressure builds in my head as Nikolai tries to press

his way into my mind. My eye twitches so much that I close it and turn away so he can't see me doing it. But Luka sees me. He watches me as intently as ever, studying everything about me like he'll learn something he doesn't already know.

Nikolai touches my cheek, forcing me to turn back to him. I blink a dozen times, the pressure in my skull finally subsiding. Touching the back of his hand to my forehead, he acts like he'll be able to tell if something is really wrong with me. "I think you're right."

"I am?" I ask, surprise lining my words.

He chuckles, the familiarity of his laugh burrowing into me, charming me with a dozen memories of us smiling and laughing together. "You know yourself best. Plus, I know how much you hate medical attention. You have to be on the verge of dying before you relent to let someone help you."

I release a breath and turn to Luka. "See?"

He furrows his brows in response, still not believing all is right with me. And that's fine by me. The only one who I care that believes me is Nikolai. "You're too easy on her, Nik."

I glower at Luka.

"Have you considered you might be a little overprotective of Skye, seeing as you've been promoted to her guardian?" Nikolai asks, a teasing lightness raising his voice.

Silence falls around us in the hall, and it takes Nikolai's gaze boring into the side of my face as I watch Luka to kick myself into action.

"I think you're right, Nik," I say, smiling. "If he's like this now, I can't imagine how he'll be when we have the actual ceremony."

Nikolai beams me a smile. "I was hoping to surprise you, my girl."

"Apparently Luka couldn't wait to tell me."

Nikolai turns his gaze away from me and to Luka. Sienna silently stands by his side, her hands tucked into the pockets of her lab coat. I push the feelings of unease away and try not to lose myself to the fresh memories of dying over and over again by her hands.

"Well, at least there are still many more surprises in our future," Nikolai says, sliding his arm over my shoulders. "Now, if you'll excuse me, I have some things to discuss with Sienna for our upcoming initiation ceremony." He leans his head closer to mine, sending a wave of pressure through my head, and I force myself to crack open my guard. *I'd like to meet later for a session. It's time for you to return to your duties.*

"After dinner? I have some things I'd like to do."

"Only if it includes leading a meditation session for the newcomers and a training session for the guardians," he responds, pressing more into my mind.

"I'd love to," I think to him.

He nods and steps away from me and toward Sienna. Patting Luka's shoulder, he leans in and whispers into his ear. Luka's gaze flicks to mine, and I wish with everything in this moment that I had super hearing. I want to know everything that happens between them.

Turning on my heels, I speed walk away from them all, my nerves now a jumbled mess. I hate that Caretaker Sienna got under my skin and how I have to pretend everything is okay. I hate that I'm not convincing enough for Luka, and I'm afraid our connection will unintentionally be the cause of our undoing.

The memory of Avery swirls through my mind again and how she accused me I'd do anything for Luka, called me a liar for denying it, and now I'm starting to believe she was wrong despite the hurt flowing through me at just the sight of Luka's presence sneaking up on me.

Because obviously I didn't drop everything to save him. It took me a year to end up in the basement. I let Luka suffer through over two hundred deaths—Gemma and Avery, too.

Warm hands hook around my waist, slowing me down. Luka rests his chin on my shoulder, strolling with me. "You're a pain in my side, you know. I don't understand how it's okay for you to always worry about me but you flip the hell out if it's the other way around. You're lucky I love you."

A whisper of a smile plays on my lips, remembering all the times he's made sure I know how difficult I can be. "You've just learned to tolerate my bullshit."

He chuckles, the annoyance slipping from his voice. "Which should prove to you how strong and capable I am."

I turn and kiss his cheek. "I've never doubted it."

"Good, because the last thing I need is you to start doubting what he's capable of." A strange, familiar feminine voice tugs me into my memory, drawing me away from Luka as he nudges me down the hall and toward the meditation room. It's getting harder and harder to stay present with my mind constantly unraveling. And I let it.

"I know what he's capable of doing. You have no idea what I've been through," I snap, glaring at the mirror, though I'm not looking at myself. I'm staring at the girl who now haunts my memories as much as Luka. It's like seeing her on the beach triggered a part of my past to reveal itself, but I hate that she pretended like she didn't even know me.

"We've all been through a lot, but it doesn't mean we can just drop everything for one person."

"He's my soul mate."

"I don't think you get it."

I fling my hands up. "I do! Why do you think I'm not rushing back? Why do you think I abandoned Luka in the forest? I don't know what else I have to do to prove that I'm all in. I was this close to taking care of Knezha, you know. If you had come sooner, I'd—"

"So, you blame me?"

I heave a sigh, my vision blurring. "I blame him."

"I hope so. I hate it when you're pissed at me," she says, hugging me. "Your form of silent treatment is torture."

I smirk. "I could say the same. Want to work on breaking through our shields?"

"And then combat."

I laugh. "My favorite."

Someone knocks on the door of the room, drawing both our attention away from our reflections in the mirror. I wish the person would go away. If I could control the memory, I'd yell at them to leave us alone. Because something about this girl, who feels more familiar by the second, ignites a wave of emotions similar to the ones Luka stirs in me—we have some sort of bond. Not a bond with our souls, but something else. She feels like family. Like how the Knezha Family should feel to me. She almost feels like Angelica.

The door cracks open, and I reach over to the vanity table and grab my hairbrush, chucking it at whoever is on the other side. "I didn't say you could come in!"

"*Skye, I—*" Luka's thought sneaks into my mind, ripping me away from my memory of the girl who seems to have all the answers. He holds his hand on my door, pressing to it as I shove against it to keep him out.

I blink, the memory flitting from my mind. Confusion rushes over me, and I startle. I don't even know how I got to my room. I release the door and step back, hugging myself. "Luka, I'm sorry. I didn't mean..." I let my words trail off.

He frowns. "I hope you're not mad at me for—"

I shake my head. "I'm sorry. I just—I need a moment alone."

His lips pout, tilting downward. "Oh, okay."

I huff a breath, trying to pull myself together. The memory felt so real, so much so I thought it was my reality. I can't help the annoyance flowing through me that Luka forced me away from it.

I glance behind me at the balcony leading to the lawns and forest outside the property. "Actually, wait," I say. "Can you show me Avery's room?"

He crosses his arms over his chest. "You know the way."

I groan. "I meant, will you walk me to Avery's room?"

A line forms between his eyebrows. He clearly doesn't believe me, but instead of calling me out on it, he holds out his hand to me. I take it, lacing our fingers together, offering him a smile I hope he accepts though my whole face begs to frown.

Luka leads me from my wing of the estate and down the hall to his room, located next to a few other bedrooms. Unlike my plain white wood door, Avery's door is hard to miss. A corkboard hangs in the center of it with dozens of pictures tacked to it. My heart falters catching sight of a photo of her and me, and a third person with their face scratched off, though I'd recognize Gemma's red hair anywhere.

I tap it with my finger. "Who's that?"

Luka presses his lips together. "No one."

I wrinkle my nose. "No one?"

The door swings open, cutting off all my questions about Gemma. Avery greets me with a smile, offering me a hug while simultaneously pulling me into her bedroom. Luka doesn't follow us in, and Avery waves to him while closing the door.

"Luka can't come in?" I ask.

She giggles. "I know you like to break the rules, and Nik lets you get away with it, but I'm not losing my privileges to let your boyfriend in my bedroom."

I guess she's right.

Pulling me to her bed, she pats the spot next to her, motioning for me to sit. "I'm so glad you came to visit. I heard you'd be leading meditation today. I'll walk with you."

I purse my lips. "I'd like that. But first, I was wondering if you could show me where you did your..." It's hard for me to spit the rest of my words out with the way she pouts, looking at me.

She doesn't respond.

"Never mind," I say, turning to glance around. I spot another corkboard on the wall, filled with dozens of photos. Getting up from the bed, I stand to look at them. The hairs on my arms rise, looking at all the pictures of Gemma with her face scratched out. I also notice that none of the photos contain Luka.

"I've considered taking all those down and putting new ones up, but I love the ones of us together."

"Why is Gemma's face scratched out?" I ask, deciding not to avoid her name like I did with Luka.

Avery jumps to her feet, reaching out to cover my mouth with her hand. "Shhh!"

"What?" I mumble against her fingers.

"We can't talk about her. She's no one."

I blink the confusion from my face. "No one? How could you say that?"

"How can you not?" Avery drops her hand to her side, glowering at the pictures on her corkboard. Reaching out, she snatches it from the wall and rushes to shove it into her closet.

"Because she's—"

Avery covers her ears, her eyes wide. "Maybe you should leave."

"What? Why? We're alone. You can talk about it with me."

Thrashing her head back and forth, she spins away from

me, her buns coming undone from her head, spilling her curls over her face. "No!"

I close the distance and grab her shoulders. "Come on, Avery. Tell me. Tell me what's going on."

"Skye," she whispers.

"Tell me, please," I ask.

She shakes her head.

"Avery, tell me!"

Her eyes widen before she squeezes them shut. Thrusting her arms out, she shoves me back and into the wall. The lights flicker around us, the dresser shaking, and a few books fall off and thump against the floor.

"Avery," I say, holding my hands up. "Calm down."

She releases a shrill scream, startling me, and then freezes. Her chest heaves as she catches her breath. *Help me, Skye,* she thinks to me.

A second later, the panic and agony crossing her face disappear. She opens her eyes and blinks a few times. "We should probably go. Everyone will be waiting."

I stand in stunned silence. What just happened? It was like a part of Avery was breaking through. But now, that part of her is gone, and I don't know what to do.

Everything about Avery's bedroom suffocates me. The whole estate seems to close in now. I feel like I'll die if I don't get out of here and do something. I want so badly to pressure Avery, to badger her until she breaks for me, but I'm scared. I'm afraid of what that might do to her. And now that I know something about Gemma triggered her, I can't sit back and wait for Nikolai to finally release her. I'm not even sure he would. He's turned her into no one.

Taking a deep breath, I nod my head. "Yeah, sure. Why don't I meet you there? I forgot something in my room."

Avery bobs her head. She crosses the room and opens the door. "Okay, see you soon."

I wait for a second for her to leave and rush to the window instead of the door. Easing it open, I climb out and stand on the ledge, glancing at the one-story drop. I kick off my heels and let them fall before me.

Taking a deep breath, I jump.

I have to get out of here. I have to find Gemma.

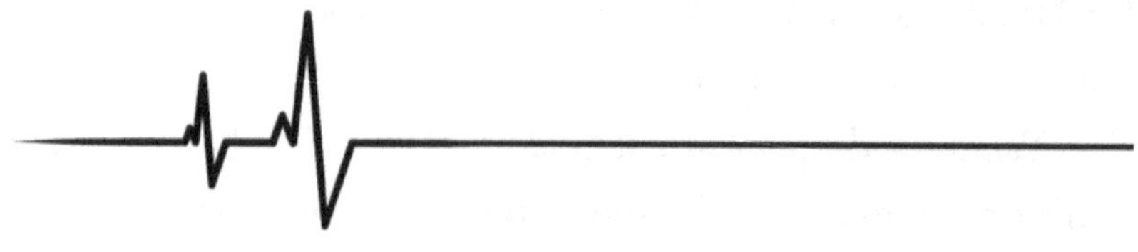

Chapter 5

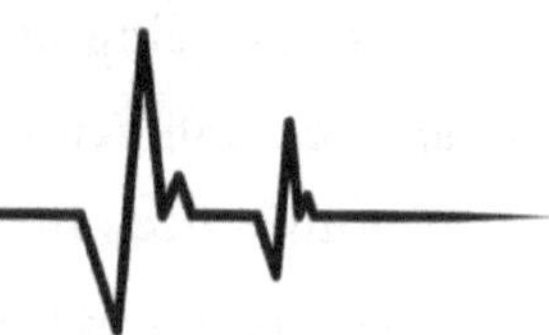

HOW THINGS ENDED

A THUMP SOUNDS to my right, and I roll to scramble to my feet. Luka huffs next to me, pushing on his hands to stand up. I search around the grounds for a dozen guardians to swarm us, to tackle me and drag me back to my room, but we're alone.

Luka scoops my shoes off the grass and hands them to me. I don't bother slipping them back on. They'll only slow me down, and I have to run.

He reaches down to help me up, but I ignore his hand and get up myself to search the area. Still, no one lurks around.

I curl my hands into fists and position myself into a combat stance. "I don't want to fight you, Luka, but I will if you try to make me stay. I need to go somewhere."

His face morphs between a frown and a smile, confusion lining his eyes. He doesn't know how to react. "You think I'd fight you?"

I shrug. "Maybe."

He presses his lips together to stop a smile from sneaking onto his face as he tries to act seriously. "No, definitely not. I don't want to get my ass kicked."

I laugh. I can't help it. I had expected him to say he wouldn't fight me because he didn't want to hurt me. "I'm brutal, aren't I?"

The smirk fades, never turning into a full-blown smile. "You have to be."

Shifting on my feet, I peer around again. "Well, okay. I'm going to go then. I'll be back...I think."

I turn my back on Luka but don't get far before he comes up to my side. He strolls with me, probably testing to see what my reaction will be. I'm not going to stand around and argue with him, especially if he actually wants to leave with me. I won't leave him behind if he's willing to go. Because where I'm going might spark something within him—within me, too. Maybe we can light up the darkness and finally see things the same way, at this moment in time.

When I don't do anything, he clears his throat. "Where are we going exactly?"

"I told you I wanted to go to the mountains today."

He sighs. "I'm sorry. I forgot to arrange it. You can't wait until tomorrow? You have duties to take care of. If Nik—"

"Luka, if you're so concerned, then go back and lead meditation and training for me. I'm going to the mountains. There's something I need to see for myself," I say.

"Does this have to do with how you've been acting?"

I shrug. "No, it has to do with how *you've* been acting."

Lowering a brow, he tightens his jaw, thinking about my statement. I'm nearly certain he's about to argue with me and try to convince me to turn around like a good little Knezha, but he doesn't. He releases a puff of air from his lips, sending a cloud between us, and says, "Can I at least grab our coats?"

"Afraid of a little snow?" I ask, teasingly.

He laughs. "Fine. We'll stop along the way."

"Really? No protesting at all?"

"I'll even borrow a car from someone. We'll be gone before they can verify."

"You have no idea how much this means to me."

"Well, I did promise you we'd go, and I never break my promise."

If only he promised to remember.

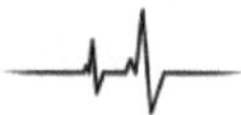

I almost don't believe my eyes.

A quaint cabin sits nestled in the forest of sugar pine trees a half mile off the main road. Luka parked the Subaru Legacy, one of the many Knezha Family's vehicles, at the beginning of the driveway where a snow truck cleared a path, though the rest of the street hasn't been shoveled or salted yet. It's clear that no one's been here since the last snowfall.

Hugging myself, I stroll forward. My boots crunch over the snowy gravel, and I scoop up a palm full of snow into my bare hands. "It's just like I remember," I say, tossing the powdery snow into the air to scatter over me, melting into my hair.

"It's hard to believe we ever lived here. I mean, look at this place." Luka says it like a bad thing, sending an ache through my heart. Nothing can compare to the Knezha Estate in his eyes now.

I clench my jaw so I don't sneer. "How can you not love it? We have a lot of good memories here, don't we?" I ask, refraining from telling him how much his words get to me.

He stops at my side, glancing at me in his peripheral vision without obviously staring. "You must've blocked out all the bad stuff."

"I wish. I wish I could forget how things ended here."

"I wish none of it happened at all."

I wonder what he's referring to. He doesn't remember how I shot him by accident. How I abandoned him in the snow and ran away. How he was taken by Caretaker Sienna and kept in a basement, killed over and over again for almost a year until I showed up in the room next to his with only the memory of my death. No, those memories, while horrible, never ruined our life together according to him. Nikolai put something else in his head to despise this place.

Strolling forward, I head toward the tree line and to the pine where I remember a stray bullet hit when I was attempting to murder Nikolai. It's still there. It gives me hope knowing that there are some things Nikolai can't touch. He can't take every little detail from me.

I touch my finger to it. "Yeah, if none of it had happened, we'd still be here and free of the Knezha Family." I cringe at my words, wishing I'd kept them to myself. I couldn't help it seeing the cabin before me, knowing the history I have here. I remember the good times more than the bad now.

A muscular hand grips my shoulder and spins me around. I meet Luka's worried eyes. "Why would you say something like that, Skye? Nikolai saved us. He protected us."

"I'm sorry. Just drop it and forget I ever said anything."

Grimacing, he tugs me closer and wraps his arms around me. "I can't. Where is all this coming from?"

Anger rolls over me, stiffening my muscles. The freezing air bites through my sweatshirt, which isn't exactly snow-proof, and I shiver. "Maybe it has to do with the fact that I shot you near here because of him," I say, my voice rising through the air.

His eyes widen. "Shot me? Skye, you never shot me."

I blink. "I did. You just don't remember. I shot you and abandoned you."

"Now that's ridiculous. You'd never."

"I did!" I smack my hand against the tree, my racing thoughts overwhelming me as Luka makes me feel like I'm crazy.

Stepping back, he raises his hands in surrender, twisting his lips to the side. "Hey, okay. It's okay. Come on. Let's go in. You're shivering. We can talk more about this."

I glare at his outstretched hand. I don't want to talk more

about this. I just want him to believe me and help me find the basement. I want him to remember no matter how awful that particular memory is for the both of us. I should be afraid that if he remembers it right now, he might hate me, but I still have to hope for it. Because horrible memories are better than false ones created by a master manipulator.

Sighing, he grabs my hand anyway and guides me forward. We make our way to the front porch where he pulls out a set of keys from the combination lock box hidden in a storage container. He opens the door, and my heart sinks to the floor seeing how much the inside of the cabin has changed, no longer matching any of the memories I have of it. On the wall above the fireplace hangs the letters KF twisted into their shapes by black metal. A white leather sectional replaced the old couch, and the glass coffee table in front of it is now a black ottoman. The place lacks the warmth and comfort I had expected. It lacks anything I can use to help Luka remember—to help me remember more.

Luka motions for me to sit on the couch. He disappears into the kitchen through a swinging door. From my position, I glimpse the updated stainless steel appliances. This cabin, which I was certain would feel like home, now feels like another place from a time I don't belong.

Taking a deep breath, I fill my lungs with the wintery air, trying to calm my racing heart. As much as I want to run from this place, it's better than being at the Knezha Estate. I'll give myself a couple of minutes to acclimate and adjust to Nikolai's changes, and then I'll find the basement.

A cupboard slams, drawing my attention back to the swinging door in the kitchen. Avery steps through, carrying a tray of steaming hot chocolates. I blink my eyes, unable to push the memory away. I stay frozen as an onlooker like I'm trapped in a movie where I have no control.

"I couldn't find him at the Knezha Estate," Avery says, setting the tray on the glass coffee table I remember. The memory ignites a wave of anger and sadness in me, and my eyes blur at her words.

The world turns dark as I rub my eyes. "But Nikolai does have him."

She nods her head. "I think so. I heard him mention his name to a guardian, but if he is at the estate, Nik's hiding him well."

I groan. "You checked the basement?"

"There's no basement, Skye. All the realignments happen in the building around back. I should know. Nikolai mentioned how it could be good for me and he showed me the empty rooms."

I suck in a breath. "That's a façade to show people. There is a basement, but you can only access it from his office. Maybe you should take him up on his offer."

She glances at the front door. "Now you're talking crazy. I'm not you. There's no way I could make it out with my mind intact."

"You can. I made sure of it."

"You haven't seen Nik lately, though. Your 'poor behavior,' as Nik called it had freaked him out. He's told everyone you were on a personal journey, but I overheard him mention to a guardian that he was afraid you wouldn't change your mind."

"And I won't."

"He's starting to believe it's more than about Luka."

I rub my hands on my knees. "Ugh. Not good."

A knock on the door sends Avery rushing to answer it. An unfamiliar boy stands on the porch, bundled up in winter gear with a scarf pulled over his mouth. Avery yanks it down and kisses him, pulling him inside.

"All good, Cooper?" she asks the boy.

He nods. "Skye definitely knows what she's doing. I just can't wait for all this to end so you can come home already."

My vision blurs with tears. "Soon, I promise."

Avery crosses the room to hug me. "Stay safe, okay? We'll get everything fixed and can flip Nikolai off and blow up his damn compound."

I laugh. "I can't wait."

After Avery and the unfamiliar boy, who I now know is Cooper, leave, I hug myself and sob into my hands. Screaming out a string of curse words, I take the mug of hot chocolate and smash it into the coffee table. Glass cascades everywhere in a chocolate mess, but I don't move from my spot.

"Skye?" The memory fades away with the sound of Luka's voice. "You're spacing out."

I blink a few times. Luka flips the top of the ottoman over, turning it into a table, and sets down two cups of hot chocolate in the same mugs Avery had used. I realize that tiny glimpse of the time after Luka was taken has given me the answer I've needed all along. The basement isn't here on this mountain, but being on this mountain showed me where it is.

"The basement is real," I blurt, leaning my elbows on my knees. "I can prove it to you."

He sighs. "Is that what this is all about?"

"Yes—no." I groan. "It's about you and Nikolai. About everything."

He stares at me without saying a word.

I can't stand the silence, so I say, "I know you think something is wrong with me, but it's not me. It's the world. Our supposed family. You, Luka. Something is wrong with you."

"Me?"

I nod, holding his gaze. "I've failed you. I was supposed to protect you from all this. I almost succeeded, but then—"

He leans forward, cutting off my words with a kiss. *"You're under a lot of pressure,"* he thinks to me, still brushing his soft lips against mine.

And I let him. Because kissing him feels like even if the world is collapsing around us that we'd still survive in the end. That we'd still be okay no matter what. Kissing Luka is like gasping for air after almost drowning—painful but necessary to live.

"Nik's been working you too hard," Luka continues in my mind. *"I told him you needed a break."*

I jerk back. "A break?" My hands tremble the longer I stare into Luka's eyes.

He tries to kiss me again, but I press my hand to his chest, nudging him back.

"I can't do this, Luka," I say.

"What do you mean? You know I love you, right?" he asks.

I back away and head toward the door. "I'm sorry. I have to go."

"Please, don't leave. It's freezing out there."

I grab a stranger's jacket off the coat rack by the door. "I don't care."

"Let me take you home. We can talk to Nik. He'll get you—us—through this."

"That's not my home. I don't even know where my home is," I say. "I thought this was it, but I was wrong."

"Skye..." He shuffles closer, raising his hands up like he's afraid any sudden movement will make me attack like a frightened animal. And I just might. Because everything feels so wrong.

"I'm sorry," I say.

"Don't leave me. You promised me," he says.

My heart aches at the desperation in his voice. "I know I did. That's why I have to figure out how to find you."

"But I'm right here."

Physically, yes. He's right about that. But it's not what I'm talking about. I need answers I can't find in this life or in this cabin. I need answers that only reveal themselves to me in the galaxy world where I feel like I lost the key to opening the door at will.

Rushing to kiss him, I brush my lips to his once more. "I'll find you. I promise."

Without waiting for Luka to argue or seeing what he'll do

to make me stay, I sprint from the cabin and into the forest of snow-covered sugar pines, ignoring the gut-wrenching pain of abandoning my soul mate again.

I curse the universe for doing this to me. I curse the stars and Nikolai for ruining everything.

It takes everything in me not to look back when Luka calls my name.

I keep running until everything turns white and the world disappears.

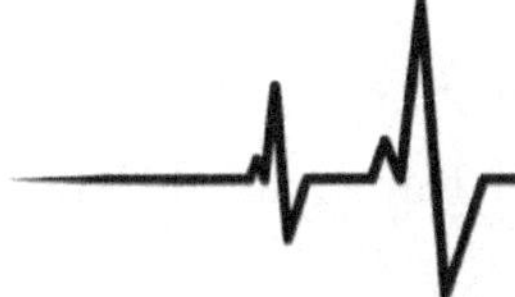

Chapter 6

LOVE TRANSCENDS FAITH

"YOU'RE HERE." THE brilliant stars of the galaxy world sparkle around me. I turn to Luka and extend my hand out to him. I can't remember much of what happened after I left the cabin, but I didn't stop running until I couldn't take another step. And now I'm here with Luka.

Luka runs his fingers over my cheek. "I'm sorry."

Shifting to face him straight on, I gaze into his intense eyes. "What for?"

"For forgetting. For letting you down. For letting Nikolai get to me," he says. A tear sparkles in the corner of his eye, but he blinks it away.

"But you're here now. You followed me."

"Because I love you, Skye, and even if things are different in life, that will never change," he says.

"You sure about that?" I can't help asking. Because even though I know Nikolai got to Luka, it's hard to deal with the fact that he sometimes looks at me like I'm out of my mind. Like I'm wrong for asking questions—for questioning the Knezha Family and Nikolai.

"Absolutely. My love for you is more powerful than the beliefs Nik has put in my head." He leans over and kisses me so softly, a whisper of his soul against mine. Melting into him is easy.

"Skye, sweetheart, that's because love transcends faith. As much as Nikolai wants to deny it, when it comes down to it, if your heart and soul belong to someone, you'll choose them over everything." The familiar voice rings in my ear, pulling me away from Luka and our galaxy.

"That's stupid. I'm not going to turn my back on our eternity for a boy," I say. It's been a while since I've thought about Angelica, but something in Luka's words triggered this memory that didn't feel so important until now.

She chuckles, pulling me into her arms. "That might be true, but you never know. That's why I'm telling you this. Love comes in many forms. Remember that."

"Is this because of the dreams?" I ask. Dreams of Luka before we met. I don't have detailed memories of them, but I recall conversations about them from the time before Luka, before the Knezha Family, when it was only me and Angelica and the door to the galaxy world.

She shrugs. "Yes and no. I want you prepared for anything, including the journey your heart leads you on, wherever that may be."

Angelica knew what my journey was all along. She did everything she could to try to prepare me, but I didn't see it then. I was too young. I wasn't thinking about love or soul mates. I was thinking about survival, about family—everything Nikolai promised me.

"Skye?" Luka asks, forcing me from my thoughts. "We can't stay here."

I suck in a deep breath, expanding my lungs with the very essence of the galaxy world, of Luka, and how it feels when our souls collide.

"So, you want to go back? Even if you can't remember?"

"We'll figure it out," he says.

My bottom lip quivers. "And if we don't?"

"We will. If I can't, you will. I know you better than anyone."

"Even better than me," I say. Because it's true...at least in this moment of clarity that I wish Luka would hold on to.

He kisses me. "Get ready."

He pulls us toward a void, a black hole amid the stars where the door to the living awaits. My skin tingles, buzzing with everything good in the universe I want to bottle up and keep with me on this journey.

Five.

My ears ring.

Four.

Iciness travels from my toes to my head.

Three.

My heart jumpstarts, ripping me from Luka.

Two.

I snap my eyes open and gasp, my breath too cold to fog in front of me. Groaning, I flop to my side and peer around. Snow floats through the air like a soundproof barrier, silencing everything but the blood pounding in my ears.

"Luka?" I ask. "Luka, where are you?"

No response.

Pushing my hands into the frozen ground, I get to my knees and then use a tree to stand. My icy hair clumps to my cheeks. I'm so cold I can't feel my hands. I spin around, searching the white forest. I don't even know where I am. I can't see anything beyond a few feet of me. Except for something dark red peeking from a mound of snow.

Blood? No.

A jacket.

"Luka?"

I step closer and find Luka curled on his side, hugging his knees to his chest. He releases a quick gasp. Bolting upright, he screams my name, struggling to get to his feet. Snow veils the space between us, stealing the sound of my name on his lips away. I kick through the frozen terrain and fall to my knees at his side.

"Why did you leave me?" Luka asks, his teeth chattering

from the cold.

"I'm sorry," I whisper. "I couldn't stay there."

He shrugs his shoulders, and it takes me a second to realize he's wearing a backpack. With unsteady hands, he drags the zipper down and pulls out another jacket. He drapes it around me and reaches into the bag and retrieves a heat pack for me to hold.

With trembling hands, he lifts me onto his lap and scoots back into what looks like a snow cave.

I frown at how prepared he was. I don't know how long it's been since I lost myself to the snow storm, but it was long enough for Luka to create a shelter he didn't bother using. "I don't understand. You did all this, yet you died," I say.

"Like you gave me a choice," he snaps.

Warmth explodes in my chest, pushing the chill from my bones. "Don't blame me." Anger lines my words, and I can't help lashing out at him. He acts like he didn't have a choice when it was obvious he did.

"You knew I'd follow you, Skye. But why put us both through this? What has gotten into you? Just because we can access the stars, doesn't mean we should. It's a gift meant for our family to share. What would happen if something went wrong? You're risking our everlasting eternity together with everyone."

As much as I want to shove him away and scream at him, I can't. Not only because his arms lock around me, hugging me against his solid body, but because I know he would be hurt if I held this against him. It's not his fault he can't remember or that he's treating me like I'm the one with something wrong.

I close my eyes. "Do you trust me?"

"Yes."

I savor his immediate answer. He didn't even have to think about it, and because of that, I know he's not lost to me yet. "Then believe me when I say I'd never abandon you or put you through something without reason."

"And what reason do you have that I had to search for you in the stars? You know we're not supposed to enter the door on a whim. It's sacred."

My heart picks up pace. "You remember the galaxy?"

His silence extinguishes the flicker of hope I lit within my heart. "I—"

"Come on, Luka. Remember."

He blinks a few times. "It's all a blur."

Shifting in his arms, I position myself in his lap with my legs wrapped around his waist. I press my forehead to his, our lips close enough to touch, but I don't kiss him. Instead, I bring my thawing hands to his temples and gently press them against his head. I stare at his closed eyelids, wishing I could somehow discover what Nikolai did to him so I could reach into his memories and break them all free.

But I can't. I can't even do that for myself.

"Let me in," I think to Luka, pushing my thoughts into his head.

"You're always welcome in my head. You know that," he thinks back.

"Then remember."

Luka yells, thrusting me off him and into the snow. His body jerks as he thrashes, breaking the wall to our snow cave. It collapses, separating us from each other, and I sit up, shaking snow from my freezing hair.

Digging my hands into the snow, I search for Luka, who now lies utterly still. The sound of sirens pierces through the quiet of the forest. The snowstorm dissipates, leaving everything a glittering white in the pale beams of winter sunlight breaking through the looming clouds.

The rustle of leaves draws my attention from Luka, and I stiffen, reaching for an imaginary gun I haven't had since the day everything changed. It's a reflex ingrained in me being out here in the familiar sugar pine forest. A coyote yips from a distance before dashing away, and I huff out a huge, shaking breath. I don't think I'll ever shake the feeling of being chased or followed. Of being in danger.

Luka groans.

"You better get up before you die again," I say, shaking his shoulders. Snow dusts from his bluing face, and I lean down and press my cold lips to his.

He doesn't open his eyes.

Sliding my arms under him, I yank him from the snow mound. I shouldn't be surprised by my strength because Nikolai insists that everyone should know how to defend themselves, but I haven't trained once in weeks. I skipped, just like I did today. I don't leave my suite if I don't have to unless it's to get away.

"Luka," I say again. "Come on. Get up. This isn't funny."

Fear slithers through my chest, knotting around my heart.

"Luka!" I project my thought as hard and as fast as I can into his head.

He bolts upright, yelling out my name again, and then our eyes meet. Slowly, he reaches out his hand and runs his gloved fingers over my chin before pushing my snowy hair over my shoulder. His dark eyes hold mine, a sparkle of something familiar in them, yet he doesn't do anything except stare at me.

I clench my jaw, trying to summon something—anything—to say to break the silence veiling over us, over the forest, maybe even the universe.

"Luka," I whisper. Saying his name seems to be the only thing I can manage.

He leans closer. "You can't stay here, Skye."

I frown. "What do you mean?"

"You should've never remembered," he says without answering my question. "You should've left me."

I swallow, trying to suppress the panic turning the edges of my vision dark. "Luka..."

His hand drops down, and he grabs onto the front of my open jacket and shakes. "Leave me."

"I could never."

"Then forget."

"But Luka—"

He scrambles to his feet, putting distance between us. "It's the only way, Skye."

"I—"

"Leave!" he yells, turning his back to me.

I don't move. All I can do is stare at his back, his body taut, his hands curled into fists. "Luka," I whisper once more.

He doesn't turn around. A chime rings through the air, and I startle at the sound of Luka's cell phone. His shoulders relax, and he reaches into his pocket, pulling it out.

Holding it to his ear, he says, "Hey Nik. Yeah, I found her. She's a little distraught, but nothing I can't deal with."

The boy who yelled at me to run is no longer the boy standing in front of me. Luka shifts on his feet, glancing over his shoulder to smile at me. Something strange flickers in his eyes, the boy who wanted to protect me now gone.

He nods his head. "Yeah, we'll be home soon," he says, continuing his conversation with Nikolai.

His words kick me into action, and I scramble to my feet. Concern knits Luka's brows together, and he quickly hangs up the phone without saying goodbye. He steps closer while I step away. My back hits a tree, and snow rains down on us from the high branches.

"What's wrong, Skye?" he asks.

I maneuver around the tree, walking backward. "You told me to leave."

He grimaces. "I did? Why would I do that?"

"Because it's the only way to save us."

He slowly raises his hand to me, like any of his sudden movements will frighten me away. And they might. "Skye, come on. It's cold. We'll get this sorted out."

I shake my head. "That's what you keep saying."

"Nikolai will know what to do. You don't have to feel this

way." He tries to grab onto me, but I jerk away.

"Stay back, Luka. Just trust me, okay?"

"I do trust you."

"Then come with me." My voice lowers, pleading with him. Something about his strange reaction to me pressing into his mind, asking him to remember, claws at my own memory. I know if I can take a little more time, maybe I can figure out how to use my telepathy to rebuild what Nikolai broke.

"Come with me." The voice trickles from behind me, yanking my attention away from Luka. Gemma stands at the door to the cabin, her arms across her chest. "If we stick together, maybe we can fix things. Avery didn't show up at our checkpoint, and I'm worried."

Tears shine in Gemma's green eyes, tugging at my heart, summoning a world of grief through me as I watch the memory unfold through blurry eyes.

"I know she didn't." I turn my gaze toward the window.

"You knew?"

"I felt the block slide into place this morning."

She covers her face with her hands. "Damn it, Skye! How do you expect me to return now? He will come for me next."

"And you'll be ready. You can handle Nikolai. You're strong."

She groans, shaking her head, her wild red tresses whipping around her face. "Please, you have to come back with me. Nikolai will forgive you. If you just act the part, maybe he'll release Luka. We can create a new plan."

I sigh. "Impossible. Going back is a last resort. I'm dangerous by his side. Remember what would happen to Sam if I do." Sam? The name sounds familiar, tickling my mind, trying to put a face behind the boy.

"He'd be like us."

I shake my head. "He'd be like Nikolai. I'm sorry, Gemma. We can't change the plan now. You have to go back. You have to make sure Nikolai trusts you. Tell him I contacted you if you have to. He needs to think I'm not coming home as a form of rebellion. Don't give him a reason to doubt your loyalty."

She grimaces, twisting her lips. "I don't think I can."

"You have to. This is for the sake of our eternity. He's robbing us of everything. He's robbing the world. He's breaking our family. He'll destroy this life if we don't stop him."

"You're selfish, asking me to do this. Trying to guilt me."

"I'm sorry." Her words get to me. Maybe she was right. Maybe my selfishness is what pushed me forward all along.

"I'm sorry," Luka says, ripping me from the memory. "I can't."

I blink my eyes. Only seconds have passed. "Luka, please. I'm begging you. I don't want to go back with you like this. I want to help you. Trust m—"

Luka yells out, startling me. A look of agony crosses his face, and he squeezes his eyes shut, pressing his hands to his ears. "Run!" he screams. "Skye, run. Leave me."

I spin on my feet, dashing away from him through the trees, following my instincts to decide which direction to head in. My Luka somehow managed to break through, and while I know I should be happy, the desperation in his voice pierces through my soul. Pain expands in my head, behind my eyes. Someone's trying to test my resolve. They're getting stronger— no, I'm getting weak. Luka was right. I shouldn't have remembered. I need to forget. If I forget, Nikolai can't get to me.

The crunch of tires on gravel breaks through the quiet of the forest, and I push my legs to run faster in the direction of the nearby road. My heart aches abandoning Luka like I have, but what else am I supposed to do? There's a reason I need to escape while I can. I can feel the need deep in my bones, my mind, my soul. Because staying with the Knezha Family wasn't part of the plan.

The plan? I squeeze my eyes shut, trying to summon something, anything. But whatever plan I think I have evades me.

I spot the blur of a semi truck barrel past, and my heart soars at the sight of my escape.

"Hurry, Skye," a feminine voice says, coaxing me along. *"You can do this."* It's the girl from the beach, the one trickling into my memory. I know it.

"Skye, stop!" Luka yells from behind me.

His loud voice nearly sends me crashing to the ground. He's fighting with himself. Fighting against whatever Nikolai did to him, and what I'm trying to do. I couldn't get into his head to shake his memories free, but I must've put a crack in the wall trapping him. But I can't tear the blockade down now. I can't pass up my opportunity to figure things out. To remember completely. Something I know I can't ever do with Nikolai.

"Skye!"

I peek over my shoulder at Luka chasing me through the

trees. A car horn blares, startling me, and I spin in time to see bright headlights flash in my eyes. Pain explodes through my body, the car knocking me off my feet and onto the hood before I smash into the window. The driver hits the brakes, and I roll forward and back onto the hard ground.

The last thing I see is the brilliant blue sky.

A sky without stars.

Without escape.

Without me.

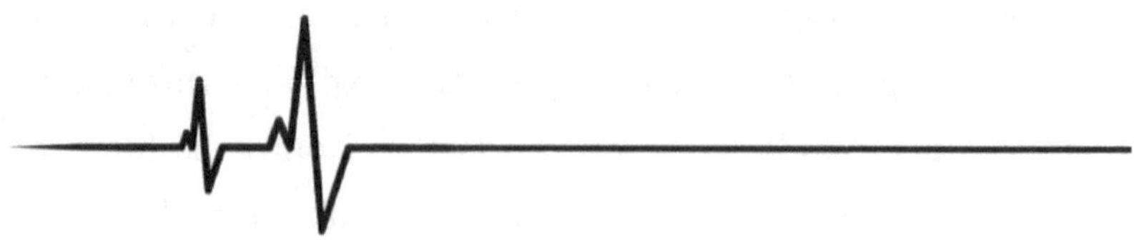

Chapter 7

ONE FLAW COLLAPSES A MASTERPIECE

"**B**RING HER THIS way." Nikolai's deep voice pulls me from the recesses of my mind.

With every one of Luka's steps, pain burns through me. I can't tell how badly I'm hurt, only that I know I can't walk, and I keep passing out.

To my dismay, Luka refused to let the poor driver of the Honda Civic I ran in front of call an ambulance. I thought if maybe I could immerse myself back into the world outside the Knezha Family, I could manage to find someone to protect me from Nikolai while I sorted things out. Maybe find the answers my memory tries to hand me but can't completely. But Luka scooped me up, pressed my face into his jacket to muffle my screams of pain, and ran back into the forest and away from the road before anyone could get to me.

"Why here?" Luka asks, pausing in his tracks. "She needs to go to the infirmary."

I force myself to open my eyes. "I want a hospital. Please, take me to a hospital."

Nikolai leans down and into my face. "You don't need a hospital, my girl. This isn't something we haven't dealt with before."

I groan, turning my head away from Nikolai to hide in Luka's jacket. How can I argue with him when I know he's right? We both know well enough that because I can open a door to the galaxy world and travel between life and death that I acquired the ability to heal my body through my spirit. It's one of the reasons Nikolai needs me so desperately. Control the one who can access death and control death and life—eternity.

I try not to think about it much, but when Nikolai speaks of our eternity, he means it. Spiritually, we're immortal. There is life beyond this one, but I choose to stay. We all do. It's the Knezha Family's purpose. Fatality is rare, and those who move on from this life are considered saintly—like Angelica. She's not dead and gone. She's supposedly another star. But now? She doesn't feel like a star. She is dead. Gone. Thrown from this damn journey Nikolai creates to ruin my faith and everything I love. The false prophet.

"You're going to be fine, Skye," Luka says. "Sienna's a fantastic doctor."

Reminding me of the caretaker, who killed me over and over again while locking me away in a basement, sends an explosion of anger through me. Even if she can't remember ever doing those horrendous things, I'll never forget them, and there's no way I'll ever let her put a hand on me again. I'll fight like the last time.

Nikolai clears his throat. "Doctors are for those transitioning into our family. All Skye needs is our family's support in these trying moments." Trying moments? More like acts of rebellion. He wants to say it, but then he'd have to accept that he failed. That's the last thing I want. He can't know he failed.

"You mean..." Luka's voice trails off as Nikolai's words sink in. I pray that he doesn't mention I dragged him there today and yesterday—that I've grown almost addicted to death because with dying, I remember. Luka remembers. Death is the key to this life if only I could turn the lock...no, I must not open it.

"Exactly. Now, come on. The others are waiting."

Nikolai leads the way into a grand room. Not just any grand room, but one used for ceremonial purposes. The last time I can remember being here was my first death that brought me into the Knezha Family. It hasn't changed much. If it weren't for the streak of light cutting across the floor, I wouldn't be able to see every member of the Knezha Family surrounding a small pool on a platform. The door closes behind us, leaving us amid the room solely lit by candlelight. The winter sun set on the way home, lazily disappearing on the horizon early enough that I'd hardly call the time of day the evening. In that moment, I yearned for the long summer days from another time with Luka.

"Help her into the pool," Nikolai says, staying at Luka's side.

I dig my fingers into Luka's shoulders. "No. Luka, please. I can't do it alone."

"Of course you're not alone, my lovely. Our whole family is here," Nikolai says, intervening in my pleas to Luka.

And I can feel them. Dozens of minds press against the block protecting me from them. I can feel each person as if we're connected. Maybe we are. Doesn't make me want to open my mind, to travel to the galaxy world, leaving me open. Not with Nikolai standing in waiting. He hasn't had an excuse before this—like Luka said, opening the door and entering is supposedly sacred. It feels less than sacred right now. It feels utterly wrong. Blasphemy.

It takes everything in me not to thrash in Luka's arms until he drops me, but I'm in enough pain as it is. Even if I somehow manage to drag myself away, there are dozens of people who would stop me. They'd blame my injuries for my sudden lapse in cooperation and force me into the ceremonial pool regardless of how much I fight.

"No, I can't," I say.

"Maybe we should give her time to heal." Something shifts in Luka's demeanor. He's gone from following Nikolai's instructions to freezing in place, gripping me tighter against him.

Nikolai touches Luka's shoulder. "There is no healing from the injuries she sustained. I don't want to prolong her misery."

A mercy killing—healing. It's what the Knezha Family does. Bond by acts against the living world, gaining power from the beyond. And with power comes opportunity. Nikolai won't pass it up. He's all power, controlling. He'll rule life and death before long. He'll decide who's fit for the Knezha Journey. All else will be the stars.

The door to the grand room opens again, cutting off anything more that he was going to say, and a silhouette saunters through the light. Flashes of a memory from my past dance through my head. I remember a distraught man with a gun screaming that he was going to save me. I remember Angelica falling to the ground after he accidentally pulled the trigger and killed her. I remember the panic in the man's eyes after he shot me when I fought back. I'll never forget the man's acceptance of his own death the second Nikolai turned the gun on him, the gunshot echoing through the air before the man died with me—though only I came back to be welcomed into the Knezha Family.

"I brought what you asked for, Nik," a familiar woman says, ripping me from one of my darkest memories.

"Thank you, Sienna," Nikolai says, reaching out to take a small vial from her hands.

I can almost taste the poison dripping down my throat. This wouldn't be the first time Sienna poisoned me, but I'd rather fight than submit to such a horrible way to go. I shouldn't even be here. I should've tried harder to run and make Luka go with me.

I tense in Luka's arms.

"You're scared."

I keep my eyes trained on Nikolai's silhouette as I mentally respond to Luka's thought by saying, *"Yes."* But it's not for the reasons I assume he thinks.

"You won't be alone. Nikolai will be there to support you," he thinks to me.

I was afraid of that. *"Luka, please. Don't let them do this to me. I just want to heal naturally."*

"Skye, you know it's not possible. You're dying already."

A dizzy spell washes over me, and I blink in and out of consciousness.

"Skye? Skye, can you hear me?"

I moan. "Luka, please. I can't do this."

A hot hand touches my forehead. "We must make her as comfortable as possible and hurry with her ascension into the stars. Such a traumatic death will wreak havoc on her for days. It's bad enough as it is lately. I'm afraid she won't recover if we let her journey from our world end naturally."

"No," I whisper. "Don't touch me." Nikolai's right about one thing. I am dying. I know it. I've died so many times that I can feel my body slowing, unable to keep up with my mind. It's getting harder to focus. I hate being out of control because while my body dies, my mind is more alive than ever.

"Calm down, my girl. You've been too hard on yourself. We can't risk more damage to your spirit." It's Nikolai's voice in my head this time. I couldn't keep him out.

God, I need to keep him out.

My breath quickens, my chest aching with every gasp. Panic seizes me, shaking the world around me. I'm afraid of what he'll do to me. What he'll do to my mind now that I've accidentally let him in.

This can't be happening.

"Get out!" I scream, wriggling in Luka's arms.

I catch Luka off guard, and he nearly loses me before sliding to the ground to stop me from pushing away from him. Chaos breaks out, and I summon my courage to fight against my soul mate as much as it kills me to do so. But it's something he'd want if he had any of his good senses left.

Swinging my arm out, I punch Luka in the jaw. Someone else grabs me from behind, dragging me off Luka. My voice rips through the air, the high tone deafening all other noise. It's almost as if I'm alone by how quiet everyone else is.

"I call upon the stars in the name of the Knezha Family to shine down on our beloved Skye in this moment of great peril. Please give her the courage to accept this blessing you've bestowed on her." Nikolai's voice sends a shiver through me, cutting my scream off. His commanding voice demands attention from the room, from even me, and I can't help but stop to listen to everything he has to say.

"Blessed the stars for this gift to Skye," a few people add.

There's nothing more I want to do than scream. But I don't. If I resist too much, Nikolai might intervene. His words are intended to bring me comfort. To remind me nothing is permanent, and I have the strength of the Knezha Family behind me. Behind his words lies his charm, his mind manipulation. He can't know whatever he did to me is slowly wearing off. That my spirit is realigning, and I'll soon be completely me again.

"I just want the pain to stop," I whisper.

"Then accept the strength of our family into you," Nikolai says. The strength that'll surely break me.

"I can't do this alone," I whisper.

"I'm here for you, my girl. We can go together," he says.

"I want you to stay in this life with my body. Make sure I come back. Please." The last thing I want is for him to ruin my galaxy world.

"Please, Nik. Stay." My words sound in my mind, pulling me away from the ceremonial room and back to a time I couldn't recall until this second.

"Of course, my dear. I'll protect you here. Just leave the door open for me." Nikolai's thoughts remind me of a moment from the basement when I died and Luka couldn't follow me into the galaxy world. It was when I learned I could open a door without going through. If only I could remember how to do it now.

"It's always open for you," I say.

The memory blurs, and I don't know what the reason was for me to touch death. All I know is that it was for Nikolai in a time that I trusted him, believed in the life he had given me. A life I was content with until something changed—I changed.

"I'll go with her," Luka says, pushing away the memory completely. "I'd be honored."

"But Luka—"

"I knew you'd always be a fine guardian, Luka," Nikolai says, cutting me off. Shadows cross his face as the candlelight flickers around us. He doesn't give any of his feelings away.

As much as I don't want Luka facing death under Nikolai's scrutiny, I'd much rather it be him crossing through the door rather than Nikolai.

"Thank you, Nik. You can trust her journey with me," Luka says, brushing his lips against my temple.

Nikolai hands me back to Luka, only letting me go when he's certain I won't fight Luka again to escape. I consider it, but what's the point? No one listens to my wishes, and I'm prolonging my agony longer than necessary—pain that at one time would have made me utterly incapable but now reminds me of my strength. Pain I've experienced so often I can work through it with my mind intact even when my body fails. If I get this over, I can retreat to my room and come up with another plan. A well thought out plan. Something the girl I used to be would be proud of. Because from my memories, I know my impulsivity is something new.

Luka holds me gently yet firmly to his chest and climbs the steps to the platform with the pool. He lowers us in together, the warm water easing the pain in my leg as I gain buoyancy. One by one, the candles snuff out, leaving us with only the waxing moon shining overhead through the glass ceiling.

"Blessed the stars, please guide Skye and Luka on their journeys. Instill in them the power to strengthen our family to ensure our eternity in this life," Nikolai says, his voice echoing through the air with such command that the stars will surely bow before him.

"Open your mouth, Skye," Luka thinks to me.

Something hard and cool—glass? A vial—touches my bottom lip. *"I'm not drinking the poison."*

"Poison? When have we ever been poisoned? It's a sedative to help."

"I've never had to take one to cross. Just do it."

"Skye..."

Before I have a chance to argue, the hum of some sort of machine sounds through the air. Fear rips through me, the already claustrophobic pool suddenly getting smaller as a cover slides toward us. Luka wraps his arms around me, pulling me under, and I realize what's happening.

"I just don't see another way around it. It's my duty, Luka." The sound of my own voice cutting through the air yanks me away from the infinite blackness. Another memory breaks free, giving me a reprieve from a moment I wish wasn't happening.

Luka touches my chin, raising my head to meet his dark brown eyes. Sun haloes over the ocean behind him as we sit on a concrete bench on a familiar beach near his house before we ran. The salty sea breeze swirls around me, lifting the blond hair from my neck.

"Aren't you scared that maybe you won't come back?" he asks. "I don't know what it was like for you, but dying was the scariest moment of my life."

"If I don't come back, then it means my journey in this life has ended, and it's time to move on to the next. There's nothing scary about that," I say. "I'll be the stars."

"But what about me?" he asks.

I press my lips into a line. "I wish I didn't have to do it, but Nikolai needs me to. He counts on me. It's a dangerous world. The only way to survive is to expand our family."

Luka shades his eyes, looking away. "I count on you, too, you know."

I don't say anything as I think. I bet at the time I was surprised by his words, though I'm not now. Not as I'm watching a memory of us unfold. One that stirs excitement within me, hugging me to the goodness I so desperately need.

I smile. "Really?"

"Yeah," he says. "That's why I don't want you to go back there."

My smile quickly morphs into a frown. "What? I don't understand. You want me to abandon my family?"

It's his turn not to respond. "Would you? My mom wouldn't turn you away if I asked her if you could live with us. You wouldn't have to..." His words trail off, and I wonder how much he knows about the Knezha Family in this memory. How much I know. Because it feels like I'm ready to give Luka a million excuses not to leave.

A tear escapes from my eye, and I swipe it away. "You say it like it's so simple."

"It is."

"It's not."

The memory, one from what feels like so long ago, hugs me close, reminding me of one of the very first times I met Luka. Then, I still had it in my head that I was Skye Knezha, Nikolai's perfect gatekeeper, the perfect adopted daughter who wouldn't be influenced by the outside world—a world I still don't know, one that's supposedly dangerous and at war. A world I'm not a part of. My world was the Knezha Family—and then Luka...after that, when both those worlds imploded, I have no idea.

"Skye, come back to me." Luka's voice sounds from behind me, and I blink the memory of us away.

Stars dance around Luka, and I reach out and lace my fingers through his. "I had assumed that I chose to leave the Knezha Family on my own to protect you, but you asked me to leave them first," I say.

His brows crinkle together. "Yeah, because I didn't want to join them. But you turned me down at first."

"I made you leave your mom," I say.

"That was Nikolai, Skye. We'd have never run if it weren't for him." I know Luka's right. Everything always comes back to Nikolai, the man playing a game with me like I'm a little doll.

"Because he wanted you," I say.

Luka shakes his head. "No, he wanted you. He knew he'd get me as long as he had you. But something changed, and you suddenly wanted nothing to do with the Knezha Family."

I nestle my head against his shoulder. "You changed me."

He shakes his head again. "It wasn't me. It was something else. Because of someone else. But you never told me who or what. Only that Nikolai betrayed you in the worst way and that you couldn't share the same journey with him any longer. You promised that once you had prepared me, we'd start a new one together with a new family."

A new family? I wonder if he means Avery and Gemma—the couple from the beach, maybe. I wish I remembered.

The feelings from my memories tell me something different than what Luka's telling me now, but it doesn't mean what he's saying is untrue. Each facet of my life is like a stone on the path I follow on my journey in this life. Nikolai and the rest of the family each work together to follow the same path, but something must have happened to my stone. It turned to point me in a new direction. Luka's stone fell into place next to mine. Avery and Gemma's, too. All of our lives were veering away from Nikolai Knezha, the man who thinks he's fit to guide us. And he might guide us but in the wrong direction than what my instincts tell me.

"What I don't understand is how Sienna and Avery play in this game of Nikolai's. Gemma, either. She's still in the basement, Luka. I know where to find her. If I can get to her, I can break Nikolai's hold. I know it. It only takes one flaw to collapse his masterpiece."

"Is she worth it?" Luka asks. "Don't you remember how awful she was?"

I frown. "Luka, she's my friend. She tried to help me save you. That's how she ended up in the basement. I remember more and more from my life outside here apart from you."

He groans. "This can't be good. If I know Nikolai, I know he'll use it against us."

I nod. "I know, and I'm scared. He got into my head. Death weakens me to him, but it makes me stronger as well. I just—I need to figure out how to put all the versions of myself together. Something—maybe Nik—broke me into pieces and scattered me around. Until I can know everything for certain, I'm at risk of being pieced together improperly.

"He's going to try, and I think I'm helping him. He's using me to see you as you are. He knows I can get you to let your guard down," he says. "You have to stop it. You have to resist me. This isn't the basement anymore, Skye. Whatever I do outside the stars isn't for your benefit."

"This kills me, Luka. I'm afraid I'm not strong enough. I'm afraid I won't keep my memories straight for much longer. Avery showing up messed with my head. Your constant questions don't help, either."

"I've failed you, Skye," he says, his voice lowering.

I know in my soul Nikolai went to great lengths to arrange everything and steal my memory away. He continues to do so, testing me at every opportunity. And I'm losing. This is worse than the basement because I'm already at a disadvantage. And that plan I had, the one that involved sending Gemma and Avery here—the plan that had me turn myself over is long gone, and I think my old self forgot to create a backup plan.

I rub my hands across my cheeks. "No, I've failed everyone."

Luka holds me closer. "I won't stop trying to remember. I felt something shift in the forest, but the pain that came after was too much. It's like my love and this faith Nikolai instilled in my head is battling it out."

Realization settles into my mind. "Because love transcends faith."

"Huh?" Luka asks.

It's something Angelica mentioned to me long ago. She said that love would guide me on my journey, and it's my love that always leads me back to Luka, but what if my love could lead him away? What if it's what I need to fix what Nikolai had broken?

Love is the one thing the Knezha Family lacks.

"Luka, our connection is what returned part of my memory to me, and I think I can use it to help you, but I'm afraid I can't do it here with Nikolai. Every time I open my mind, he sneaks in. You sneak in. I need to get into yours."

"I'm always open to you," he says.

I shake my head. I hadn't known it until this second that he's not. It's always him asking me to open up to let him in. In the forest, I had asked the same of him, and it hurt him. It was like he wasn't capable of it.

"You're not," I say, sighing. "And I don't know how to make you. God, Luka. What do we do? I can't just keep acting like everything's okay. Nikolai notices when I'm not acting like his perfect girl. I'm afraid he'll mess with my mind, and I won't be able to fight him again like in the basement."

"Then run. Get away. You know it was our plan all along," he says.

"What about you? You won't remember any of this, and I can't just leave you. I can't make you go, either."

"I'll follow you," he says. "I always do."

As much as I want to argue, I can't. I don't want to mention that Luka will try to drag me back to the Knezha Family like the last time or that he'll lead Nikolai to me.

This is why I left him before. I know it. But how could I have? It hurts my soul thinking of it.

"Do it for him." The foreign thought sneaks into my essence, drawing my attention from Luka.

I push the feminine voice away. It shouldn't be able to reach me. Not here. I can't lose myself in strange thoughts. I need to block the world out.

"There has to be another way."

"There's not," the girl says again.

"Skye?" Luka questions. "What is it?"

Something stops me from telling him someone else accesses the galaxy world. "I will figure out another way," I say out loud in response to the thought, to myself, to Luka, too.

I'll have to figure out a way to make him remember so he doesn't follow me like a guardian under Nikolai's influence. Luka wasn't immersed as deeply as I was in the Knezha Family way of life. Even now, it's still ingrained deep within me. I love the galaxy. I can't deny the journey I'm on toward creating our perfect eternal life, but I don't imagine it with the Knezha Family. I see it with Luka, together as soul mates, forever.

"I know you will," he says.

"Now, you better listen to me and let me in."

A new intensity lights his eyes as he stares at me. Ever so slowly, he guides me closer until he brushes his lips against mine. Our souls light up through the glittering galaxy world, shining red through my closed eyelids.

Reluctantly pulling away, dreading my next words, I say,

"We need to get back before Nik realizes something is wrong."

He sighs. "I never thought I'd hear you say that."

Tears blur my eyes. "I know, but we made a promise to each other, right?"

"Right."

There's nothing I wouldn't give to stay here with Luka, to survive on the feelings of our souls colliding, but that'd be too easy. It goes against what I know we both wanted—a life in the world we were living in.

And I'm willing to fight, to do what I have to. Just like always.

Maybe this time, it'll be enough.

It has to be.

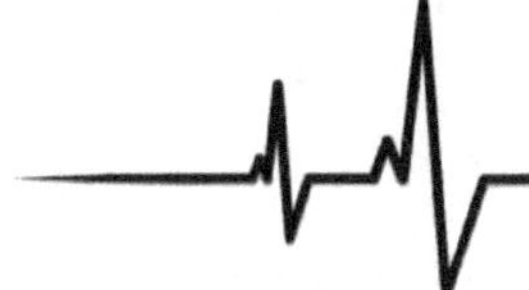

Chapter 8

COMPASSION FOR THE UNDESERVING

"*THAT'S IT, MY girl.*"

I snap my eyes open, the sound of Nikolai's voice intruding on my thoughts. A bright chandelier shines in my eyes, startling me. Bolting upright, I search my surroundings and fear snakes up my spine.

I've been relocated, dried off, and dressed. Soft music drifts through the air, and it takes everything in me not to scream. Because waking up in my own room without recollection of what happened after going to the galaxy confuses the hell out of me. It's like falling asleep in one place and waking up in another, but I'm not a child being moved to my room after falling asleep on the couch. No one should've relocated me. It throws me off balance and disorients me. Nikolai knew this. He purposely did this.

"Nik?" I ask, rubbing the heels of my hands into my eyes. I release a heavy sigh, because at least the pain of getting hit by a car is no longer radiating through me.

"Feeling better?" Nikolai asks, drawing my attention to the loveseat positioned in front of a glass coffee table in my sitting area. Beyond him lies my open window, still darkened by night, so at least I know not too much time has passed.

"Much," I say. "Is Luka...?" I know Luka's alive. I think I'd know otherwise, but I do want to know where he is and why he's not with me.

"Luka's fine, and you can see him in the morning. You both need your rest." Nikolai stands and glides across the room to my bedside. He waits for me to motion that it's okay for him to sit beside me. I only do it to be polite, because I feel awkward enough as it is. I should hate Nikolai. I should despise him. But part of me wants to hug him, to let him comfort me like he did in my memories of him. My gut tells me how awful he is, but my heart doesn't necessarily agree. I'm at war with myself, and my mind just didn't want anything to do with such a losing battle on both sides.

"I'm not tired," I say, slightly whining like a child.

Nikolai chuckles. "Good, because while you do need your rest, I have something I need you to do."

"It can't wait until tomorrow?"

"I'll let you decide if you're up to it," he says. I don't think

I'll ever be up for anything Nikolai asks of me, but even though he's pretending to give me a choice, I know it's not really one. Saying no to Nikolai is nearly impossible. Look where it got me.

I don't react or respond. He takes my silence as a cue to continue.

"We have potential family members in the guest quarters. I need you to visit with them. Feel them out."

"You can't do this?"

"I need you to convince them to stay."

"Oh."

We stare at each other for a long moment before he says, "Is that a problem?"

I whip my head back and forth, my hair flying around me with the movement. "Of course not, Nik. I'll go right now. Just let me get dressed."

Nikolai pats my shoulder, stands, and then leans down to kiss the top of my head. I don't move from the edge of my bed until he clicks the door closed behind him. Strolling across the room, I head to my wardrobe full of clothes I'm sure I loved at one point, but now? None of them feel like me. The only pants to wear are of the athletic variety, and Nikolai would mention something if I suddenly decided to wear track pants all the time. It's not proper clothing to meet with newcomers, and I'm too nervous to ask for jeans. For anything for that matter.

I run my fingers along the tops of the hangers of all the dresses, then the blouses and skirts. Heels sit in perfect rows on the shelves, and an array of jewelry hangs within a built-in, glass-fronted jewelry box.

I sigh and pull a silk shirt with pearl buttons off a hanger and pair it with a mid-calf pleated skirt. I refuse to look at the heels and decide to remain barefooted. Opening my jewelry box, I pick out a small sapphire KF brooch and nothing else, pinning it over my heart.

"Luka?" I ask, sending my thoughts out to hopefully find him. *"Are you awake?"*

The deafening silence of him shutting me out squeezes me, or maybe it's me who finally keeps him out.

I consider calling to him again but decide against it when I see a flash of light through the crack under my door. The guardians are doing a room check. They'll sweep the entire property after to make sure our family is safely tucked away for the rest of the night until our morning vows just after dawn and before breakfast.

Steeling myself, I pad across my white rug and wait at the door until the lights vanish. I peek into the empty hallway, not in the mood to stop and chat with the guardians who sometimes feel more like prison officers than family members, even if I don't have to follow the same rules as those just welcomed into our household.

Comforting silence greets me. Small nightlights offer me a path to follow as I make my way to the opposite end of the mansion where much smaller bedrooms keep people who want to join the Knezha Family. Outside the main estate, two dozen or so family homes create a small community within the compound. There is even a small dormitory for those who quit public school like I had to study under two teachers who've apparently been here since before my induction.

Soft voices hum through the air, and I hold my breath to listen through the door of one of the guest bedrooms.

"We'll ask for a ride to town tomorrow," a masculine voice says. I think it belongs to a guy only a few years older than me. Samuel? I think he prefers Sam.

Sam. The name prods at me, reminding me of a memory with Gemma from before. She asked me to return to the Knezha Family with her. She thought if I did, Nikolai would give Luka back to me, and we could create a new plan. I mentioned what would happen to Sam if I did. I'd have murdered him to turn him into another piece of Nikolai's army. He still hasn't been inducted after all this time because I wasn't here...but now? Oh, no.

Nikolai mentioned newcomers were having doubts and needed me to convince them to stay.

Another muffled voice sounds out, drawing my attention away from my thoughts. I can't make out what the other person is saying or who it is.

Straightening my shoulders, I knock, despite wanting to run back to my room.

"Oh, God. They bugged the room. He's never going to let us leave. Coming here was a huge mistake." The thought belongs to a woman—Deborah—who has been coming to Friday night dinners since I escaped the basement. It wasn't until last Friday that she decided to stay.

"Deborah? Sam? It's Skye. Can I talk to you?" I ask, pressing my ear to the door to listen to the whispers between them.

Their panicky thoughts are all over the place, giving me a headache, so I force them from my mind.

Their voices dissipate, and the door clicks and swings open. Only Sam stands on the threshold, blocking my view of the room. I recognize him from morning vows, but I never put much thought into him before. He hasn't said a single word to me once, and I wonder if past me has done something to him.

His gaze sweeps the dark hallway behind me. "Hey, is everything all right?"

I stand on my tiptoes to try to peer over his head, but I can't see anything. "Is Deborah in here?" It's against the rules for people to hang out together after midnight without permission or taking promising vows that are basically like marriage, but instead of pledging life to each other, they pledge their journey together.

He furrows his brows. "No, why would she be?"

"Because you're planning to leave," I whisper. "Don't worry. I won't say anything, but you have to let me in."

Sam's eyes widen, and he motions for me to step in. I look around the hallway once and enter his room, closing and locking the door behind me as if Nikolai or the guardians don't have a key to every lock on the estate.

Unlike my room, Sam's doesn't have a seating area. It's barely large enough for the queen-sized bed, dresser, chest, desk, and nightstand. A sheer curtained window, which faces east on the property, shows a glimpse of the solar lights that pepper the greenery of the vast landscape.

I don't see Deborah, but I know I heard her thoughts. I

doubt it came from another room, but maybe I was wrong.

"May I?" I ask, motioning to the desk chair.

Sam hesitates. "What will Nikolai do if he finds you here? I don't want to get in trouble."

I keep my face expressionless. If he were to find out that Nikolai sent me, then there would be no possible way to make him believe that I'm not the one out to get him. My sudden need to protect him overwhelms me—but not in a romantic way. My sudden need blossoms with thoughts of Gemma. She tried to help me with Luka, and now look where it left her. Look where it left Sam. "He won't."

He runs his hand through his cropped black hair and rubs the back of his neck. His Adam's apple bobs in his throat. I shift, now as uncomfortable as he probably is by my unannounced arrival. "Then why are you here?" he asks, flicking his gaze past me.

I take a deep breath. "Because I want to help you." I shift in the seat to face the closet. "And Deborah."

The closet door slowly creaks open and out steps a woman old enough to be my mother. Her hands tremble as she closes it behind her. When our eyes meet, hers glass over like tears will spill down her cheeks at any second. Sam crosses the small room to her and hugs her.

But not in a romantic way. It's the kind of hug you give a family member. A mother.

"Are you Sam's—"

Deborah shakes her head before I can finish my sentence, cutting me off. "Samuel's my nephew."

I stare between the two of them for some sort of resemblance, which I see in their eyes. Both a shade of brown I didn't know I liked until this second. It's light and bronzy unlike the chocolate depths of Luka's.

"And you've come to take him home? It's why you've been coming to Friday night dinner?" I ask even though I know it's the truth. Deborah wouldn't have been the first person to try to persuade someone to give up a chance at eternity with the Knezha Family. My first death resorted from the aftermath of a father unable to convince his daughter, who wasn't fated by the stars to become one of us. If it were easy, then the whole world would become a Knezha if Nikolai had a say in it.

She blinks the tears from her eyes. "It's not like that. Samuel called me. He asked me to get him. He wants to leave."

"It's true," Sam says. "After what happened with Gemma, I just don't know how I can be a part of this life and family."

Hearing her name on his lips ignites a mixture of emotions in me—relief and happiness, yet grief sneaks in my mind. Avery flipped out at the sound of Gemma's name, basically cursed her existence. And Luka? He didn't want to talk about her either. Nikolai messed with their heads in regards to Gemma. They both believe she abandoned the Knezha Family, which means she's been shunned, though I know it's more than that. Nikolai doesn't forget and let go.

But Sam? Nikolai couldn't get to Sam in the same way. He can tell him Gemma ran away all he wants, but the boy isn't a Knezha. His feelings for Gemma shine on his pouty face as he brings her up to me. *Love transcends faith.*

"You know what happened to Gemma?" I ask.

He tilts his head, frowning at me. "I'm surprised to hear you say her name. I thought it was forbidden to speak of those who turn away from the Knezha Family."

"Oh," I say. "I'm kind of a rule breaker." My hope dwindles, hearing him confirm that he was told Gemma was shunned. And there's nothing I can say to convince him otherwise. It's too risky. Nikolai assigned me a job to do, and like before, I have limited options. The last thing I want is to put Sam or his aunt in danger by helping them. It puts me in danger, too.

"Of course you are," Sam says, sarcasm lining his words. "Must be nice to get away with whatever you want. Leave and come back whenever without having to face the same consequences as everyone else."

I'm taken aback by the heat in his voice. He has no idea what I've been through. If I didn't think he would possibly use my secrets against me, I'd tell him how I've been manipulated. How Nikolai ruined everything I wanted. How I'm just as imprisoned here as he is. How we need to stick together and find Gemma. How we need to fight.

But I can't say any of that. Instead, I say, "And do you know why that is?"

"Because you're training as a guide," he says, rolling his eyes. "You're the key or whatever."

I shake my head. "No. It's because I believe in our eternity and believe I have control over my own with or without the Knezha Family." *Definitely without Nikolai Knezha,* I add silently to myself.

"She's like everyone else here, hon." Deborah touches Sam's shoulder, drawing his gaze from mine. *"Tomorrow might be too late to leave. God, help me. Please help us get away safely."*

"You know, you can leave at any time," I say, addressing her thoughts. We don't go around showing off our special abilities to the uninitiated, because those uncertain of the acquired are not ready to see, to know, what goes on outside of morning vows, Friday night dinners, and day-to-day activities. A person must see the stars themselves to experience a real Knezha Family gathering. "No one is holding you hostage. But you only get one chance. We don't accept those who can't commit to our faith undoubtedly." I'm such a liar, but I'm afraid to say anything otherwise. This is how the game works from the dozens of memories that flit through my mind as I tell those who decide to leave what they want to hear, using their doubt against them.

Deborah's hand flies to her mouth. "I've heard the whispers..."

"About what we have to offer once you commit to the Knezha Family and the stars?" I ask her telepathically. *"Because it's all true. We're not some cult. We're a family, and not everyone who wants to join can join."* If only everything were under different circumstances...

Sam looks back and forth in between us. "What's going on?"

Deborah ignores him and says, "Oh, my God."

It worked, like always. Her thoughts spin in a whirlwind through my mind, confirming that she wants to know more outside what Sam has told her and what she has seen.

"Auntie," Sam says. "What's wrong?"

I reach out and grab his hand. "I think it's best if you leave, Sam. Tonight. I'll get you out of here, and you can find Gemma." I don't know why I mention her, but I want nothing more than to keep Sam's doubt alive even if he can't truly leave. Because Nikolai would never allow it.

He bobs his head. "I do want to find her. I know she's waiting for me."

I frown and then force my lips to smile. "Maybe."

Deborah's lip quivers, and the second I meet her gaze, I know I got to her. Sam doesn't stand a chance. Because she's not going to want to leave. "No, wait." She reaches out and touches Sam's shoulder, a new expression softening the features of her face. "Maybe we can wait a few more days."

As much as it makes me want to throw up to play these kinds of mind games—how awful I feel for twisting Deborah's mind to go against Sam—I'm doing it to save Sam's life. Gemma isn't out in the real world. Sam would never make it. All I can do is try to push things out, keep them safe, and hope I figure out what I'm supposed to do.

"No, Auntie. We need to leave now," Sam says. "We need to find Gemma."

"We can't go after Gemma, yet." The memory yanks me away from Sam and Deborah, plopping me in the middle of a familiar room, though I don't know where I am.

"But she slid the block in place," I say, turning toward the familiar girl with dark hair and black eyes.

She places her hands on her hips. "And you know it'll keep her and the rest of us safe. That's what it's there for. She knew the importance. Do I need to remind you?"

I sigh. "Of course I know, but it doesn't make this easier. I just—" I groan into my hands.

"Would you feel better if I attended a Friday night dinner? He doesn't know me. I can sneak in and out," the girl says.

I thrash my head back and forth. "No way. I'm not losing you, too. I just—I'm failing. I'm taking too long."

"It's been long enough," Sam says, dragging me back from my memory. "She's not coming back to ask for forgiveness like I was hoping." He side-glances me. "Which I'm not sure they'd give."

Deborah releases a small whimper. "She'll return, and they'll forgive her."

I frown. "I'm sorry, Deborah. He's right. It's not how it works. This isn't some joke or game. Once you leave..." I let my voice trail off, though I want to say that once you leave, especially as an uninitiated, things get messy. There aren't realignments for people like Sam or Deborah. Not like they'd want such a fate.

She nods. "I know, and it's not to me. Not anymore."

"My family is important to me, and I'll not risk—"

Deborah drops to her knees and wraps her arms around my legs. Tears burst from her eyes, and she sobs so loudly I'm sure the stars can even hear her. Fear lines Sam's eyes, and he kneels down next to his aunt, patting her shoulder like he has no idea what else to do.

He looks up at me. "What have you done, Skye?"

"I haven't done anything," I say. Except manipulate the situation to protect them.

Deborah stifles her sobs with her hand, pulling herself together. "She showed me, Sam. She showed me what it means to be here. I want to stay."

Sam's eyes narrow. "That's crazy, Auntie. I called for your help, not for you to fall for these false ideologies. I told you what happened to my girlfriend." He scrambles to his feet, like the words that came from Deborah's mouth were the last things he expected.

And I feel bad. Because I've already gone further than I wanted to. I already feel like crap that I fulfilled Nikolai's want for me to get them to stay despite knowing deep down that they don't belong here.

I'm conflicted between doing what's right and what's right for me.

"Maybe you weren't meant to journey together," I say, swallowing the lump in my throat. "There's a reason people won't say her name."

Rushing to the door, he flings it open. "Her name is Gemma! Do you hear me Knezhas? She doesn't deserve your bullshit! It's Gemma!"

"Gemma!" My own scream rips through the air. The memory steals me away from Sam and Deborah, dropping me in front of a beat-up Toyota Camry with peeling window tint, damage to the front bumper, and a cracked windshield.

Someone hidden behind a ski mask blares the horn at me,

inching forward when I don't move out of the way. I press my hands to the hood of the black car, staring into the driver's strange eyes.

"I'm not letting you take her!" I yell, holding my ground. The driver can't reverse with the looming eucalyptus tree behind him. At least I think it's a man—broad shoulders, wide chest, a thick neck. His eyes narrow at me—one brown and one blue—a strange feature that digs into my mind.

The driver honks the horn again, motioning for me to move.

I don't. Instead, I stare at the figure in the backseat. *Gemma.*

Closing his eyes, he stiffens in his seat. The car lurches forward, ramming into my knees hard enough to knock me back. My screams rip through the air, the agony in my voice making me want the memory to end. I don't want to see what happens next.

Pain explodes in my lungs, and I suck in a sharp breath that refuses to give me the oxygen I need to breathe. A cloud of dust hazes my vision, and pieces of small rocks shoot at me from the tires as the man speeds over me, running over my leg in the process.

I scream again.

"Skye! Skye! Where are you?" Luka's voice cuts through the sound of my screams, tugging at my consciousness.

"I don't know but Gemma. You have to help her. She's been taken."

"Skye, calm down. You're having a nightmare."

But I'm not. I'm wide awake and in pain.

"Sam, stop!" The sound of Deborah yelling rips me from my own memory and drops me back in the present. Sam straddles my stomach, slamming me into the carpet hard enough to wind me. "Sam, let her go!"

The second I realize what's happening, my body reacts, and I swing my arm up and punch him in the nose. Sam hollers as blood splashes my face. He jerks back, giving me the opportunity I need to shove him off of me and onto the carpet.

"Skye!" Luka calls in my mind again.

I ignore him and scramble to my feet. "What were you thinking?" I ask Sam. "Violence isn't tolerated in our family. You have to—"

The door to the room swings open, smacking the wall. Luka enters first with Nikolai behind him, and they both pause to assess the situation. Sam pinches his bleeding nose with his shirt, and Deborah stands between us, tears of panic rimming her eyes.

"He's so sorry," she says, making me wince.

I hold my hand up to Luka before he can charge. "This is my fault. I lost control of the situation, but everything is okay. Right, Sam?"

Sam glances between me and Luka and then to Nikolai. "Right."

Deborah lets out a breath. "It was very nice of Skye to come out of her way to talk to us. I must admit I had my doubts, but I now realize how silly they were."

Nikolai turns his steely gaze to me. "Are you certain everything's okay, my girl?"

I nod. "It's fine, but I must admit to harming Sam. I accept any and all consequences."

Nikolai turns to Sam next. "You know, it's unlike Skye to react unprovoked. Is it true what she says?"

If Sam says yes, everyone will know he's lying. If he says no, I'm not sure what will happen. Guilt grips at my heart. I should've just let them leave and risked Nikolai realizing I'm not his little doll.

"Nik, please don't question my lapse in judgment," I say.

"Was it another episode?" Luka asks, cutting in. I'm surprised he does.

His quick thinking might have saved Sam from a fate I feared. "Yes. My mind is playing tricks on me, making me remember getting hit by a car."

Nikolai's hard eyes soften. "Oh, my dear. I feel at fault. This was too sudden. Your state of being is still fragile."

I nod. "I think I need some rest." I don't know what else to say or do. I'm not even sure Nikolai believes me. Death makes me stronger, not weaker, despite what kind of havoc it wreaks on my spirit.

Nikolai turns to Luka. "Would you mind escorting both Deborah and Skye back to their rooms? I need a minute of Sam's time."

I keep my face expressionless, though everything in me wants to scream for Sam to run. My blood pounds in my ears, the sound of him yelling Gemma's name still radiating through me. And the memory it stirred? It was terrifying. I have no idea what happened and who took Gemma, but it wasn't Nikolai or the Knezha Family. It was someone else. I only wish I could remember more.

Luka offers out his hand to me and motions for Deborah to exit. She pats Sam's shoulder, kisses his cheek, and then follows Luka's silent instructions. I don't move to follow. I can't find the willpower to leave, not unless Nikolai comes with me. I'm afraid of what he'll do the minute he glimpses inside the boy's mind.

I twist my hands together, releasing a long breath. "Actually, Nik, I was hoping you'd walk me back to my room." I can't shake the feeling of unease leaving Sam alone with Nikolai.

Nikolai smiles, and I know I've won. I haven't asked for Nikolai's guidance or company since I've arrived, and I'm sure he's noticed. We were close once. "Of course, my girl." He turns to Sam. "Luka will escort you to the infirmary to make sure your nose isn't broken. We'll talk later."

Sam nods and follows Luka out.

Nikolai waits for the others to disappear down the hall before he offers his arm for me to take.

If I wasn't worried about Nikolai doing something to Sam, I'd have agreed to go with Luka. I want nothing more than for Luka to take me back to my room. But I need to protect Sam. He knows things and refuses to accept that Gemma would abandon the Knezha Family. Doubt leaves him open to persuasion. His anger will fuel him to stay out of line, which I desperately need for Gemma's sake. For Luka and Avery, too. He might be the answer to my questions.

Nikolai guides me along without a word until we reach the foyer. He pauses, turns to face me, and rests his hands on my shoulders to make me look into his icy blue eyes. A blip of pain radiates from behind my eyes, and I can feel him trying to search my mind. It's almost as if he's taking a needle to a balloon in my skull, but the balloon is made out of thick rubber instead of latex, and instead of popping it, he's slowly releasing a tiny bit of air at a time.

I clench my jaw to hide the discomfort. "I think I can see myself the rest of the way."

"Is Samuel worth the consequences, Skye? I know he provoked you, and you were only defending yourself. Deborah's thoughts said it all," Nikolai says.

I knew I wouldn't be able to hide that fact from him, and I don't even care that he knows I tried anyway. "You're mistaken, Nik. I provoked him."

He laughs, like what I say is ridiculous. "You always have such compassion. Even for the undeserving. You know, if I didn't think Sam would be a good fit here, I'd have cast him out tonight for laying a hand on you."

"Nik..." My words trail off as I think of how to respond or if I even should. "Maybe we should just let him go. He's not as receptive as his au—"

Nikolai raises his brows. "His aunt? Of course that's the case and an easy fix. She must go."

My forehead crinkles. "What? But she wants to stay."

"Outside blood bonds ruin our familial bonds. Samuel's devotion will sway toward Deborah. If one doubts, the other will follow. I can't allow that kind of risk and devastation within our family."

"Then let Sam go so Deborah can stay," I say.

He shakes his head. "I need Samuel."

"Nik, be reasonable and give them a chance. Do you want the others to see you cast out someone who has done nothing wrong except come from the same blood? You'll cause fear in those already blood bound here."

He heaves a sigh. "Don't be ridiculous, my girl. Those circumstances are vastly different. Mother and child. Brother and sister. They came together. They accepted the stars together. They never doubted our journey together as a whole."

"And if they didn't?"

His jaw tightens. "They'd let me know so they could have their journeys readjusted."

"Like Avery?" I ask.

He doesn't respond.

"Like Gemma?" I just can't drop it. "Where is she? I know you better to know you would never give up on Gemma. She's family. This isn't like with—"

"You're out of line, Skye," Nikolai says. "I think it's best you return to your room to calm down and reassess your thoughts before you say something you might regret."

All I wanted to say is this isn't like what he's trying to do with Deborah. Maybe that's why I could never believe him about Gemma, about how she ran away. Because I know better. He's showed me that once you're a Knezha, you're always one.

Pain explodes behind my eyes, and I wince. He's trying to

get into my head again, and I refuse to let him.

"Nik, please," I say, nearly a whisper.

He glares at me for a second before stepping back. His shoulders slump and he huffs, "We can discuss this all tomorrow after morning vows."

I tilt my head to the side. "Really?"

He nods. "If it's that important to you, then yes. I don't want to fight. You just have to understand why I'm so cautious. I don't want our family getting hurt."

"They won't."

"That's all I can hope for," he says. Nikolai pulls me into a hug and kisses my forehead. "Now, you need to rest and meditate. Open up your mind and let the stars in. It will help you. I can help you if you'd like."

I slowly pull away. "I'm not a little girl anymore, Nik."

He hugs me once more. "You're right about that, aren't you? But still, you'll always be my beautiful girl.

I force my mouth to smile. "Always."

He releases a small breath, touches his fingers to my heart, and says, "Until tomorrow."

I can only nod and watch him stroll away.

A pit of dread sinks in my stomach when our gazes lock as he peers at me from over his shoulder. But I can't tell if it's because of me or the situation with Sam and Deborah. All I know is things are about to get worse if I don't try to fight. If I don't do something more than try to remember.

I'm not the old me. I can't stay quiet anymore. I'm not sure if anyone will listen, even if I yell and scream. I guess I'll have to wait and see who's more powerful. Me or Nikolai.

Hopefully me.

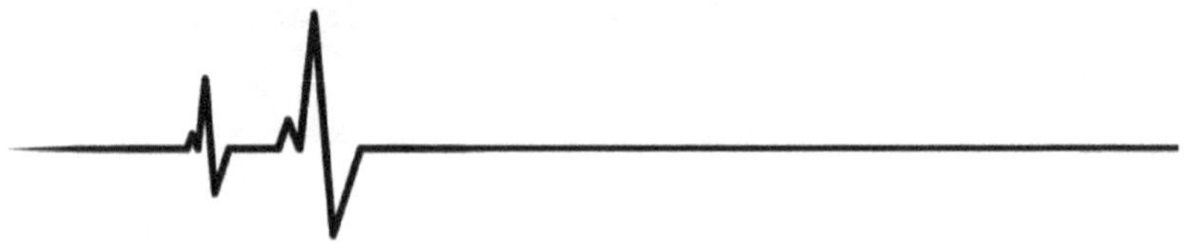

Chapter 9

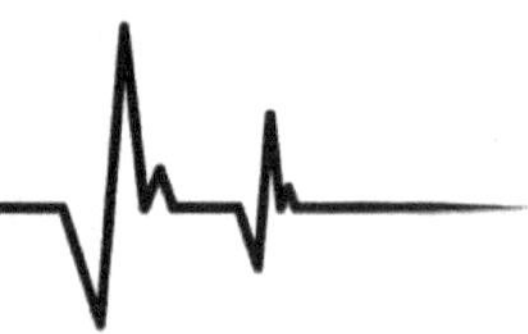

BREAK HIM

I SIT ON the edge of Luka's bed in his dark room. I shouldn't be in here because it's against the rules, but I didn't want to be alone after my confrontation with Nikolai.

Staying away from Luka should be my goal, but under Nikolai Knezha's influence, I need to be with someone familiar, someone connected to me, someone in my past who isn't toxic, despite what Luka might be to me now.

Unlike my suite, Luka's resembles one of the guest bedrooms. He doesn't have a personal bathroom or a sitting area, but he has a window seat and enough room for a bookshelf, which is full of a variety of things from journals to hardbacks. I've never paid much attention to them, though. I can't risk losing the fragile line of my sanity I hold onto. The material items and trinkets belonging to Luka contain a fantasy life tailored to me.

Nikolai found me as an empty shell to fill up, and it's too easy to believe things I can't remember. Like the photo Luka has on his night table of us together supposedly from the weeks before I ended up in the basement.

The possibility that they could be real and everything my mind is creating is wrong does nothing but smash me piece by piece.

But the logs for Luka in the basement said a year.

I'm regaining memories Nikolai couldn't have possibly altered during that time...I think.

"Remember, Skye." A familiar, feminine voice trickles into my mind, and I stiffen.

Maybe I am confused.

Maybe I am experiencing things that never happened.

What if Nikolai was right?

Shaking the foreign thought from my head, I whip my hair against my face and cover my eyes.

"My name is Skye Kne—" I groan and tap my hands to my temple. "Stone. My name is Skye Stone. I'm seventeen years old and from Los Angeles, California." Oh, crap.

My name is Skye Stone.

Skye Stone.

"Luka?" I ask, sending out my thought. *"Luka, can you hear*

me?"

I shouldn't open up the telepathic line. I know better. But the confrontation with Nikolai got to me. Falling into line, doing what he asked, risking both Sam and Deborah felt all too familiar. I hate it.

I need a good familiar.

After a few more minutes without Luka, I climb into his bed and bury myself under his blankets. He should've been back by now, and because he's not, I'm worried. The estate is big, but not big enough for it to take him more than fifteen minutes to walk Sam to the infirmary.

"Luka?" I ask again. *"Where are you?"*

"Where are you?" he thinks back to me.

I release a breath into his lavender-scented pillow. *"I'm in your room waiting for you."*

Five minutes later, Luka's bedroom door clicks open, and he peers around the room until he finds me on his bed. Looking over his shoulder once, he enters and flicks the lock over. The only light comes from the moon and the solar lights outside his window, creating a veil of shadows across him.

My heart picks up pace, and I clutch the sheets in my hands, gazing at him.

We don't speak as he crosses the room to me. Something feels different between us since our last visit to the galaxy world. It's a good different, one that burns through me, destroying all the negativity left behind by Nikolai. Like everything we've been through has pushed us closer together even if there is a vast space created by Nikolai to keep us apart.

"I wanted so badly to come to you sooner," he says, his voice nearly a whisper. "It should've been me making sure you were okay when you came back from the stars. Not Nik."

Closing the distance, Luka sits on the edge of his bed and leans down to kiss me. He runs his fingers through my blond hair and rests on his elbow to hover over me. I remain on his pillow, my hair spilling around my head, and he smiles down at me.

All words bury away in my throat with his soft breath on my lips. My body reacts, tingles rushing from my stomach to my heart, and my guard crumbles. It's almost as if the Luka, who is in front of me, is the same boy from the galaxy, the same boy from the basement, from the cabin. It's like all these versions of Luka have finally come together to complete the boy who is my soul mate. Something about his brooding intensity, the hatred lined in the way he says Nikolai's name, everything in this moment tugs me closer to Luka.

I never knew how badly I needed this closeness until this second, because a deep ache inside me grows at just the thought of any sort of space between us. My soul can't handle being apart from him.

I kiss him harder, like our lips brushing together can somehow crack the locks that have imprisoned us. Like the kiss we share is the answer to every question burning deep within me, waiting to be snuffed out before my world is set ablaze.

Shifting the blankets around me, I pull Luka on top of me. One of his legs rests between mine, but he doesn't put his full weight on me. His mouth wanders from my lips to explore the sensitive skin on my neck.

His fingers move from my hair and to my shoulder while mine slide up his untucked dress shirt to glide across the heat of his skin in search of the heartbeats inked into the taut skin of his back. He pushes down the sleeve of my nightgown and kisses my bare skin, trailing his lips in such a way that makes me gasp and hug him closer. With the heat of his breath, the way his fingers explore my curves with gentle intensity, I can almost forget everything that has happened tonight. That has happened the last few weeks. The world doesn't feel so wrong just feeling things for Luka I had forgotten about.

I run my hands back down to the hem of his shirt. After tugging it over his head, I trace my fingers along the sinewy muscles of his broad shoulders and to his chest. If I hold my breath, I can hear the sound of his heart beating for me. The quick thrums pulsing in a rhythmic melody better than my favorite music, because we're alive, just being together, like how we should be. How we were meant to be.

"I've missed you," Luka whispers in my ear.

I breathe into the crook of his neck. "You can't miss me when I'm here."

His hands trail over my bare legs where my nightgown hikes up to my thighs, and he slowly tugs it higher to touch the flawless skin of my hips, moving to my stomach, grazing over spots no longer scarred by the torment my body experienced in the basement.

"I know, it's—" He snaps his mouth closed, not finishing his sentence.

I stiffen. I can't help it. "It's what?"

He shakes his head. "It's nothing. Never mind." He tries to kiss me again, but I turn my head. "It's been a crazy day. I just want to be with you, okay?"

But it's not okay. I realize that nothing is okay, and this familiarity I've found in Luka still can't compete with all the other things clouding my mind. I can't use Luka as a distraction as much as I want to. I can't ignore that even though he feels like the boy I met, a part of him is missing. A part of me is missing. Kisses can't really heal and make everything better as much as I pray for them to. I can't even do that.

"Yeah, okay," I whisper.

Instead of letting my desire for Luka control me, I lean away from him and motion for him to lie next to me. He doesn't protest. He doesn't even complain. All he does is slide his arm under me to pull me close to him. I rest my cheek on his bare chest, running my index finger in small circles around his navel, trailing it up to the puckered scar of a bullet hole he swears never happened. Unlike my scars, Luka's remain a whisper of the truth no matter how he claims he got the scar.

"I'm sorry," I add, the silence growing between us but not awkward silence. Just silence. A silence that clears the fog in my mind.

"For what?"

"For failing you," I admit. "For not fighting harder."

He shifts me up so I have to look at him. "What are you talking about?"

I meet his dark eyes. "Nothing."

"Skye..." His brows furrow, confusion taking hold of him.

"What's the point? Telling you won't change anything."

"Change what?"

Instead of answering, I kiss him again. I kiss him with desperation, with frustration, with every bit of turmoil and hope and fear that rushes through my veins. I kiss him in hopes of remembering something more, anything that can help me to help him. To help us.

"Remember," I think, sending the thought to Luka in the process. *"Remember, or just make me forget. I can't do this anymore."*

Luka freezes mid-kiss and pulls away. His wide eyes speak a thousand unsaid words between us. "Skye, it's going to be okay."

Tears spill from my eyes, and I turn away from Luka. I'm tired of him telling me it's going to be okay when it's clearly not.

"It won't be," I argue. "Not until you remember."

"Skye," he says again, like saying my name over and over will make a difference.

"Just stop."

"Skye, I—"

I flip over and glare at him. "I said stop!"

He blinks a few times and slowly raises his hand to smear the tears across my cheek. "Just listen to me."

"I don't want to listen. I want you to remember!"

He chuckles, catching me off guard. "Stop being a pain and let me talk."

I freeze, my lip quivering. He sounds like the boy from the basement. "Luka? Do you..." I'm afraid to utter the words.

He nods. "I remember."

"The basement?"

He nods again. "Monster Sienna, Avery, and Gemma. Everything."

"Even when I shot—" I'm afraid if I recount the memory that led him to the basement I'll lose myself to the pain of it again.

He sits up and yanks me into his lap to hug me against him. "Like I've said before, it wasn't your fault."

"God, Luka. I don't understand. How? I was so scared you'd never remember again." More tears blur my eyes, and I hate myself for crying. I feel so vulnerable. Pathetic even. This is a moment I need to be strong.

"I know the feeling," he says, wiping more of my tears away with the pad of his thumb. And he does know. He's had to deal with me having no memory of him at all. "But I knew you'd figure it out. You've cracked whatever block Nikolai put on my mind. I forgot what it was like to let you into my mind, but now that you're here, I know we're going to be okay. "

I sniffle, holding his face in my hands. "But how long will this last? I don't even know what I'm doing."

"I don't know," he whispers. "I can still feel him, Skye."

I groan. "We need to leave. Now. If I can get you out of here—"

He shakes his head. "Everything in me says not to, Skye."

"That's Nikolai." I hate to think it, but hearing Luka say

that his instincts tell him not to leave, might make getting him to follow me impossible. I'm afraid I'll have to fight Nikolai for control, but then what?

"Better to break him yourself than let Nikolai."

I squeeze my eyes shut, forcing the thought, one that sounds like my own but not, from my mind.

I don't reveal my worries to Luka. I don't think I have to. I can see the same fears in his eyes reflected back to me. We hold onto our fears for a moment, and then my lips find Luka's again, and I kiss him just like the first kiss we shared in the basement together, and like our first kiss when we ran away from Nikolai. It's another first kiss to remember, one I'll fight never to forget no matter how hard Nikolai tries, or how hard life tries. I dare the universe to try.

The sound of a door slamming pulls my attention away from Luka and his love that reminds me of when our souls collided the first time in the galaxy world. My body kicks into action before my mind, and I hop from the bed, rushing to crack his door open to hear the commotion in the hall.

It's the guardians.

"Take him to the assessment center." Nikolai's voice booms through the air, and I catch sight of him standing behind his wall of human shields.

My heart sinks into my stomach. He's instructing the guardians to take Sam. He's going against our agreement, against my wishes. I knew I couldn't trust Nikolai, and this proves it. But what now? I can't just go storming into the hallway to make him stop. If I make a scene, it'll reflect badly on me. Not to mention I'm breaking a rule just being in Luka's room.

Hands grab my shoulders and tug me back. Luka quickly closes and locks the door before anyone notices us through the commotion. He presses his index finger to his lips, holding me against him like I'll run away from him and into the chaos. But I'm far beyond acting irrationally. I'm beyond listening to my muddled instincts that seem to be off caliber.

"Intervening won't help Sam," Luka whispers.

Sam's yells sound through the thick door. He's fighting.

I press my face into Luka's bare shoulder. "I know you said that everything in you doesn't want to run, but we need to run, Luka. We're in over our heads. Nik is too powerful, and I'm afraid you're going to forget everything at any second. You have to trust me."

He holds me tighter. "I do, Skye. I'll pack a bag now. We'll buy whatever else we need in town."

Luka drags me with him to his closet and opens it to reveal his neatly hung wardrobe. Before he has a chance to pull any-thing off the hangers, someone knocks on the door. I rush into the closet, hide within the clothes the best I can, and partially shut the door.

My heartbeat pounds in my head when I meet Luka's gaze through the crack. Nikolai unlocks the door without warning and glances from Luka to his unmade bed. They share a silent conversation, and Luka grabs his shirt from the floor and shrugs back into it.

"Go pack your bag, Skye," he thinks to me. *"As soon as I'm*

done helping Nikolai, we're out of here. Meet me in the forest by the back gate."

"Be careful," I think to him. "And remember, you made a promise."

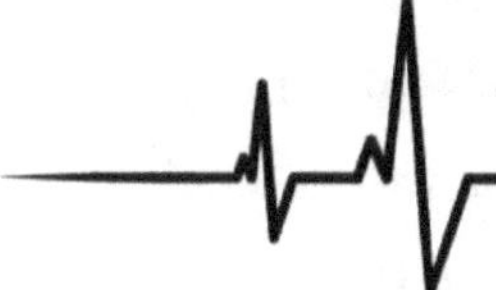

Chapter 10

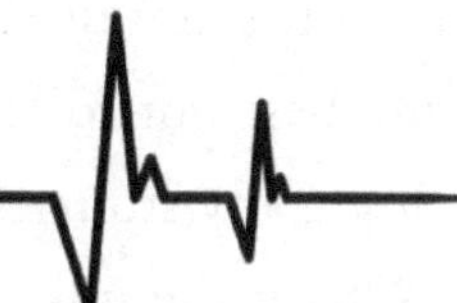

LIGHT BETWEEN TWO DARK PLACES

I PACE IN figure eights around the looming eucalyptus trees, their smooth yet flakey bark shining white in the setting moon. Thankfully, the soft dirt beneath my feet silences my footsteps, because if it didn't, someone would surely hear my anxious commotion. It's been an hour since Luka left me in his room. I'm afraid that whatever he has to do will mess up our window of opportunity to leave, and we'll have to wait another day.

Soon, people will rise for morning vows and notice my absence, especially if Luka's missing, too. We won't have enough time to get out of town before the guardians flood the area in full force to drag us back. If they do? I have no idea what'll happen. Nikolai will discover I know he's playing games. I might even end up back in the basement or worse. Locked forever in my room to be used as a tool at his discretion.

"Luka, you need to hurry," I say, thinking the thought to him.

"Hurry for what? I thought you were sleeping."

A small guttural noise escapes my mouth, and I grip the trunk of the closest eucalyptus tree. I squeeze my eyes shut, trying my best not to let my sudden, overwhelming despair make me sick as my stomach heaves. This can't be happening.

Why is the universe so cruel to tease me with hope? Have I done so wrong that this is my eternal punishment? Maybe the stars have realized I'm unworthy of my journey, unworthy of what they have given me, including Luka, that they strive to rip everything from me until I'm an empty shell obeying orders from a man who believes he will lead us to eternal prosperity in this life.

"Skye? Are you there? Answer me," Luka thinks to me.

But I don't want to answer. I want to blame him for breaking his promise to me, even though I know it's not his fault. It's mine. Whatever I did to bring back his memories just wasn't good enough. I'm not good enough.

"You'll never be good enough if you continue to hold so tightly to your grief, my girl. You know Angelica would've never wanted you to mourn her like this." Nikolai's voice drags me into a memory that leaves me wanting to curl up on the floor. It's the same feeling I had after I had accidentally shot Luka, but it's different. That one was also full of anger. The need for revenge.

Now, the memory is raw enough that I can barely breathe.

"It wasn't supposed to be this way. Why would the stars even allow for such a thing to occur, and on my birthday?" Tears cloud my vision, blurring my memory.

"Have you thought maybe the stars wanted to make room for greater things on your journey? Angelica knew you had filled up your journey with such devotion to her you didn't leave enough room for anyone else," Nikolai says.

I stiffen at his words, my grief turning into anger. "I have plenty of room, Nik."

"Then why push me away when I'm trying to help you?" he asks.

I shrug and turn away. "I—I don't know. I don't mean to. I'm just angry."

"And that's okay. You need to use it for something else instead of lashing out at those who will give their lives to see to it you're safe, Skye. You're so lucky to be surrounded by such a wonderful, loving family."

I sniffle. "I know. And I'm sorry. It sometimes feels like the stars have gone out and are suffocating me with darkness."

"That's because you're the light. You only see the dark because you shine so brightly. But the others, they see you. You are their beacon of light. You're the sun in our universe. Don't forget that." Nikolai grips my shoulder. "Understand?"

I nod. "Thank you, Nik."

Nikolai hugs me once, and I leave his office to gather myself in the hallway. A girl stands a few feet down, facing a water-color painting of the ocean on the wall. When she turns, surprise runs through me. It's Gemma.

She runs her fingers through her auburn hair and meets me with a stern expression. "Careful, Skye. You don't want Nik to question your devotion to the family."

I roll my eyes. "He has no reason to."

"You sure about that? I saw you leave through the back gate yesterday. Where were you going?" she asks.

"None of your business," I snap in a hushed whisper.

She leans closer. "You know, Nik's going to want to meet this mystery boy."

I clench my hands into fists. "Careful, Gemma. Don't think your fondness for Samuel has gone unnoticed."

She narrows her eyes. "Leave Sam out of it. He'll join our family soon enough."

I grab her hand and pull her farther from Nikolai's office. "He's going to ask you to leave with him."

Her eyes widen. "You listened to his thoughts?"

I lean even closer. "Hard not to when he basically screams them out loud."

She glances over her shoulder. "Think Nik knows?"

I shrug. "Possibly."

"Can you do something to help shield Sam?"

I shrug again. "Depends."

"On what?"

"I need something in return."

"Name it."

"I need you to help me leave."

"Skye? Why won't you answer me?" Luka's voice pulls me from the past and drops me in the present. I don't want to be in either place, but it seems my mind isn't giving me a choice. The memory of Gemma plays over and over again in my mind. Without having to know for sure, I can guess that whatever I asked her to do led her astray from the Knezha Family to join my side. Everyone's fates seem entangled in mine.

A soft thud echoes from behind me, and I turn to find Luka standing among the forest of trees. He stares at me, worry in his eyes. Crossing his arms over his chest, he waits for me to say something, to make the next move.

But I'm afraid even to blink. Because once I do, everything becomes utterly real, and I'll know for certain that I failed Luka once again. I failed Avery and Gemma, too. And now Sam.

Sam. I must find him.

"What are you doing out here?" I ask Luka.

"Looking for you," he says. His silent question about why I'm out here in the first place hangs in the air, but he doesn't ask it.

"I needed some air," I say.

He glances at the backpack near my feet. "You've packed a bag."

"I know. Where's yours?"

Luka stares at me, his dark eyes intently searching mine for answers I'm not willing to give. *"Skye?"*

"We were supposed to go to the beach for the sunrise, remember? Did you not see my note?" I ask, knowing well enough my

overly stuffed backpack contains too many things for a beach trip. But what am I supposed to say? I'm afraid of how he'll react if I tell him we were supposed to run.

"I'm sorry, Skye. I forgot. It's been a little crazy with Sam and Deborah," he says.

I knew about Sam, but his aunt? "What about Deborah?"

His brows knit together. "She was asked to leave and didn't take it so well."

I suck in a sharp breath. "I don't understand."

"She only came here to try to take Sam from us," he says.

No. This can't be happening. I knew that's why she came, but now that I ruined her, and Nikolai discovered the truth, panic seeps through me. "Is she gone?"

"She's packing her bag now," he says.

Dashing past Luka, I leave both him and my bag in the forest. I race across the vast lawns now lightening with the break of dawn. It's still dark enough to see the stars, though the sky morphs from dark blue to purple by the second. The solar lights will soon blink off, and the world will light with another day. Another morning with the Knezha Family. Another morning vows. Another day lost to Nikolai.

"Skye!" Luka's voice rings through the air.

I ignore his calls and run toward the side entrance to the mansion. It's the quickest way to get to the guest wing. Flinging the door open, I rush inside and ram into a solid body. We both crash to the floor, the girl screaming as she slams her back into the marble floor. I meet Avery's wide eyes. She clutches her chest, trying to catch her breath, and I roll off her and stare at the ceiling.

She groans. "What the hell, Skye?"

I pull myself together and sit up. "I'm sorry, Avery. I'm trying to catch Deborah before they take her away."

"I saw a guardian outside her door," she says. "She might not let you talk to her if they are even still there."

I don't have time to argue, so I push to my feet and head through the sunroom and to the hallway that leads to the guest quarters. It's empty. I'm too late.

A hand rests on my shoulder, and I turn to look at Avery. Her bottom lip puffs as she watches me in her peripheral vision. It's a friendly gesture, one I know I might've experienced with Avery dozens of times before, and it sends my heart sliding into my stomach. It's a different kind of familiarity than what I have with Luka, but familiar all the same.

"You're worried about her," she says.

I push my hair from my face. "She should be allowed to stay."

"She wasn't good for our family. She was trying to get to Sam. You know he's been so vulnerable since—that girl changed him."

"That girl's name is Gemma," I say

She scrunches her nose, her lips tilting into a sneer at the sound of Gemma's name coming from my mouth. "Don't say her name. She betrayed us all when she ran away, Skye."

"You really think that? Didn't I run away?"

"You were never planning to stay away long. I knew your plan. Nikolai allowed you to sway from our path to bring Luka in not be persuaded by the outside world to leave. She endangered us all."

"Skye, there you are," Luka says, coming up behind me. I swivel on my feet to face him and to stop him from distracting me with a hug. I can't get swept away on Avery's anger or Luka's love. I need to stay focused. I need to find Sam.

"You know where they're holding Sam?" I ask.

He holds his face expressionless.

"Please, Luka. I want to make sure he's okay because of Deborah," I say, pleading with my eyes.

"It's probably a good idea, you know, since the incident," Avery adds. She doesn't have to say it for me to know she's referring to Gemma.

"You can say her name," I snap. "It's Gemma, and she was our friend."

Luka nearly hisses for me to shut up, and the heated look he gives me is enough to make me take a step back. It's not the kind of look I'm familiar with on Luka toward me. He always saved that look for Nikolai.

I hold my hands up, blinking tears away. "Chill out, Luka. It's just a name." I turn to Avery. "Do you think we can talk later in my room?" I have an intense need to try to poke into her head next. Maybe I can make something stick that I couldn't with Luka. I so desperately need someone on my side.

"You have people on your side."

Avery beams me a smile, pulling my attention away from the voice now haunting me more and more. "I'd like that. I could use your guidance again since Nikolai realigned my journey."

I grimace while nodding, pulling Luka with me back toward the sunroom. Over my shoulder, I call, "I'll try my best to help you."

If only I can succeed.

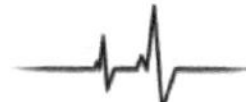

"Wait outside and warn me if someone's coming," I say to Luka.

He opens his mouth to protest, but I stop him with a wave of my hand.

"I'll be five minutes, okay? We'll have enough time to get to morning vows, and then you'll be taking me to the beach like you promised. We can have breakfast or something." Standing on my tiptoes, I kiss his cheek, hating that I've woven a lie to Luka to fit in this stupid supposedly perfect world. It's easier to explain he forgot he promised to take me to the beach than run away.

All he does is nod and watch me open the door.

Sam doesn't move from the metal chair in the middle of the stark, cell-like room. I click the door closed behind me, wishing there was a lock on the inside, but the door is meant to keep people in, not out, just like the prison it feels like. But a prison cell might be better. At least there'd be a cot or something to lie on. In here, you have the chair or floor. I wonder if this is the isolation therapy Avery mentioned, though I know she never actually went through it. Nikolai can't actually murder Sam over and over again to condition him into complying like he did us.

I shuffle closer, my bare feet squeaking on the pristine tile. "Sam?"

He still doesn't lift his head to acknowledge me. I don't blame him.

I close the distance and plop down on the floor, resting on my bent knees. He doesn't flinch or lash out when I slide my hands over his, holding his fingers in mine. "I know you don't want to hear this, but I'm here for you."

"Like you were here for me when Gemma left?" he asks.

I purse my lips. "Gemma didn't lea—"

"She could be halfway across the country now. I'll never find her. And now my aunt? You ruined that, too. She was going to help me find Gemma." He covers his face with his hands. "Now, what? Nikolai thinks I'm the bad guy. Skye, I just—Gemma is my world. That's something you should understand. Wouldn't you do anything for Luka?"

I swallow, the back of my throat burning with unshed tears. "I would," I whisper. Our souls are one. We're aligned.

"Then you can imagine how painful it is to me to have her gone. Like a piece of me is missing. It doesn't make sense. She used to talk about aligning our journeys. Vows. Everything. Then she abandoned me. I can't wrap my mind around what went wrong. I can't stay here without answers."

My chest clenches, hurting as much for him as me. "Gemma didn't run."

"What? How do you know?"

I squeeze my eyes shut, summoning the courage to break my façade to let Sam know that his instincts about Gemma are right. "She..." No matter how much I try, I still can't spit them out.

"You mean?" He yanks his hands away. If his chair wasn't bolted to the floor, I'm sure he'd push it back from me. "He did this, didn't he?"

I glance over my shoulder at the door. Grabbing Sam's hands again, I bring them to my chest and look into his light brown eyes. "You must never think those words. I need you to build a huge wall around yourself. Don't let anyone in. Not even me, okay?"

His lips disappear as he clenches his jaw. "That's the last thing Gemma said to me, but I don't understand."

Of course Sam doesn't understand. He has not touched the stars yet.

Reaching out, I press my fingers to his temples. He doesn't take his eyes away from mine, staring at me with a mixture of confusion and anger, but it's not aimed at me.

"Don't let anyone in your head," I repeat.

"I don't think I can," Avery says. Her voice pulls me away from Sam to drop me into a memory.

Gemma touches her fingers to her temple. "Imagine a wall."

I nod. "And build it block by block."

"Fill the cracks with steel," Gemma says.

Avery closes her eyes. "I think it's working."

"Now push me out," I think to her.

She squeezes her eyes shut. "Did it work?"

"Push everyone out," I think.

She gasps, pressing her hands to her temples. "Ouch!"

"Do it, Avery!"

She screams. "I can't."

"You have to. Do it! Block me out. Block me out, and the pain will stop."

She screams again.

"Skye, stop," Gemma says, grabbing my hand to pull me away from Avery.

"She needs to block me out. Everyone. We'll fail if she can't."

"She says it like I can control—" Sam's thoughts pull me from the memory of Gemma and Avery, and I remember the panic seeping through me until I finally managed to get Avery to build the shield to protect her. But I wasn't good enough. I still might not be.

"Sam, block me," I think to him, repeating exactly what I did with Avery.

He grimaces, groaning at the sudden pressure I create in his mind. "What the hell, Skye?"

"Block me."

He hollers, jerking back. *"Make it stop!"*

"Do it, Sam. Block me. Imagine a wall. Close yourself off."

"What's wrong with her?" he thinks about me.

"Sam. Block me."

"Skye, stop! I can't do what you want. Please, stop." Teardrops escape Sam's eyes to trickle onto his shirt.

"Block me."

His yell turns into a full blown scream.

"Block me!"

Sam slumps over, falling out of the chair and onto me. We crash to the floor together with his unconscious body on top of me. I huff, the air knocking from my lungs from the force. Stars sprinkle through my vision, a wave of dizziness washing over me.

The door to the room swings open, smacking against the wall. Luka rushes in, dragging Sam off me. He kneels next to me, running his hand over my temple and to my cheek. Something warm drips on my top lip, and he presses his sleeve to my nose.

"You're bleeding. What happened?"

I scramble to my knees, dripping blood from my nose onto the tiles. Sam lies unconscious next to us, blood seeping from his nose as well. Panic rushes through me, and I press my fingers to his throat, relief flooding over me at the thrum of his pulse against my fingers.

"Sam? Sam? Can you hear me?" I ask.

He doesn't respond.

"Sam?" I question telepathically, my eyes blurring at the effort.

Again, no response.

I think it worked. He shut me out. But at what cost? My head throbs, and I'm sure his does considering I knocked him unconscious. And now, Nikolai might know what I've done.

"Skye, come on," Luka says, grabbing me by the arm to tug me away from Sam and pull me to my feet. "We have to get out of here. If we're caught—"

"Let's go," I say, cutting him off.

I shift my gaze around the room, letting Luka pull me toward the door to leave Sam on the floor, bleeding. Luka locks the door behind us and drags me down the hall to another room that looks more like a medical office than anything, except there's a glass door leading to a walled-in patio.

I release a long breath outside, the cool air clouding my sigh. Luka spins me around and gently pins me against the concrete privacy wall just tall enough that I'll have to jump up or have Luka help me over.

"You drive me crazy, you know," he whispers into my ear, leaning in so close that he's pressed against me. "Testing your luck against trouble. What were you trying to do?"

I kiss him lightly before pushing him back enough that I don't feel trapped. "Nothing, really. I was trying to provide Sam with some guidance. Maybe trying to keep you alert to my kind of trouble to help you with your guardianship."

"I'll need all the help I can get," he says, kissing me again.

I suck in his bottom lip between my teeth, making him inhale a quick breath. "I think you're capable."

He smiles. "Yeah?"

"But I don't need a guardian."

"Nik thinks so."

"Of course he does."

"But he doesn't know you like I do," he whispers, leaning forward to rest his forehead against mine.

I smile against his lips. "And he never will if I have anything to do with it."

A loud bell rings through the air, announcing the coming morning vows. I want nothing more than to convince Luka to skip them, but I don't want Nikolai getting suspicious. He knows he broke his promise to me, and I'm sure he knows I'm aware of it by now. He wouldn't expect anything less than another confrontation.

And he's about to get one.

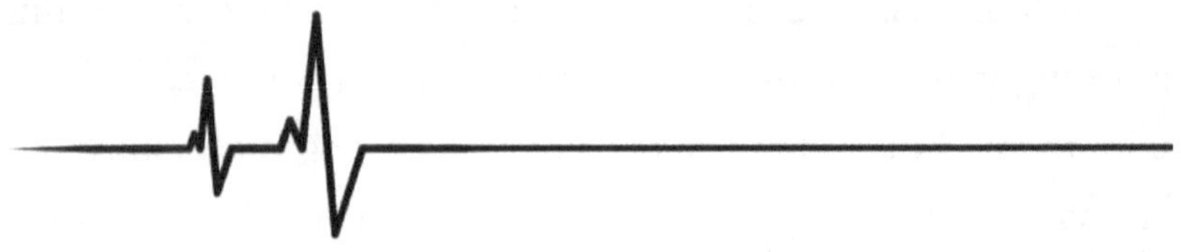

Chapter 11

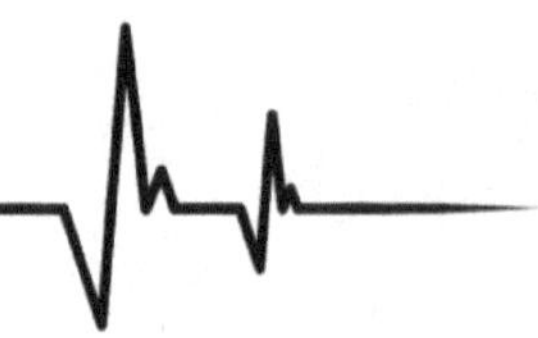

LOST

"GOOD MORNING, SKYE," a man by the name of Cedric says as I let Luka tug me toward the group of people ready for morning vows. They're a few minutes early but already in the circular formation, anxiously waiting to start the day.

"Good morning to you, too," I say, letting him kiss my cheek. He greets Luka next, and the others all smile and wave if they're too far away, and if close, they hug or kiss my cheeks, some just offering a simple pat on the back or a touch to my heart.

Goosebumps prickle over my skin. I wish I had thought to

grab a sweater to pull over my blouse. It doesn't help that I didn't stop for shoes either, and the dewy grass is frosted over in the early winter morning air.

Luka notices me shiver and shrugs out of his coat to drape it around my shoulders. "I can grab you your shoes," he says, looking me up and down like he's taking in my appearance for the first time this morning.

"I can do it," I say. "Have Nik start without me."

Before I have a chance to turn back toward the house to take my time in getting into something more cold weather appropriate, a throbbing sensation shadows my vision. Someone's trying to get into my head.

I carefully let my guard down enough to hear Nikolai say, *"Skye, my girl. I need you to take over today's morning vows for me and then meet me in my office when you're through."*

I frown, wishing with everything in me that I could run back inside and not have to do this. *"Okay, Nik."* Being invited into his office sends my mind whirling. I haven't been in there since my memory told me about getting access to the basement in the only place in the mansion I don't have complete access to. Only Nik has a key to his office, which no one is allowed in uninvited.

I had planned on confronting him more about Sam. I had planned to try to persuade him to keep Deborah around for his sake. But now? He'll know I'm up to something with how I left Sam. I have no idea what I'll do. I need to comply with whatever it is he wants so I can figure out how to find Gemma. I feel like if I can find her, she'll tell me what I need to know. She'll confirm my truths. Seeing the basement will cement my questionable reality. And then, I might be able to fully escape.

"We can have breakfast together."

"I'd like that," I respond, trying to keep my mind from racing at the thought. He found Sam for sure. There is no other reason for him to want a meeting. What if this is it? He could lock me back in the basement. Play with my head some more. Hurt Luka. I can't stand the uncertainty. I can't stand not being in control and feeling like I've failed everyone I love.

The pain in my head disappears with a few blinks. Standing in a completed circle, the others watch me with smiles, almost like I deserve their special attention. I push away the annoyance threatening to have me cancel morning vows, but I wouldn't dare. Not now. Not if I have to face Nikolai right after.

Luka touches my shoulder, slowing my racing heart. "You better hurry if you want to make it back in time."

I sigh. "I'll survive. Nik asked me to take over the vows this morning."

"What an honor for us, Skye," Cedric says from his spot, clearly not ashamed he was listening in on my conversation with Luka. *A family without secrets remains strong...*

I force myself to smile at the older guardian. "Indeed it is." Ugh. I sound like Nikolai.

Offering one hand to Luka and the other to Cedric, I enter the circle mostly filled with those unwaveringly devoted to the Knezha Family and those who want to join.

"Why doesn't everyone join us for morning vows?" My

own question pulls my attention away from the circle of people and to a past from long ago, where Angelica was still alive, right after we moved into the Knezha Estate, and things were so much simpler.

Angelica squeezes my hand. "They do, just not always physically. You don't have to be present in the circle to be a part of it. Those Knezha Family members present are here to guide our newcomers onto the same path we journey, Skye. They need not only the spiritual assurance of our love and devotion for each other, but one of corporeal feel of our unity as well until they realize we're beyond flesh and blood in our family." That's why everyone's minds must remain open for vows.

From my spot in the circle, I gaze around at a few familiar faces. Nikolai leads the vows from the center of the circle, and I follow along with Angelica, suddenly gripped by sorrow at the memory of my lost guardian. What I wouldn't give to have Angelica back with me to ask her every question that travels through my mind, questions she always tried her best to answer no matter how obvious or sometimes stupid they may have been.

"Just beautiful." Before I have a chance to realize what's happening, I'm yanked from the memory of my first morning vows at the Knezha Estate and pulled into a hug by Cedric. I blink the tears from my eyes, caught up in the raw emotions consuming me. To my relief, even though my mind wandered to my past, a part of me continued on and completed the vows like I've rehearsed them a thousand times, and my mouth knew to go into autopilot.

The group disperses to head to the dining hall to join those not physically present for vows for breakfast. Luka hugs me from behind as I watch them leave without moving from my spot. He nuzzles his chin in the crook of my neck, breathing in a soft breath of the cold winter air around us.

"Where'd you go?" Luka asks, hugging me.

I turn in his arms to face him. "Was it that noticeable?"

"Just to me, but I'm the only one who can feel the shift in you when your mind decides to go elsewhere, and this time, it felt awful," he says.

"It wasn't the memory that was awful. It was realizing I'll never have another new one like it. I miss Angelica is all," I say.

His brows furrow. "Angelica? Who's that?" In the basement, Luka had no idea who Angelica was either, because I chose not to tell him about her for the sole reason that it was probably too painful a memory. But now? I'm not so sure. She was supposedly a big part of the Knezha Family. It's strange that Nikolai would leave her out of people's new memories.

I pull away and lace my fingers through his. "No one important now. Walk me to Nik's office?" If I don't change the subject, my mind might be too weak to stand a chance against Nikolai, and I need to be strong—not just for the others and Luka, but for myself.

"So no beach day?" he asks, strolling alongside me.

"I'll make it happen, but first I must have breakfast with Nik."

Luka's quiet the entire stroll back inside the mansion to Nikolai's office. I knock on the door, waiting for Nikolai to answer. He doesn't respond, so Luka motions for me to sit on the bench seat with him outside the office.

Shaking my head, I touch my hand to the door, gathering my courage to turn the knob. It twists open and surprise washes over me. He left his door open. I can't recall the last time he's done so, but never in the last few weeks. All I can do is thank the lucky stars and enter.

"Skye, what are you doing?" Luka asks.

"Waiting inside."

"But Nik's—"

"He invited me. It's fine. If you're too good to be a rule breaker with me, then you can wait here outside. I don't mind."

He follows me in with a sigh.

I close the door behind us and flick the lock into place like it could keep Nikolai out when he has a key. I don't care, though. I need time to hear him if he does come to interrupt my need to investigate. Luka hovers in front of the door, making the perfect shield if anyone were to enter.

Peering around, I take in the walls of built-in shelves, the KF emblem created from twisted metal hanging on the wall near the seating area, Nikolai's neat desk with a computer and phone, and...nothing else. There's no other door in here.

The access to the basement must be hidden. Maybe in the walls.

"Where would you put a button to a secret door if you had one?" I ask Luka, peering at him still standing in front of the door with his arms crossed.

"At my desk where I can easily access it." He says the words without much thought, not getting that I'm searching for something in Nikolai's office since I haven't done more than glance around.

"Seems too obvious," I say, heading to Nikolai's desk anyway.

Moving around it, I sit in his leather chair, rocking back and forth as I stare at the computer and phone. I wiggle the mouse, staring at the background picture of a group shot of the Knezha Family, my heart nearly faltering seeing my smiling face between Nikolai and Gemma. Unlike with Avery, he didn't try to erase her, which speaks volumes to me. If she were shunned, I'm sure Nikolai wouldn't keep this picture.

Glancing at the rest of the family, I notice Luka's not in the picture. Nikolai probably wasn't expecting me to go through his computer.

"Skye, really?" Luka whisper hisses at me.

I shrug. "I'm on a mission."

"Mission for what?"

"To find the door to the basement."

His brows furrow while he crosses the room to me, clearly thinking I'm having another episode. "We don't have a basement."

"We do," I argue.

"Skye—"

"I'm not doing this," I snap. "Believe me or don't, but the Knezha Family has a basement, and it's where Nikolai's keeping Gemma."

"This is about Gemma?"

"It's about—"

"You're wasting your time. He can't see the bigger picture. He's lost." The strangely familiar feminine voice trickles into my mind, sending nerves bunching in my stomach. The voice, while annoying, feels nothing like a Knezha as it sounds through my head. Instead of breaking down my guard, it's almost like it's always been here, quietly whispering to me like a shadow I couldn't see in the blinding light.

"About what?" Luka asks, pressing his palms to the top of Nikolai's desk.

I shake my head. "I'm wasting my time."

"Talking to me?" Hurt lines his words. "If you'd explain, I could—"

"Luka, please. Let me think. This is important that I—"

Luka smacks his hand on the desk, startling me, and a strange beep sounds through the air. We frown at each other and peer around the office. No secret door slides open from the bookcases or floor or anything.

"I don't understand," I say. "You heard that, right?" I glance up at Luka, who studies the row of windows that beam in light from outside.

Then I see it. One of the windows, hidden behind a heavy curtain, doesn't display the glow of sunlight like the others. Racing from the desk, I cross the room with Luka behind me and tug the curtain away, recoiling at the sight of a blue-painted door within a wall. It hides in plain sight. Had I looked out one of the other windows, I might have noticed the extension of the building. And the blue door freaks me the hell out.

"Oh, no," I say, bumping my back into Luka's chest. "No. No. No."

"No?" Nikolai says from behind me, and I spin around at the sound of his voice. "Well, why not?"

The memory rushes over me in a hot wave, stealing my breath while snatching me away from Luka. "It's your space. I don't want to intrude."

"My beautiful girl, it's our space now. I know you've been having trouble concentrating lately, which makes you sloppy, so I figured you could use the space to practice. I've tailored it especially for you to work on your skills in a safe, private environment." What does that mean? If only I had asked in the moment. But I probably knew.

Panic seeps through my bones. What if the basement was mine? What if I was like Caretaker Sienna? I know I've done horrible things for Nikolai—I've killed for Nikolai—and I can't rule anything out.

I hate to think that could possibly be the truth, either. If it were the case, I deserve all that comes my way.

I slide one of my arms around Nikolai, half hugging him. My soul screams at the memory, though I know I'm smiling at Nikolai. I see my reflection in his silver pin on his lapel. "Thank you, Nik. I think you're right. I just worry what the others will think of me sometimes. Our purpose is clear to us, but you know how others can't necessarily see."

He kisses my forehead. "Never worry about judgment from our family."

"I wish everyone could see when they step into our home. I

sometimes wish you didn't allow outsiders. They would think I was a monster."

"The world they come from is riddled with demons. You, my beautiful girl, are an angel. They flock to you. Now, how about we explore?"

"I'd like that," I say.

He grins.

I touch my fingers to the door. "And Nik, the blue door's the perfect accent color for your office. I like it."

He chuckles. "I thought you might."

"Skye? Skye, come back to me. I heard—"

"And I was worried things have changed between us," Nikolai says, his thoughts intruding my mind, erupting pain behind my eyes. *"I'm happy to see you sneaking in here again. It's been weeks since I've caught you. I thought you decided your bedroom was more suitable for practicing."*

Spinning around, I face Nikolai with one of the kitchen staff pushing a cart into the office. He nods to the man, motioning him away, and watches him go. He wouldn't dare say anything in front of an employee. Very few people apart from the Knezha Family understand our way of life, but money buys compliance. Fear does, too.

"Nik, I'm sorry," Luka says before I can respond to Nikolai's thoughts. "The door was open, and Skye—"

"Is welcome to come in my office whenever she wants," Nikolai says, strutting forward. "Now, if you can excuse us, Luka. Skye and I need some privacy to discuss a few family matters."

Goosebumps prickle over my skin at his remark.

Luka kisses my temple and leaves when Nikolai shoos him away. I'd give anything to have Luka stay, but he wouldn't disobey Nikolai over something so trivial as me not wanting to eat breakfast alone with a man who I have no proof to show he had been messing with our heads. To Luka and the others, Nikolai is generous, loving, and almost godly. They can't see him as the false prophet that I do.

"My girl, I have all your favorites," Nikolai says, lifting one of the covers on the trays of food. He wheels the cart to the sitting area situated in the corner.

I remain near the blue door, crossing my arms. "Thanks, Nik, but I'm not very hungry."

He turns his head from the tray of food to look at me. "You're angry." It's not a question.

"Of course I'm angry." I'm more than angry. I'm terrified. "You promised we'd discuss Sam's situation before you acted."

Nikolai sighs and saunters to me. He wraps me in a hug and squeezes me against him, reminding me of hundreds of fatherly hugs he's given me before. Pulling back slightly, he forces me to peer into his icy blue eyes. They lack the cold, calculated expression I've seen in them nearly every day for weeks and are now filled with what feels a lot like compassion—an emotion I don't want to associate with Nikolai. I don't want to be reminded we've shared a lot of good memories, ones I can't deny. Ones I'm certain are as real as all the other ones breaking free in my mind.

"I'm sorry, Skye. I made the promise to you before I had

worked everything out. Putting you in such a position was an error in judgment. Had I known about Deborah's intentions, I'd have never gotten you involved," he says.

"But I am involved now," I argue. "And I think you're making a mistake. Please, you have to change your mind."

"Her soul is disjointed. She'll never be able to fully commit to our journey, and an uneven stone on our path would cause problems for everyone. It'd have an ill effect on Sam. He's been here for over a year, waiting for his time. I will not have an outside influence mess things up for him so close to his induction ceremony. We protect our family no matter what. You know this," he says.

I do. It's one of the first vows. But in Sam's case, it shouldn't apply. "But Nik, Sam doesn't want to be a part of our family."

He wags his head slightly, smiling. "That's where you're wrong. He was confused, but now he sees...thanks to you, my beautiful girl."

I tense, and Nikolai steps back to put space between us. "What do you mean?"

Tilting his head, he studies me. "I thought you could tell me."

I swallow, stepping back. My hand brushes the curtain concealing the blue door, and even now it stirs paralyzing dread within me. I don't know if it's because of Caretaker Sienna or because it's the door I saw that threw me from the basement and into the winter forest—either way, I want nothing more than to run out of here. Nothing good lies beyond that door.

But Gemma.

"Gemma is lost, Skye." Rubbing my hands over my eyes, I push the thought away.

"She's not lost," I say out loud, the sound of my voice echoing through the air. "She didn't run away. I know she's here. I'll find her."

"Find who?" Nikolai asks.

A string of curse words trickles through my mind, a mixture from my own thoughts and someone else's. "Gemma." My voice barely sounds above a whisper.

"What was that, Skye?"

"Gemma!" I scream. Swiveling sideways, I lock my hands onto the curtain covering the blue door and rip it down, rod and all. I swing it in Nikolai's direction, causing him to raise his hands up while stepping far enough back that I don't clobber him with it.

The blue door swings inward without me even touching it, sending panic through my very soul. I hold my breath, staring into pitch darkness, half expecting it to explode in a lightshow of stars from my familiar galaxy. The darkness doesn't change.

"Gemma," I say again, stepping forward.

A clammy hand grabs my arm. Jerking away, I stumble forward, and the ground drops out from under me. I scream, my voice cutting through the air, piercing my ears. Just when I don't think I'll ever stop falling, I land with a thud on something soft but still hard enough to wind me.

I groan, sitting up on my elbows. "Gemma?" I ask again. I can't stop her name coming from my mouth. "Gemma?"

"Skye, calm down. I'm here." Nikolai's voice intrudes my thoughts.

"Where?"

"Open your eyes."

Haze clouds my vision, and I blink through the light shining in my eyes. One second I was lying in pitch darkness and now I'm lying on my back in the middle of Nikolai's office. My head swims with dizziness, and my stomach heaves when I try to sit up.

"Careful, my beautiful girl. Don't let your mind get ahead of the rest of you," Nikolai says.

Huh?

"Yeah, Skye. That's how you nearly passed out the last time," Gemma says, bumping me with her shoulder.

Confusion washes over me as the memory unfolds. "Well, how am I supposed to train my body to keep up?"

"Push it to its limits," Nikolai says.

"I don't know what those are."

"Now's a great time to find out."

Pain erupts in my head, my eyes watering, and I scream. The world flashes from dark to light, my mind jumping between the past and present both under Nikolai's influence. Agony steals my breath away, and I cough, reaching for something, anything to hold onto.

Fingers wrap around mine. "Take a deep breath, Skye. It's all over."

Oh, no.

I'm no longer in the basement or Nikolai's office. I'm lying in my own bed with the comforter pulled up to my chin. "What happened?"

Nikolai squeezes my hand. "You were distraught. I did what I've always done for you. You needed my help."

A wave of ice drips through my veins. I have no idea how much time has passed—hours? Days? I can't be certain. But I should've expected it. I knew Nikolai would know something was wrong with me when he found Sam.

I rub the heels of my hands into my eyes. "I—"

"There's no time for talk, Skye. I need you to do me a favor."

Everything's happening so fast. It's hard keeping up. "Yeah, sure." I blink, trying to sort through my memories. *My name is Skye Knezha."* Something's wrong. *"Luka?"* He doesn't respond. I'm losing control.

"...you know how it goes, so Sam requested Deborah not be allowed to contact him anymore." Nikolai's words cut through my racing mind. I tuned him out and missed parts of what he was saying.

"What?" I ask.

"I need you to make sure that she doesn't contact Sam," he says. "Or can do anything to harm our journey by any means necessary. Understand?"

I swallow the dread tightening my throat, making it hard to breathe. I don't like what Nikolai's implying, but I'm also afraid to ask him to clarify what he expects from me. Because I know what he expects of me. This isn't the first time he asked me to guarantee a person never returned to the Knezha Estate or the first time he swore someone was a threat. And I've vowed always to protect the Knezhas.

Nikolai's testing me. I can't afford to fail. Not now. Not after the...the basement. I can't lose any more time. I also know I can't live like this anymore, always in a state of confusion, of memories, of trying to figure out what's real. Everything's getting to be too much. I had opened my mind to Nikolai in the basement for the same reason. Maybe I was right all along. Maybe life is easier if I just followed the journey Nikolai laid in front of me...

"It is not your journey."

"I—" I pause for a second, pushing the rogue thought away. "Can't someone else do it? I'm not feeling so well."

He scrunches his forehead. "There is no one else, my dear. I know it's a lot to ask, and a burden to carry, but I am here to help you. Like always. Okay?"

The sudden stern look he gives me, icy eyes so cold they burn my very soul, stops me from arguing or saying anything else. I just suck in my bottom lip to prevent it from quivering and nod my head.

"Okay," I whisper, turning away from him to lie on my side in bed. I just want him to leave my room. I want to lie down and try to grasp what's going on. What I have to do.

"And Skye?" Nikolai says, touching my shoulder.

I don't turn to face him. "Yes?"

"Luka may give you a ride, but you must confront Deborah alone. I'll be with you in spirit. You must keep your mind open. No more shutting me out."

"No more shutting you out," I repeat.

Because I can't shut him out if he's already in my head.

182

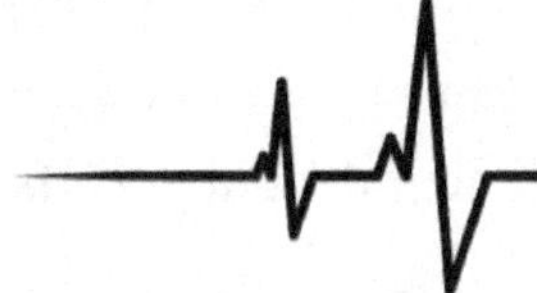

Chapter 12

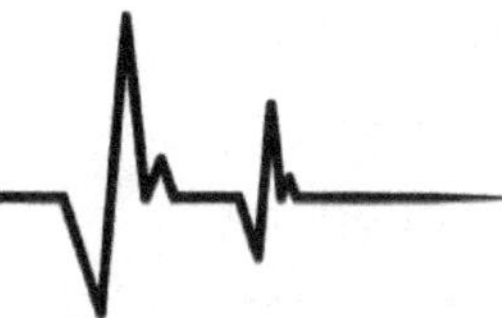

SOUL BOND

I SIT IN the front seat of an SUV, watching Luka pump gas. My mind spins circles, leaving me restless and confused. Angry. My head will burst at any second if I can't focus on something real, anything to keep me from losing my mind completely. I feel Nikolai's presence, and no matter what I do, I can't shake it.

"My name is Skye Kne—Stone," I say to myself. It's getting harder and harder to automatically say Stone. I have to concentrate on my last name to do so. If I don't, Knezha slips out, and the last thing I want is to be Skye Knezha. I'm not even sure I want to be Skye Stone. She's useless, too.

If only I could be Skye Nobody without having to worry about anything in the world. What I wouldn't give to face the real world I can't even remember. The only world I know is the Knezha Family and Luka. My memories refuse to take me beyond what's in front of me. I know there's a big, wide world beyond the compound, beyond the cabin in the woods, but I'm afraid I'll never know it or what it meant to me. Even in this car, sitting at the gas station, the world around me feels tainted. Corrupted. Nikolai owns this town and who knows what else.

Fury grips me, and I slam my fist against the dashboard. It does nothing to help the turmoil in my soul, and I'm not sure anything can. Shifting in the seat, I lean my head back and curl my knees to my chest. I hug myself.

Piece by piece, Nikolai chips away at my armor. How can it protect me if it has enough holes in it to be a sieve? What good am I? I can't fall apart. If I do, there is no one to put me back together again the way I need to be. Not even Luka. If I fall apart, I'll fall together perfectly for Nikolai.

"Skye? Let me in," Luka thinks to me through the door, pointing at the lock I must've hit.

I want to scream I already have let him in, but instead, I jab my finger into the button to open the door. Luka slides behind the wheel without saying anything. He closes the door and rests his hands on the steering wheel.

I can't take it. I need air. Thrusting my door open, I step out and peer around.

Looking at Luka hurts too much when I'm feeling so lost and out of options. He knew in the basement how much despair Nikolai brought in my life before we ran away. He knew how much it made me hate myself. But now? He's driving me to face Deborah to do Nikolai's bidding. Something I can't see getting out of unless I fight Luka and run away. And I can't do that, either. I bet he doesn't even care what I'm going through now. He'd probably tell me exactly what Nikolai did—that this is how we protect our family. But who will protect me from myself? Luka would if he could, but he can't. I can't.

Because if Nikolai wants something done, it gets done. I know this. I used to be okay with this. But whatever happened after I accidentally shot Luka changed me—maybe I was already changing before.

"Don't give Luka so much credit. You changed yourself."

"Why are you haunting me?" I ask, thinking back to the shadow of a voice.

The voice doesn't respond. I wouldn't doubt it's all in my head.

"Just unlock the door, get in, and leave. It's not that hard." I snap my eyes open to catch my reflection in the window of a car. The memory occurs so suddenly that I startle myself. And something's different about this memory. It's hazy, like I'm peering through fog. Instead of feeling connected, like watching a movie through my own eyes, I feel like I'm standing next to myself to witness the memory unfold. "This is what Luka would want."

Snowflakes dance in front of me, sticking to the metal roof. The sugar pines glisten in the haze, like they've been dusted with glitter.

As for my reflection, I look more like the me I remember seeing in the glasses of Caretaker Sienna in the basement. My steely eyes line with worry, but they also contain a darkness unlike the memories from my past with Luka in the cabin or with Angelica in the apartment we shared.

"This is how it has to be. You know if Nikolai forces you back like this, it'll all be over. He'll steal away everything good in you," I say to myself. "He will destroy everything you want from this life. You can't let him use you anymore. He is not who he claims to be. He turned you into a monster. You have to do this, Skye. You have to. He took Luka. He took Gemma and Avery. He will come for you next. He will break into your mind and see who you've left him for, who you refused to return for. You can't let him hurt them." Them? I want so badly to know who I care for so much to have to argue with myself over the right thing to do.

I shove the key into the lock and open the car door. The fog follows me into the car, blurring the rearview mirror and my reflection. I grip the steering wheel, sucking in deep breaths to settle my nerves. It doesn't work.

So I scream.

My wail cuts through the thick silence of the memory, slicing through the fog hazing everything until the world around me clears. Like the wind blowing away the clouds, my sudden outburst rips the veil free, and I remember exactly what happened that day. It was the day I decided to give everything up and return to Nikolai Knezha for Luka. But I wasn't letting Nikolai near my very essence. It was the day I thought I'd make it out unscathed. The day I thought I could beat Nikolai at his mind games.

"Nikolai can't steal what he can't find!" I scream to myself, staring at my gray eyes in my reflection. "He can't. You won't allow him to. Luka would agree with you. He'd want you to do this. He'd rather you forget about him to protect the others than remember him and lose everything."

Hearing my words out loud sets off a wave of emotion through me. I thought Nikolai had erased my memories when I died from head trauma or that my mind gave me a clean slate to deal with what I was going through, but now, I realize it was me all along. No one messed with my head. I did something to myself to wipe away everything I had ever known. I put a block on my own memories. The year missing between Luka being shot and me waking up in the basement, I protected them the most. I'm not even sure they'll ever return. But why? Who was I protecting?

"*Skye?*" Luka's voice cuts through the memory, but it doesn't disappear. I cling to it like it's a life raft in an unforgivable storming sea, threatening to drown me.

"Just do it," I say to myself in the memory. "It has to be this way. The stars showed it. Luka would want you to be brave. Do it! Don't let him steal from you anymore. One mind to save many. You are that one mind, Skye. One soul. Don't let him destroy you. Don't let him control you. Do it now!"

My head spins, the world shifting and moving, blurring, and then disappearing. A shudder runs through me, starting from my toes before crawling up to my head to dig into my mind. Heat rushes over me, followed by ice, and my heartbeat thuds in my ears.

"Skye!" Luka's voice rings over the sound of my screams, pulling me from the darkness and into his arms.

He holds me against him, cradling my body to his like I'll somehow float away if he doesn't. Moaning, I sag against him, and we both sink against the backseat. Luka must've dragged me back into the car. The world spins for a minute longer, and my stomach heaves a few times trying to rid the last thing I ate.

"Luka," I whisper, my throat suddenly dry as the memory still warps my mind, like it might try to reset itself again. Maybe that's what I need. If I forget, I can restart Nikolai's game. It won't be over. "I—"

"What was that?" Luka asks, interrupting me. His fingers lock around mine, pulling my hands up to touch his temples. "You've never done that to me before."

I blink a few times, trying to push the fog from my head. "What do you mean?"

"You projected something into my mind, and I couldn't stop you. The darkness—"

"That's my truth, Luka," I say.

"I don't understand."

"I'm made of darkness. It's what Nikolai has done to me."

Luka frowns, cupping my face. "That's not all I saw, Skye. Yes, I saw darkness, but I also saw light. It felt incredible. Everything felt so clear. I could remem—" He presses his lips together.

I stare at his dark gaze, trying to peer beyond his intensity to see what he saw. Feel what he felt. "You remember?"

His eyes glass over, and he blinks. "I—what was I saying?"

Groaning, I bury my face in his chest. "Nothing."

"Come on, Skye. Please, you can talk to me."

I raise my finger and press it to his mouth. "I wish I could, but..."

His jaw tightens, something shifting in his gaze. From my memories, I know I used to be able to read him. I could tell what he was thinking without even having to glimpse into his mind. But now? Nothing. I don't recognize him half the time.

"Nikolai won't let you," he says, catching me off guard with the heat lacing his words. He doesn't want to bring up what Nikolai asked of me. His hesitation gives me enough hope to pull myself together long enough to ease away from Luka.

"I wish I didn't have to—"

He clears his throat and thinks, *I hate it. I wish you didn't have to, either. If I could, I'd do it myself.*

"I'd never ask you to carry that kind of guilt."

"Always protecting me. Maybe you should let me do the same."

"Then don't take me. Let's just drive and never stop."

He groans, rubbing his hands on his temples. "I can't, Skye. It's not what you want. But I'll help you through this. I'm your guardian. It's what I'm for."

He's not my guardian. He's my soul mate. If only he could see it. If only I didn't fail him. Fail us. I gave up my mind and all our memories, and for what? Supposedly to protect whatever world I have—had—outside the Knezha Family. But it's not good enough for me anymore. I want things to return to something I can deal with.

And I can deal. I have to. Maybe if I can accept that this is how my life is supposed to be, I can finally be free.

I sigh. "I know. I just—let's go and get this over with."

"You're going to be okay, Skye," Luka says.

"He's right." I push the whisper of a thought away.

I need more than empty hope. I need the light Luka mentioned seeing in my mind. I need clarity. Without those things, I'm afraid I'll never be Skye Stone again.

In this moment, I can't even remember who she was. Who she is.

Right now, I'm Skye Knezha. Skye Stone died at the hands of a monster.

She died at the hands of me.

As for Skye Knezha. She's ready to live. She's ready to do whatever it takes.

⎯⅄⎯

The silence surrounding the rundown motel burns my ears. It's the type of quiet that sends fear trickling down my back and leaves the hair on my arms standing on end. The type of silence found after a brutal death.

"Skye?" Luka asks, his voice cutting through the silence. He startles me, causing me to jump. "I can come with you."

I stop in my tracks, one boot already on the concrete stairs leading up to the second level of the building. "I'd rather you didn't."

"Why?"

"Because I need to protect you," I say.

"Protect me? I can protect myself from anything Deborah does."

I release a shuddering breath. "Not from her. From me."

Standing here, preparing for a confrontation I want nothing to do with, breaks free memories from my past I try so hard to forget. Glimpses of unfamiliar people flash through my mind, and I concentrate on pushing them away.

Screams rip through the air, making me wince, and it takes everything in me to remind myself that the screams aren't real. If only this whole situation wasn't real either.

"Nikolai Knezha really messed you up." I peer at the space next to me at the sound of the feminine voice. "I can help you, you know."

The strangely familiar girl places her hands on her hips, glancing at me up and down. Her dark eyes don't hold the same intensity I find in Luka's but they're mesmerizing all the same.

"Why would you want to do that?" I ask, crossing my arms.

"Because that's what family does. True family."

I scrunch my nose. "My blood family abandoned me. The Knezha's are my true family."

"You're not a Knezha. No one but Nikolai is a Knezha, the poor lost little boy who breaks instead of builds. Who destroys instead of creates. He cannot stand in comparison to you, Skye."

"You say that like you know me."

"I do."

"How?"

She jabs her finger to my chest. "You don't feel it?"

"Feel what?"

"Our soul bond. We all share it."

I sneer, stepping away from her so she can't touch me. "I have a soul mate already."

"So do I. And he thinks I should just knock you out and drag you home."

Fisting my hands, I prepare to fight.

She laughs. "The universe played a massive prank on me with that one. I'm not going to drag you anywhere. But I wanted to meet you and let you know that you have a home outside of Nikolai Knezha if you want one. We could use someone like you."

"A monster?"

She rolls her eyes. "A creator. A key. A healer. A badass combat fighter. You can define yourself however you want."

"A Knezha," I say.

She sighs. "A monster is better than that."

It's my turn to sigh. "Honestly, I don't want to be anyone. I don't want to follow some journey or let the stars guide me. I just want to hang out with Luka and stop letting Nikolai control my life." My hand flies over my mouth. I don't think I meant to say that as I watch the memory unfold.

The girl smiles. "Then come with me."

"I can't."

"Just for the night. I'll show you what true family is, and then you and your soul mate can decide."

"Nikolai would never allow it," I say.

She closes the space between us and rests her hands on my shoulders. "That's why you need to. You'll regret it if you don't. Just think about it. I can help you. You have so much potential."

"For what?"

"You'll see. Just protect your soul mate until you do, okay?"

"I always do," I say, anger rolling through me.

"Then protect yourself."

A door creaks open, drawing me from the strange memory that felt like it was full of answers if I could just let it play out in my mind. But something stops me. It's like pieces are missing.

"Skye?" a feminine voice says from in front of me. "What are you doing here?"

I hadn't even realized I climbed the stairs and knocked on Deborah's motel door. The woman stands before me, holding herself. Tears rim her eyes, her nose red, and she releases a small sob before flinging her arms around me.

I don't say anything. I can't summon the words to speak.

"Was this some kind of test?" she asks, tugging me inside her motel room. She closes the door, the sound of the deadbolt sliding into place deafening. Of course she'd think this was a test to see how devoted she could be to the Knezha Family. If only it were. If only I were here to bring her back to the estate. "I know Nikolai told me to leave the area, but I didn't want to. I know my path belongs to the Knezha Family. I won't abandon my nephew."

I straighten my shoulders. "He's no longer your nephew,

Deborah. I'm here because he wants nothing to do with you and asked that it was made certain you left and never returned." My cold voice makes even me shiver.

My heart thuds in my ears, and I clench my jaw, steeling myself for Deborah's reaction. Tears fill her hazel eyes, and she holds her chest with her hand. It was cruel to allow her to kindle a spark of hope for even a second, and I wish I could just rush to the door and leave.

"My Sam wouldn't do this to me," Deborah says. "This is all your fault."

It never fails that the blame falls on me. Maybe because it is my fault.

"Please, Deborah. You must calm down."

"Calm down? No. I'm calling the police. You cannot keep me from Sam. I'm his family." She heads to the phone on the side table next to the bed.

I tense when she lifts the receiver. "Sam has chosen his family. I'm sorry it had to be this way. You knew the possibility of exclusion was there. I can't help it if Nikolai deemed you a risk to our family because you lied."

"I didn't lie! I wanted to join your journey. How dare you say otherwise. You're crazy!" she screams. "Just get out."

I don't move. It's like weights have been tied to my ankles, stopping me in place. There's a reason Nikolai wanted me to come, and I must face it. If I don't, I won't even know my real name by tomorrow. Because Deborah was right about this being a test, just not for her. "I can't. I'm sorry."

I close my eyes, listening as the dial tone of the landline

sounds out through the now silent room. Deborah pounds one number and then another. She presses the third button and gasps.

Slowly opening my eyes, I gaze at the red door in the middle of the room. Deborah slams the phone down and turns to me, wide eyes full of awe and surprise. She blinks a few times, shifting her feet. I don't have time to stop her before she touches the doorknob. The door swings out and reveals my glittering galaxy beyond it. The place where souls collide and life and death meet, a place of light and hope between two worlds of uncertainty. Without a proper guide, it's a place that can lead to a universe of who knows what.

"You want me to take you into it?" I ask.

"Nikolai would be so pissed off." It's not Deborah who answers me. My mind wanders from the motel room, from glassy-eyed Deborah, and the task at hand. "You know you shouldn't access the stars for fun." Gemma stares from me to the galaxy world and back to me.

"It's not a big deal," I answer. We're standing in the middle of my gray and white bedroom at the Knezha Estate. The red door stands tall right in the middle of the room.

"For you, maybe," she says. "My spirit isn't strong enough to adjust and evolve without a guide. I will not risk getting lost if you accidentally lose me in the stars. My journey is here."

"I've done it dozens of times with Nikolai and—" I snap my mouth shut.

She turns to me, mouth gaping like she's discovered a secret she could use against me.

I glare at her. "You can't tell Nikolai."

"Of course I won't. Nikolai would punish me because I knew about your soul mate before him and didn't say anything. I'm not getting stuck performing morning vows with the newbies," she says. "Too bad you can't summon a soul mate for me."

"That's what you get for being an accident," I say, teasingly.

She shoots me a heated glare. "Hey, the stars chose me. I'm one of the lucky."

"If you say so, Ms. Lucky." I turn toward the door to the galaxy. "Now, come on. Go through the door. I promise not to let you go."

"You better not, Skye. I trust you."

I push her forward. "Maybe you shouldn't."

Gemma's laughter sounds through the air and disappears, leaving me more confused than ever.

I stare at the open door to the galaxy and prepare to step in.

"You mean, you'll go against Nikolai and take me?" Deborah's voice rips me from the memory, dropping me in the present I don't want to be. I glare at the exact door from the memory of Gemma in our room as we went places Nikolai didn't want us to go.

"Isn't this what you wanted?" I ask. Showing her the door is my way of trying to give her some sort of peace, even if I won't actually take her through it. I won't do that to her. I won't be her guide right into Nikolai's clutches. I almost half expect that this is what he truly wants. He wants me to choose to go against what he asked to display my weakness for the family to see.

Deborah presses her lips together. "What happens when I go through?"

"The stars will decide." It's a lie, but how am I supposed to tell her that her fate lies in my hands? Her soul hovers in the middle of two dark places—death or in the control of Nikolai. I refuse to be the light to show her what hides in the darkness.

Deborah sucks in her bottom lip, just staring into the galaxy world through the door. My heart beats harder the longer she hesitates, the longer she weighs all the possibilities she thinks she has before her. But the fact is I have to decide. What action can I live with? My past is full of bloody hands and broken promises to those who trusted me all for the sake of Nikolai.

"Skye, what is taking you so long? The task is simple." Nikolai's voice cuts through my mind, sending a wave of pain exploding behind my eyes. I was too focused on Deborah that I forgot he was in my head with his promise to be here in spirit. Now I know he's testing his influence on me. Seeing if I'll comply or break.

I can't do either. *"I'm sorry, Nik. Just give me a minute. It's been a while since I've had to visit such a dark place."*

"You don't have a minute, my dear. You've grown careless. Do what I asked now and get out of there."

Someone bangs on the door, and I nearly jump from my skin.

Deborah doesn't even have a chance to answer it before Luka says, "Skye, the police are heading to the front office. What's going on?"

I flick my gaze from Deborah to the phone back in its cradle.

She brings her hands to her lips. "I didn't think it connected. I'm sure everything's okay. I'll explain that we're fine. Let me call the front desk."

"Skye, get out of there," Luka says.

"I need a minute," I say. Why can't I just have a minute?

Deborah nods, a smile crossing her face. "That's all it takes. A minute. I'm ready." She knows what has to be done to enter the door, except I don't want to take her through. I'd be disobeying and obeying Nikolai at once. The decision falls on me. Bring her into our family supposedly against Nikolai's wishes or show my family that I do what it takes to keep us safe.

"Skye!" Luka yells, banging on the door.

"Come on, Skye. I'm ready," Deborah repeats.

But I'm not. I can't do this. I can't be here. I refuse to believe I don't have a third option. Taking a step back, I put space between me and Deborah. Her brows lower on her forehead, and she blinks a few times, realization clouding her eyes. With one look at me, she spins and heads to the red door opened to the galaxy. She's going to attempt to cross alone.

"Deborah, don't do it." The door slams shut at the sound of my voice.

She wraps her fingers around the knob, yanking it, but the door doesn't budge. "Skye, you can't do this!"

"I must," I say.

"Skye!" Luka yells again. "Time to go!"

"Please, Skye," Deborah pleads. "Please."

I ignore her and thank the stars above and beyond for giving me this sign. For intervening in a moment that would weigh heavy on me if I had gone through with what Nikolai had asked or disobeyed him by bringing her to the family. Because Deborah isn't a risk to the Knezha Family. She's a risk to no one.

"I'm sorry," I whisper. "I have to go."

"Wait!" she screams. She lunges forward and locks her hands to my arms, forcing me to stop to look at her. "Don't leave."

"Don't leave me!" The memory of another person, a man, rings in my ears.

"You have to take me with you!" It's yet another voice from my memory.

A dozen screams crowd my mind, pushing into my thoughts so fast the edges of my vision darken. Deborah shakes my shoulders, yelling into my face, but I can't hear her over the memories of all the people I've abandoned before. All the people I saved instead of succumbing to doing what Nikolai had asked.

I realize I've been going against Nikolai for who knows how long. The blood of those rejected from the Knezha Family doesn't coat my hands.

"Stop!" I yell, my voice booming through the air. "You will leave and never return. You will create your own journey in life. You will be free from this!"

My ears ring, the room falling silent as Deborah stands in shock before me. The memories of the others I've sent away dissipate, leaving me to listen to the sound of nothing but one voice.

"Open the door, Skye!" Luka yells.

I do as he asks, twisting the door open.

Luka locks his arms around me and pulls me back. The last thing I see is Deborah standing in the middle of her motel room with a smile on her face.

I pass out.

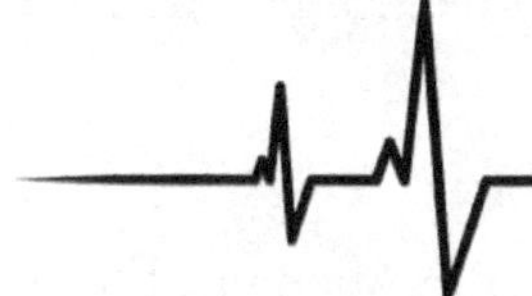

Chapter 13

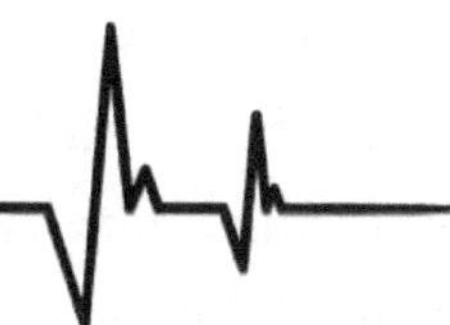

DESTROYED

"THE STARS HAVE Deborah." Luka's voice tugs at my consciousness, pulling me from my dark mind.

"And you're sure you weren't seen?" Nikolai asks.

"We were gone before the police had a chance to get to the room. It's fine. We're fine."

"But look at her." Nikolai's cool hand touches mine, and it takes everything in me to remain frozen with my eyes closed. "She's shut everyone out again. How am I to help her recover if she no longer allows me in?"

"Skye's strong, Nik," Luka says. "And stubborn as hell."

Nikolai sighs. "You're right. I sometimes forget she's not the girl I first met."

Because he ruined that girl. Destroyed her.

"Why don't I stay here and wait for her to wake up. I'll call you when she does."

"Please, listen to Luka. Please, listen to him." I chant the words in my mind, willing them to happen with my entire being.

"I do suppose I'm busy. Poor Sam is having the hardest time adjusting, and his spirit is fighting his good senses. It's been a while since I've dealt with such a strong will." Because I gave him a fighting chance. Nikolai hums under his breath. "It was you in fact, Luka. You and Skye. So admirably strong. Perfect, really. But Sam will come around like you did."

Nikolai's footsteps tap on the floor, and I hold my breath until I hear the door click closed. Still, I don't move. I just remain lying down, listening to make sure he is really gone. His last words to Luka haunt me, repeating over and over in my head. He called him strong-willed. Admirably strong. But not strong enough not to be broken.

"He's gone." The bed shifts under me, and Luka runs his fingers across my forehead, combing the stray blond strands of hair from my face.

I snap my eyes open. "You knew I wasn't unconscious?"

He chuckles. "I figured it out when you started chanting your thoughts."

I shift to sit up. "Thanks for not saying anything. I mean— about everything. You could've told Nik that I let Deborah go."

Luka slides his arm around me, gently digging his fingers into my side. "I should be offended you think I would. You're so adamant about protecting me, but you know what? You need protecting, too. I'm your soul mate. It's my job." I notice and relish in the fact he doesn't call himself my guardian.

"Even if it risks our family?" I ask.

Luka stiffens, straightening his shoulders. Even though I feel the weight of his gaze on the side of my face, I don't look at him. I can't get lost in the intensity of his eyes. I can't look at him knowing that I failed to protect him completely from Nikolai and the Knezha Family. I'm to blame for his broken will and mind.

"You know who I think truly puts the Knezha Family at risk?" His voice comes out barely a breath in my ear. "Nikolai. Because he puts you at risk."

I finally turn my head to look at Luka. "Today was a test."

"I know. It's why I made sure you passed. I overheard Nik tell the other guardians to watch out for you because he thinks you might be starting to doubt your purpose. He mentioned sending you for a realignment if you didn't perform the task he'd given you."

I stare into Luka's dark eyes, seeing the truth to his words shining back at me. "I know my purpose, and I don't doubt it. What I doubt is that Nikolai knows it. And I don't need to be realigned for our journey. What I need is for you to be here for me and with me no matter what."

His forehead crinkles. "I always am. You know this."

"Then come with me."

"Where?"

"You'll see."

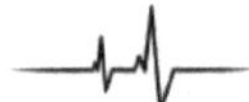

I run my fingers along the smooth, almost white bark of one of the many eucalyptus trees surrounding the perimeter of the Knezha Estate. The trees cast long shadows around us, the forest creepy this time of night with only the soft glow of light coming from the mansion to help me see. Clouds cover the moon and stars above, but they're not the universe I seek to find.

"You know we can do this anywhe—"

I raise my hand up and press it over Luka's mouth to stop him from talking. "Shhh. I need to concentrate."

He gently grazes his teeth against my palm so I drop my hand. "I can help." Sliding his hand through mine, he stands tall next to me, his shadow blending with those of the trees. An owl hoots from above, the sound of its feathers flapping loud against the silence the night brings.

A wave of peace, of warmth and love and everything good in the universe, pushes away the iciness of the winter air, and I release a cloudy breath. The red door to the galaxy world stands in the middle of the forest a few feet away, wide open with a view of the glittering stars.

My first instinct is to stay back and look at it, because something makes me hesitate about getting close enough to go through.

I glance at Luka in my peripheral vision, but he's looking into the galaxy world. Stepping forward, I close the distance to the door with Luka following my lead. My toes straddle the doorway, and I suck in a deep breath, letting the galaxy air fill my lungs.

"What now? You want to go in?" Luka's voice hums only a whisper over the sound of my heart beating in my ears.

I shake my head. "I just—I needed to see it."

"Skye, Luka. You shouldn't be out here." Nikolai's voice cuts through the quiet, and I spin around to face the direction I hear him coming from.

The door slams shut behind me, disappearing. Luka squeezes my hand tighter when a shadow emerges from the direction I know the mansion is, and Nikolai steps forward, shining a flashlight into my eyes before pointing it at the ground.

He was supposed to be busy. It's the reason why I decided to bring Luka into the forest this late to open the door I hope to find the answers I need in. Because I'm the one who locked away my own memories so Nikolai couldn't have them. But in doing so, I lost sight of what I wanted on this journey. I lost everything so that Nikolai couldn't steal from me.

"I'm sorry, Nik," Luka says, shading his eyes when Nikolai holds up the flashlight to him, purposely blinding my soul mate. "Skye wanted to get some air."

"You were supposed to come to me when she woke up." He turns the light toward the ground again.

"I'm standing right here. Stop talking like I'm not," I say, anger sneaking up on me.

"My dear, come here. Let me take a look at you," Nikolai says, ignoring my comment.

I take a step back instead of forward, tugging Luka with me. "I'm fine."

"Let me make sure," he says.

"I said I'm fine!" My voice rips through the air, startling both Nikolai and Luka.

"Grab her, Luka," Nikolai says.

"Skye." Luka's voice swirls through my mind. *"Run."*

But I don't have the chance. Despite Luka telepathically telling me to run, he pulls me closer and locks his arms around me. Nikolai closes the distance between us. He holds my face in between his hands, locking me in his stare. Pain bursts in my skull, and I cry out, thrashing against Luka's grip.

"Let me in, Skye," Nikolai says, his deep voice demanding that I give him all my attention.

"No," I say, whipping my head back and forth, forcing Nikolai to strengthen his grasp on me.

"You're unwell. You need me. I'll make things better. I know your position in our family is tough, and I know it puts fractures in your soul, and that's why you keep building your guard up. But you don't have to. You don't have to carry the burden of our whole family's journey alone." Nikolai leans forward, pressing his forehead to mine, sandwiching me between him and Luka.

His words dig into my mind, reminding me of what feels like another life. But I don't want another life. I want my life.

"Come on, Skye," he says again. "Just take a breath."

The pain in my head intensifies, sending a stream of hot tears down my cheeks. I grind my teeth, fighting with everything in me to not let Nikolai in. I've gone through too much already to give in. He will not break me again. He cannot control me. Whatever happened back at the motel room with Deborah helped me see and resist.

"You can't shut me out, Skye. I helped create you." Nikolai's voice rings in my ears, his voice coming from behind me instead of in front of me.

The memory pulls me from Luka's death grip and Nikolai's prying mind. I shift on my feet and stare at Nikolai. He presses his palms on the desk, the sunlight from his window silhouetting him in a golden halo as he stares at me.

"Angelica showed me the door," I say.

He narrows his eyes. "Angelica is gone, Skye. I'm who you have left. I'm your family."

"If that were true, then you'd stop putting me through this." Placing my hands on my hips, I steel myself from whatever conversation I was having with Nikolai at the time. From the looks of things, it wasn't good.

"I'm not putting you through anything. This is your journey. You can't shift our plans for some boy." He nearly spits the words at me.

I tense. "I'm not." I don't think I was lying despite the look of suspicion crossing Nikolai's face.

"Then bring him here. Don't make me send the guardians after him."

"He doesn't want this life."

"Then he can't be a part of yours."

"You can't do that."

Nikolai moves from his desk, making me step back. "I will not lose you. You're important to this family."

"Then don't force me to choose," I say.

"Choose? There isn't a choice to be made. Bring Luka here and give him to me. The universe didn't bestow a soul mate onto you so you could turn your back on our purpose. He should be here with us. You know that."

I press my lips together. "I'm not making him come."

"Then I will."

"No!"

My yells drag me from my memory, and Nikolai takes a step back, looking from me to Luka. Nikolai's eyes widen, and I brace myself for his reaction to me pushing him from my mind before he could get to me. But he doesn't give me one. All he does is take another step back.

For the first time ever, I glimpse a spark of fear in Nikolai's eyes. It disappears as quickly as it comes.

Clearing his throat, Nikolai says, "Take Skye back to her room. It's been a long night. We'll discuss things in the morning."

I release a shuddering breath, watching Nikolai turn to leave us without another word. Luka hovers next to me like he's afraid to speak, to do anything that might set me off. And it pains me to see Nikolai's fear reflected into Luka. Because he's afraid of me, too.

"I'm sorry," I whisper. "I shouldn't have brought you out here."

Luka blinks a few times but doesn't take his gaze away

from the direction Nikolai left in. "Skye, don't apologize."

"But you're scared of me."

"Not of you. For you. Nikolai—he's going to—" Luka can't even spit the words out.

I reach out and take his hand. "Don't worry about Nik."

"You said that the last time and look where it got us."

I blink, surprise washing over me. "Wait, Luka. Do you?"

He nods. "Everything. Whatever you did right now...I saw the light again. I can still see clearly, too. What about you?"

I try not to show my sadness. "No, but I remember enough."

"We need to run. Right now might be our only chance."

He's right. As much as I want to stay to help Sam, to find out what happened to Gemma, to bring Avery back to herself, we're in over our heads. It's not just Nikolai we need to worry about. It's his entire brain-washed family—a family I care about despite everything.

Angelica brought me to the Knezha Family to rebuild what I had lost, to give me something so special, I could never really repay her. But Nikolai, he didn't see things the way she did. And now that she's gone, he thinks there is only one way to see things. His way.

But it's his way that'll destroy us.

Continue to destroy me.

The only thing I can do now is salvage what I have left.

Chapter 14

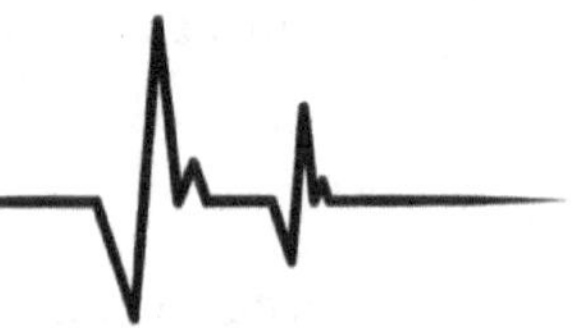

READ THE STARS

“**T**HIS WAY,” I say, heading to the east wall of the property. I can't remember the last time I've been out here, but it's like my instincts have taken over to guide me.

Luka runs next to me, and instead of cautiously sneaking through the trees, we bolt straight for the wall. With all the security cameras, I'm sure Nikolai already discovered we've decided not to head back to the house. If we keep changing our direction, he might not be able to send a guardian in time to intervene before we get to the main road leading into town.

“Skye, lights,” Luka says, huffing from exertion.

A beam of light streaks across the vegetation next to us, and I yank Luka to a stop and pull him behind the nearest tree. I press my face into his chest, sandwiching him between me and the trunk, and he hooks his arms around me. We both hold our breaths, waiting for someone to show up at any second. I'm afraid to find out what will happen if they do.

"I think they're to the right of us and getting closer. We need to run," Luka thinks to me.

I tilt my head up to gaze into his eyes. *"Ready?"*

With his nod, I grab his hand and tug him from the tree. We sprint through the forest until we come to a block wall. Flashlights set our surroundings aglow, and a few voices call out our names. If we don't hurry, we'll never make it.

Luka holds out his hands to me. "You first."

I thrash my head back and forth. I know better than to jump over first. I can just imagine Luka getting caught to save me. I won't allow it.

"Together," I say.

Jogging a couple of feet back, I charge the wall and jump, hooking my fingers onto the top. Luka swings his leg over, straddling the wall, and helps pull me up next to him. From here, we get a clear view of the forest, and I count three flashlights. That's not even half the guardians, which means Nikolai sent the others off the property. They'll try to intervene elsewhere, and Nikolai knows all the places I'm likely to go.

Luka drops to the other side and extends his arms out to catch me, easing my landing. He doesn't let me go as we peer around the landscape. I close my eyes for a second, pushing away the chaos breaking out on the other side of the wall.

Thuds sound through the air, and I catch sight of more beams of light coming from every direction we can run in.

Luka squeezes my hand. "We're going to have to fight."

"I don't want to hurt anyone," I say.

"Skye!" a voice yells. "Skye, please stop running. You're under duress. You're not acting like yourself."

"Stay back." I hold my hands up like it'll make a difference.

"Go on, fight." Nikolai's voice stabs through my thoughts, bursting pain behind my eyes. *"This is the girl I remember. Do you remember her?"*

Luka yanks my arm. "Skye, we have to go."

"I thought I had lost you, my dear. What you did for that boy was dangerous. Now, look at you. You're a mess. A weak shell of the strong girl you were." Nikolai's voice claws through my head, trying to pry open the locks I put in place to keep him out. If only he knew what I know now. I'm afraid he might discover it was for more. Something important enough that I abandoned Luka. If only I knew exactly what for.

"Get out of my head!" I scream, covering my ears.

The world shifts, and Luka throws me over his shoulder and charges through the trees away from the wall. More voices ring through the air. A flashlight stings my eyes as a guardian points it at Luka's back.

A gunshot rings out, surprising me, and Luka ducks, sending me sprawling to the ground in front of him. The star-studded sky peeks through the winter branches, and I scramble to my knees to help pull Luka to his.

And then I see the blood.

Luka clutches his side, blood seeping through his fingers. There's no way we'll make it to the road with him in this condition. Nikolai knew this.

"Skye, you have to run," Luka says.

Tears burst from my eyes. "Not again. I can't leave you again."

"I don't think I'm going to make it," he says.

I scream, my voice burning my throat, rage and despair combating to defeat my will to fight, my will to keep going. This is the forest by the cabin all over again. Luka's bleeding out, and I can't possibly carry him. But leaving him again? That's worse than him leaving me.

I close the distance between us. Another shot rings through the air, and Luka's eyes widen. He drops to his knees in the forest, and I search the trees. All the dancing beams of lights from the guardians' flashlights are now gone. Nikolai lost his patience.

And he now knows I remember. He's known all along about what I did. He's been playing my games, but he's winning. I'm not sure I ever stood a chance.

"*I didn't want to have to do this, Skye,*" Nikolai says, though I don't know where his thoughts come from.

"Stop!" I scream, spinning around.

"Skye, stand back." It's Nikolai. I managed to push him from my head again. "If you try anything, I assure you Luka's journey will end here."

Luka groans from the ground, and I search the dark forest.

Kneeling next to my soul mate, I grab his hand. "Luka, listen to me. I need you to get to your feet."

He squeezes his eyes closed. "I—I can't."

I growl, tensing. "Luka, get up!"

"You don't want to do that, my girl."

I ignore Nikolai's voice and hook my hands under Luka's arms, using every bit of strength I have in me to drag him with me. A dark streak of blood trails behind him, but I don't stop. I can't stop.

The crunching of leaves pushes me to move faster, and Luka grinds his teeth, doing his best to push up on his legs. I close my eyes, willing the universe to listen, to do something to help me. A blue door materializes in front of me, and my fear melts into panic, but I don't know what else to do.

"Skye, stop!" Nikolai yells.

I drag Luka with me to the door. Holding him as tightly as I can, I flip backwards into it, thinking about the galaxy world, about the basement, about our life before. Stars dance in my eyes, my soul colliding with Luka's, exploding in a lightshow so bright it steals away the darkness.

My back hits something hard.

The ground.

Luka moans, rolling off me, and I press my palms into the freezing ground to push myself up. Blood tints the white snow pink, and I glance around at the snowy forest. Confusion puckers my brows. I rub my temples, the pressure of Nikolai's voice gone from my head.

A warm hand grabs my leg, and I scramble to Luka's side.

He tilts his head back, staring at the sky, and I tug at his jacket, peeling away the sticky fabric.

I release a breath, noticing the gaping wounds from the bullets nearly healed. Nikolai failed.

"Skye," he says. "What happened?"

I pull him into my arms and hug him. "We escaped. You're fine. We're fine. But come on, we can't stay here."

"Did we go through a door?"

I nod. "We had to."

"But where are we?"

I help him to his feet. "I—I'm not sure."

He raises his hand and points. "That's the cabin."

I spin to peer in the direction of his finger. Sure enough, the cabin rests just through the trees. The only light in the area comes from the moon, and I heave a sigh, fogging the air. This is the exact spot I fell when I escaped the basement hell, bringing Caretaker Sienna with me. This is where Nikolai showed up with Luka to take me back to the Knezha Estate. This is the place we ran to in what feels like another life. Everything keeps bringing me back here. But why?

"We need to grab supplies and leave," I say, pulling him forward.

He stays in place, forcing me to stop. "Are we not going to talk about how we used the galaxy world to transport away from Nik?"

I shrug. "That's how I escaped the basement."

"None of this makes sense," he argues.

"Luka, we can read minds. We can come back from death.

When has any of this ever made sense?"

He folds his arms across his chest. "But how did I escape the basement?"

My lip quivers. "Nik."

It kills me to admit it. This is the first time I've had Luka's mind completely with me to discuss anything. He's the key to my past, the one who knows about who I was before. He's unlocked the best parts of me where Nikolai unlocked the worst.

"Does that really matter?" I ask. "We're free."

"It does. I remember being in a room and then I remember standing in a forest with Nik with these new memories I know didn't happen, but they still feel so real. I remember Avery and Gemma, but I know I never knew them outside the basement," he says.

I suck in my bottom lip. "But I did. And I know I destroyed all my own memories so Nik couldn't mess with them. That's why I didn't remember you in the basement. I had to protect myself and—" Something stops me from saying more.

He frowns, and I glance at a flicker of sadness in his eyes as he thinks about what I did and how I gave up everything—my entire history with him, with Angelica and even Gemma and Avery. I gave up everything that made me into who I am all so Nikolai couldn't turn me into who he wanted me to be or use me any longer.

"I did what I had to," I say.

He nods. "I know. I just wish you weren't pushed into any of this."

"Not like it matters. Nik knows what I've done. He knows

my memories are breaking free, and he's going to try to use my own mind against me like he used you against me."

Luka combs his wild hair back with his fingers, linking his hands behind his head. A million thoughts cross through his dark eyes, though none of them come to me.

I step closer and wrap my arms around him. "Don't blame yourself for any of this, okay?"

"I feel like things would've been a lot easier for us if we just complied in the first place. Nikolai doesn't mess with the people who at least pretend to believe in the Knezha Family's journey. At least we'd be together."

I press my fingers to his lips. "Stop."

"Think about it, Skye."

Goosebumps prickle on my arms, sending a chill through me. Something about his words strikes a nerve. "Shhh!"

"What?"

"Luka, look around. Something's wrong," I think to him.

He peers around without a word. *"What is it?"*

"Think about what you told me. That's not something you'd normally say."

His brows lower on his forehead, his jaw tightening. *"He's here. But how so fast? He can't go through a door without you."*

I step away from Luka and peer through the trees. The sound of utter silence greets me like someone hit the mute button. Unease tightens my chest, and I stroll forward into the forest, Luka following on my heels.

I find the tree with the bullet hole, the reminder of the most horrible day of my life. Reaching out my hand, I go to touch it. My fingers meet the rough bark of the sugar pine tree, and I gasp.

The bullet hole disappears.

"Luka," I say. "We have to go. Now."

I swivel on my boots to face Luka, my heart sliding into my stomach to fall to my feet at any second. Luka's no longer standing behind me.

"Sk-Skye."

I gasp again, dropping to my knees. Luka lies in the snow, blood seeping from his stomach to soak into the icy powder. Tears blur my eyes, and I release a small cry, my voice the only sound in the deathly quiet night.

"I don't understand," I say, pressing my hands into Luka's wound. "How did this happen?"

Then I catch sight of the gun in the snow next to me.

I freeze.

Closing my eyes, I suck in a cold breath. This can't be happening. I can't be here with Luka, reliving my memory all over again. But this doesn't truly feel like my memory. Something is incredibly wrong.

"This isn't happening," I say out loud, hearing my voice in my ears.

"Skye, ru-run," Luka says.

I snap my eyes open to look at him.

His eyes remain closed, his body shaking. The words didn't come from him—not this version of him. But where did they come from?

"Run," he says again.

This time, hearing the words in my ears without seeing his mouth move, without his eyes boring into mine, proves this isn't real. This is my memory, a memory Nikolai's trying to manipulate.

Luka heaves, sucking in one last breath. I scramble to my feet, wiping off the now non-existent blood from my hands. Snow sprinkles from the sky, turning the night forest hazy, and I spin around.

A gunshot rings in my ears.

I don't move.

"Get out of my head!" I scream, forcing the memory away. "Get out."

The pressure in my head releases. Blinking the fog from my eyes, I squint at the silhouette forming in front of me. Hands lock to my shoulders, making me yell.

"Skye? Skye? Can you hear me? Come on, my girl. It's going to be all right."

I swallow, trying to find the words to speak. "I—"

"Just take a breath."

My vision clears, the snowy haze disappearing. Nikolai holds me in his arms, the light from the mansion setting him aglow. He hugs me, and I stand frozen, confusion gripping my very essence.

"Let me have her," Luka says, his strong arms lifting me off my feet.

No. This can't be happening.

No. No. No.

Nikolai kisses my forehead and ruffles my hair. His icy blue eyes narrow for a split second before softening again. "Next time don't put up such a fight, my girl. I'm trying to help you."

I don't speak. I can't find the words.

Nikolai pats Luka's shoulder and then turns away to head toward the side entrance of the house. Luka's stare burns into the side of my face, but I refuse to look at him. I'm too confused to process anything. All I know is that we were trying to escape over the wall—we did escape—but now I'm cradled in Luka's arms right back where we started.

Did I imagine it all?

This is all part of Nikolai's mind games.

"Skye, listen to me," Luka thinks. *"We're going to get through this. We'll get out of here."*

I shudder through a breath, hearing Luka in my mind. *"You remember?"*

"Everything."

"Does he know?"

"No."

I hug him again. *"Thank the stars. Luka, do you know what this means?"*

He doesn't respond, just looks over my head at the Knezha Estate.

"You said something to me in the..." My thought trails off. The forest wasn't real. I have to keep reminding myself.

"What is it?" Luka asks.

I smile, hiding my doubt and the lingering confusion. *"It's just—we don't need to run. I know we can beat Nikolai at his own game."*

"You think so? You think that's our best option instead of running away?"

I nod. *"Don't you see? Running away takes us nowhere but back here. This is where our journey leads."*

"Skye," he whispers out loud instead of in my mind.

I press my forehead against his. "Trust me, okay? I can read the stars."

"I know you can," he says.

A red door materializes in front of us, and for the first time ever, the glittering universe doesn't welcome us. I stare at my reflection in what appears to be a mirror.

Raising my hand, I watch my reflection imitating me. "See? The door leads here. This is where I'll get my answers."

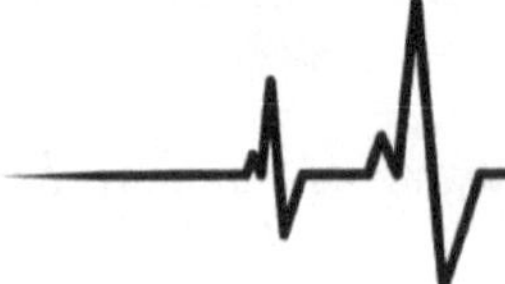

Chapter 15

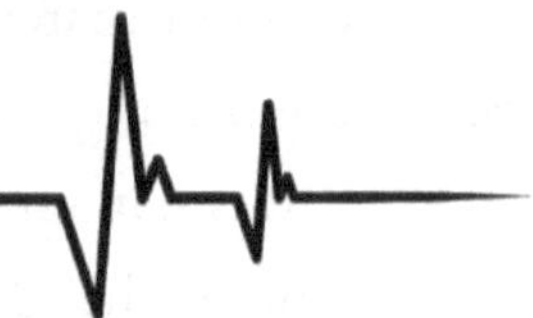

NOT A KNEZHA

“*MY NAME IS Skye Stone. I’m a seventeen year old from Los Angeles. I have blond hair and gray eyes. I’m not a Knezha.*” I’m afraid if I don’t chant the facts about myself, I might forget them, that Nikolai will get to me and change them.

I snuggle against Luka, resting my hand on his chest, feeling his heartbeat under my fingers through the soft cotton of his shirt. I don’t care if sharing a room is forbidden. I’m not sleeping alone.

“*My name is Luka Landon. I’m a seventeen year old from Carlsbad, California. I have an awesome girlfriend, who happens to also be my soul mate. She’s stubborn as hell and throws a killer punch.*" Luka kisses my temple, continuing my thoughts for me in his own words. *"But she also has a softer side—like her lips."*

I laugh out loud and playfully slap his chest. When our eyes meet, Luka leans into me and kisses the grin away. He wraps his arms around me, pulling me onto him, and I kiss him deeper, sliding my hands behind his neck until there isn't even an inch of space between us.

With the way my heart thumps against his, my breath mingles with his, my mind thinks on the same wavelength as his—it feels like our souls collide and link together even outside the galaxy world. Our very essences reflect each other like mirror images aligning so perfectly that though we're separate, we're one. A soul so painfully ripped at the seams and kept apart in the physical world that just touching eases the ache of not being together.

Luka's hands travel down my sides, touching the hem of my nightgown. Tingles rush through me, the heat of his fingers grazing over the bare skin of my thighs like a whisper, asking for permission to continue.

I know I've been intimate with Luka—I've clung onto every memory I've had of him that has come back to me so fiercely that if Nikolai tried to mess with my head, those would be the only memories to survive such an intrusion. But, remembering the girl I was before feels entirely different—I looked like her, I know I'm her, but I'm not her. She's not me. I haven't been with Luka in the way that leaves me breathless and buzzing and...

Luka's lips brush over my jaw and to my neck. Heat bursts

over my cool skin with every kiss as he leaves an imaginary trail while mapping my body. His hands glide toward my hips, playing with the soft fabric now bunching around my thighs. I kiss him harder, deeper, like kissing him will make the world right itself to realign our journeys in the direction we need to go together.

He moans against my skin, his breath tickling my shoulder. "I should stop. I just—"

I cut off his words with a kiss, because I don't want him to stop. I want to experience what I remember as the version of myself I am now. I don't want to hang onto old memories full of both love and despair without living them again. I want to create new memories, memories with the me I'm comfortable being.

"Don't stop," I think to him. *"I need you—this."*

He leans back to look at my face again, studying what feels like my very soul. "My name is Luka Landon," he whispers. "I'm seventeen, born on New Year's Day, and I'm in love with Skye Stone. If I lose my memories again, that is the one thing I won't forget. I love you, okay?"

I smile. "My name is Skye Stone, I'm seventeen, and it doesn't matter where I'm from and what I look like. All that matters is that I'm in love with Luka Landon, and I won't forget that again. Ever."

Sliding his hands up my hips, Luka tugs the hem of my nightgown, pulling it over my head. He studies me, my skin shadowed by the darkness of night with only the moon shining in through my sheer curtains to allow us to see. I don't move, just letting him drink me in, his heart nearly smashing against my palms as I rest my hands on his chest.

Luka shimmies up, sitting with his back against the wall so we're eye to eye. My legs rest on both sides of his, and he slides his arms around me and shifts me onto the bed. My fingers link to his shirt, and I tug it over his head, touching my hand to the puckered skin of a scar. He inhales a breath, putting his weight on me, so I can feel the rapid thuds of his heart beating against mine.

I suck his bottom lip into my mouth, wrapping my arms around his broad shoulders, tracing the smooth skin where I know his tattoo expands over his shoulder blades. Propping himself up, he leans back to look into my eyes again, a smile lighting his entire face.

Brushing his lips quickly against mine, he whispers, "I'll be right back."

I nod, watching him stroll across my bedroom to my bathroom, knowing exactly where I keep the protection hidden. I shift my comforter over me, pulling the warm blankets up to my chin so I can take a few deep breaths of the lavender-scented fabric. I can't believe this is actually happening or how nervous I am. This feels like another level altogether no matter how many times I remind myself this isn't something new.

Luka's silhouette hovers in the door to the bathroom, and then his shadowed figure crosses the room and back to my bed. Nerves tighten my shoulders, and I press my head into my pillow to look at the ceiling.

The bed shifts, and Luka's warm body slides next to mine.

He snuggles next to me, brushing my blond hair from my shoulder to kiss me. Pushing my nerves away, I draw Luka closer, hugging him, kissing him, arching up to press my chest to his. He rolls completely on top of me, his weight comforting and freeing. My soul ignites, setting itself ablaze like one of the billions of stars in our galaxy world still so fresh in my mind, because this is as close as I can get to Luka in this life, in this world, on this journey.

"I love you, Skye," he whispers against my lips, each kiss stealing one memory and replacing it with another I'm not sure I can ever live without. His body against mine, his heartbeat and breathing in sync with mine, his fingers linked with mine. Every gesture and kiss, every burst of desire and love and all the things good in this life pour through me, pushing away all the bad, the heartache, the disappointment, and fear—because none of those feelings have ever been caused by Luka. He's everything I want and need, more than living and breathing. More than what happens the second our hearts stop beating.

A dozen memories flash through my mind—all of Luka and me together. Our bodies entangled, our souls aligned. Every perfect moment where we're together, living one life where the world is exactly how it should be. How life should be. A world where I don't have to worry about what lurks in the shadows, about the dangers that come with being who I am, who we are and what that means.

Luka's lips touching mine bring me back from my memories. I smile into his kiss, just feeling everything good about him, losing myself in the dark abyss of his intense eyes—eyes so full of love and hope and strength, I don't know how I ever lived without them in my life.

"I never want to experience life without you again," Luka thinks to me, rolling beside me, our chests heaving. *"I mean it, Skye. Never."*

I link my fingers with his, tears shining in my eyes. I can't stop a teardrop from slipping onto my cheek. *"Never,"* I think back to him.

I know he's referring to his time in the basement, a time I'm still unsure about. But I don't want to think about that. All I want to think about is Luka and me, alone together. Happy. Yet, here I am, crying.

He turns on his side to look at me, the light from outside shining over my face, revealing my uncontrollable emotions. He frowns, reaches up, and runs the pad of his thumb under my eyes.

"I'm sorry," I whisper. "I don't know what's wrong with me." Crying after giving myself to him wasn't something I had expected, and by the look of concern flitting across his face, it's definitely something he wasn't expecting. And I'm ruining everything.

He opens and closes his mouth, words lost to him.

I swallow. "This is stupid. I can't stop." I sniffle, turning to press my face into the pillow.

"Skye," he says, sliding his hand over my side to hug me from behind. "I shouldn't have—"

Flipping back over, I cut him off with a kiss before he starts rambling on and feeling bad about something he shouldn't.

"Don't. I wanted this. I loved this. I love being here with you," I say. "This is the only right thing in my life, and I'm just so scared of what could happen."

Leaning forward, he presses his forehead to mine. "You know why Nik's trying so hard to control us?"

"Because he wants to use us," I answer.

He shakes his head. "Because he's scared."

"It's going to get worse, Luka." I hug him tighter. "I'm not sure if we'll get through this."

"The old Skye would tell you to stop thinking like that," he says.

I squeeze my eyes shut. "She's dead."

He places a hand on each of my cheeks, waiting for me to open my eyes. "And when has that ever stopped you?"

I shrug. "I don't know."

Leaning forward, Luka brushes his lips against mine. "Then how about I try to remind you?"

I smile, feeling his arms around me, his warmth soaking into my bones. "Try harder."

He chuckles. "Gladly."

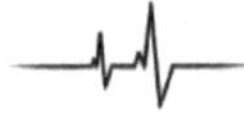

The bed bounces under me, and I snap my eyes open. Luka sits on the edge next to me, watching me in the light of early morning peeking through my sheer curtains. Reaching my arms over my head, I stretch and smile.

Luka runs his fingers over my leg, trailing them up as he leans down. Brushing hair from my face, he kisses me softly, his lips feeling like a small gasp of breath against my mouth. "I have to get back to my room."

I scrunch my nose, grabbing his hand so he can't stand. "Let me get ready real quick, and I'll go with you."

He nods without arguing.

I roll out of bed, running my fingers through my messy hair, and head to my closet to pick out an acceptable outfit for morning vows. As long as we pretend nothing is wrong, that nothing happened last night, hopefully Nikolai will think he was successful in breaking me once again.

I stroll into my bathroom to get ready. Because I showered last night, I don't do much more than comb the tangles from my hair, wash my face, and brush my teeth. I smile at my reflection, the memory of the way the moonlight lit up Luka's skin still fresh in my mind. For the first time in a while, I'm okay with greeting the day outside my bedroom walls, knowing that all isn't lost.

A door slams, drawing my attention away from my mirror. I peek out of my bathroom, my heart sinking into my stomach. Luka's gone from my bed.

"Luka?" I ask, sending the thought telepathically to him.

No response.

Rushing through my room, I fling my bedroom door open, nearly falling backward at the sight of both Nikolai and Luka standing in the hallway. Luka glances at me, his brows scrunched together, but he doesn't say anything to me telepathically. I concentrate on breaking into his thoughts, but they're sealed off to me. I can't listen in or speak to him. Hurt sweeps over me, feeling like I'm standing in front of a door, knocking, shouting even, knowing Luka's inside, choosing to ignore my pleas to let me in.

Nikolai turns his attention to me but doesn't smile. "This wasn't the kind of surprise I was expecting to stumble upon, Skye. You two know the rules." His hard gaze falls on Luka. "This is unacceptable behavior. What if someone beside me was to come into your room to find such a sight. The rules are in place for a reason."

"Most people knock," I say, anger sweeping through me. Not only because he's talking to us like children, but because memories of last night come back hard and fast, threatening to send my world spinning.

"Skye," Nikolai snaps.

Luka slides his hand around my waist. "We're sorry, Nik. Skye was having a bad night last night. Nightmares about you abandoning her."

I clench my jaw. Those don't sound like nightmares to me. "Deborah's situation got to me. I'm sorry."

Nikolai's hard jaw softens, and he offers me a smile—one almost full of pity. "You should've come to me, my dear."

I pout my lip. "I didn't want to bother you, and Luka was already here. He's going to be my official guardian, remember?"

Nikolai glances between us. "I suppose you're right. And a fine guardian at that, one I trust with your journey and life. One who sees what I see."

His words burrow into me, setting off alarm bells in my mind. Instead of responding with words, I nod, forcing myself to look at Luka, to smile at him like everything will be okay.

Like we can make it through another day under Nikolai's watchful eyes.

Luka squeezes my shoulder. "I should get back to my room. It's almost time for morning vows."

"I'll walk you," I say.

"Actually, Skye. I need you for a few minutes, if you don't mind," Nikolai says, grabbing my hand so I can't put space between us.

I do mind. I want to scream that the last thing I want is to do anything for the man who nearly broke me last night, getting into my head, re-creating the worst moment in my life all to prove that I'm no match for him.

"Sure, Nik." I stand up on my tiptoes and kiss Luka's cheek, trying once more to get into his head. "See you at breakfast?" I ask Luka.

He meets my lips for a quick kiss. "I'd like that."

Luka heads down the long corridor in the direction of his room, leaving me alone with Nikolai. Luka's dark gaze meets mine—a look so full of emotion that it screams more than his thoughts ever could. It's a look I wish I never had to see on him.

I raise my hand to wave, and he just frowns and turns the corner. Nikolai clears his throat, drawing my attention back to him. He's dressed in his usual slacks and dress shirt, a lapel pin encrusted with diamonds glittering in the overhead lights.

He holds out his arm for me to take. "We have a new visitor this morning. A man interested in joining our family."

I frown. "We don't meet new people except at Friday dinner."

Nikolai twists his lips to the side. "There are some exceptions."

"Exceptions? When?"

"Luka was an exception." Nikolai's reminder sends my heartbeat racing.

"You mean?"

"That's right. He's already like us."

I press my lips together. Nikolai doesn't mean he's a Knezha like us. He means that the man has touched death. That he's an acquired.

"Oh."

Nikolai doesn't want me just to meet this new man. He wants me to break him.

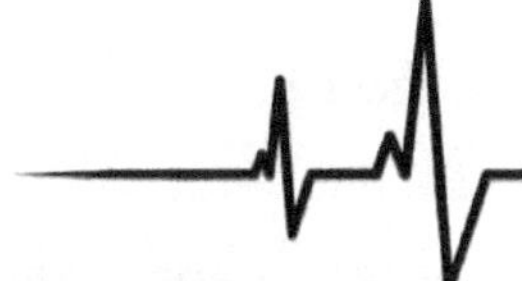

Chapter 16

AWAKENED

"SKYE, MEET REGINALD," Nikolai says, waving his arm out so I enter his office before him. Reginald, barely even old enough to be called a man, despite his name, sits in a leather chair across from Nikolai's desk. And I know him. He was the guy on the beach the other day. He was with the girl who's been haunting my memories. "Skye will be your guide today."

Reginald stares at his hands, not bringing his eyes to mine. It takes everything in me to keep my expression calm. Luka did hand him one of our pamphlets, and he could really be interested in the Knezha Family.

But the girl...

"Hi, Reg—" The second Reginald's eyes meet mine, something familiar in the green of his irises triggers a memory.

My heartbeat speeds in overdrive, the office disappearing into the familiar forest outside the cabin. But something's different. It's lush with greenery. Blue skies stretch endlessly overhead, lacking the winter chill I'm familiar with. A butterfly lands on my sleeve, and I shake it off.

Searching around, I peer through the sugar pines. A figure appears from behind a tree, making me tense. I catch sight of Reginald. He raises his arms, aiming a gun at me. I swivel on my feet and dart away, winding between the trees before hiding again.

I press my back into the scratchy bark of a wide trunk. Sweat beads on my forehead, and I gasp another breath.

"I can hear you breathing, Skye," he says.

I hold my breath, closing my eyes. Blood pounds in my head, but I try to listen for something—footsteps—over it.

"You're making this too damn easy," he adds.

The crunch of a branch sounds to my right and stops. Silence settles over the forest. My skin crawls, sensing another presence nearby. It's the same feeling I had the first time I saw Luka in the basement when Caretaker Sienna forced me into the pitch black freezer with him. The feeling leaves me buzzing with anticipation in the memory.

Sucking in a deep breath, I raise my own gun, hop from behind the tree, catching sight of Reginald feet away. I aim and—

"Skye, did you hear me?" Nikolai's voice booms through my head, pulling me from my memory.

He nudges my shoulder, and I straighten my back and smile. "Yes, of course." I have no idea what Nikolai said, but my answer was sufficient enough that he nods to me, shakes Reginald's hand, and then disappears out his office.

"I expect a full report on Reginald by lunch," Nikolai thinks to me, invading my head from the hallway.

I glance over my shoulder at the door and then to the guy. He leans back in the chair, lacing his fingers on the back of his head, and grins at me like whatever is going on happens to be the funniest thing he's ever encountered.

"You look like you've seen a ghost," he says, drawing his eyes from mine down to my bare feet.

"I—" I blink a few times, wishing another memory would break free. "I don't know. Have we met before?" I know we have. He knows we have. I don't know why I mention it. I saw it for myself, but the memory left me feeling confused. I held a gun to his face. Did I shoot him? Is that why he's already acquired? Whatever history I have with this stranger freaks me out.

"Yeah, why do you think I'm here?" Reaching into the pocket of his jeans, he pulls out the folded up pamphlet. The Knezha Family crest shines gold across it, the light bouncing off the metallic letters. "You gave this to me."

"You were walking the beach with a boy," he thinks to me, startling me. I had no idea I was letting him into my mind. I should've known he was a telepath. But why mention the beach

the other day with the weird history we share.

I clear my throat, gazing at the office door. Curling my fingers into fists, I dig my nails into the palms of my hands. Why is he here? Why now? This has to be some kind of game Nikolai is playing with me. Nikolai managed to get in my head last night. He admitted he knew what I had done, wiping my own memories. Now, he's testing me. Seeing how together or broken I am. And of course he had to ruin what was supposed to be the perfect morning with Luka.

"That's right. Luka was his name."

I push the guy out, and he winces, bringing his hands up to his temples to massage them. Fear creeps into me. How much of my thoughts did he hear? Why can't I seem to keep anyone out?

I straighten my shoulders. "I'm sorry. I don't remember you," I lie. "I meet a lot of people, and we hand those out wherever we go. We have so many people eager to get within these walls every day. But, you know, it takes real desire and commitment to see what we see in the universe." I move to the chair across from him, afraid that if I continue to stand, he'll notice my knees shaking. He'll know I've figured out the game already. The memory of us in the forest plays over again in my mind. There's no explanation except he's here by Nikolai's doing. But what about the girl he was with? She didn't feel like a Knezha. She was helping me. But why else would Nikolai ask me to be here?

I grind my teeth, steeling myself off, trying to stop myself from saying something crazy or calling him out.

"Because that's all that matters, right?" he asks. "Shun all those damn non-believers, imprisoned in their little worlds with no idea. They're just lying to themselves about what this life is all about."

I blink. He sounds condescending, almost like he's making fun of me. But I can't be certain. "We find that keeping a close-knit family helps keep the fundamentals and our foundation strong, but it's okay for others to walk their own paths and create their own journeys. We have no ill-feelings toward those outside our family, and neither should you."

He raises an eyebrow, smirking, but doesn't say anything.

"If you weren't aware, Nikolai is quite active in the community. Our doors are always open every Friday for anyone who chooses to visit the estate as long as they're not here to start trouble. We also have a few homes outside of the estate specifically for people in need in exchange for anything they can do to help us and the community thrive." I've rehearsed everything I'm supposed to say—to newcomers, to outsiders, to anyone who ever asks—that I almost believe in my words. It's something I could believe in. I want so badly to believe it.

Reginald leans back in his chair. "What happens to the troublemakers?"

I tense, trying not to show that his words make me uncomfortable. Out of everything, why focus on that? "We never really have any trouble."

"That's good to hear," he says, his eyes softening.

We stare at each other in silence. Reginald's green eyes hold mine, daring me to be the first to look away or say something. I don't take him up on his dare. Instead, I lean forward, assessing everything about him. His boots, covered in dirt, have seen better days. He's casual, more casual than anyone on the premises, his jeans and T-shirt a clear giveaway that he's new. His wild, long hair drapes over his shoulders, and he just blows strands from his face without combing them away.

"So, what do you think? Am I Knezha Family material? I have a lot to offer you, I promise," he says, causing me to grimace.

It almost sounds as if he's telling me that personally and not saying he has a lot to offer the Knezha Family.

I ignore him, trying to keep myself composed so he doesn't realize how much he's getting to me. "How about I give you a tour of the property? Morning vows should be ending soon. I can introduce you to other newcomers."

He stands up, offering his hand out to me. "I'd like that. I was hesitant about coming here at first, but hell. The universe sent me a sign. What do I have to lose, right?" A sign? I vaguely remember his thoughts saying that before, but I had no idea what it meant—I still don't.

I force myself to take his hand so he can help me to my feet. "Well, I'm awfully glad the universe spoke to you and brought you here. There is nothing to lose here, only everything to gain." I sound like I'm reading straight from the pamphlet.

"The universe gave me the sign, but ultimately you brought me here," he says, waving the pamphlet again. "And I must say, the community feel is...interesting. What do you think? Does it really feel like family to you?" He laughs. "Well, I guess it would, since you are all family."

I hold a smile, though I'm sure I'm baring my teeth. "Is that what you seek?" I ask instead of answering his question. I'm a real Knezha Family poster girl when I try to be. If Nikolai were watching, there is no way he could deny I might doubt the cause. If he wants to play games, I'm going to win every single one of them. "A place to belong?"

He shrugs. "Don't tell Knezha this, but I do have a family. They're not really into all this. But, they don't get it like you do. They're not..." His words trail off.

"Acquired?"

"Acquired? Shit, you make us sound like possessions. I was gonna say awakened. Awesome. Soul-kissed, if you're a romantic." Reginald stands in front of the door, waiting for me to make the move to open it. "You seem like a romantic."

I grimace. "And you seem like you have everything already all figured out."

"Well, I'm not exactly a newbie to the whole—" He leans in closer. *"Psychic powers life. It's a great, big world out there, Skye."*

"I wouldn't know. Nikolai protects us from the danger the outside world brings. Here, we don't have to worry about all the war and constant threats."

Reginald lifts his eyebrows at me. *"Scary stuff. That's why I like the idea of settling down. Gotta love living in a place like this, huh? Such privilege. What's the cost? Give up everything?"*

"And gain everything," I say.

Something about Reginald—whether it's his small words of uncertainty or how easygoing he feels with his messy hair and jeans, his lighthearted smile—gets under my skin, but not in some horrible way. He casts doubt on if Nikolai really brought him before me as a test. But then how do we know each other? He flat out lied to me about meeting on the beach, implying that it was our first encounter...unless he doesn't know. He wouldn't be the first person Nikolai messed with.

"Hell yeah. No wonder you stay. Easy to forget what lies beyond this compound."

I shake off his words and reach out, opening the door, before I slam Reginald into a wall to question him or try to break into his mind to unleash some sort of truth. The best I can hope for is that more memories surface or I catch him in a lie where I can force him to admit what's going on.

Sam startles me in the hallway. Grabbing my shoulder, he steadies me so I don't fall into Reginald right on my heels. Sam steps back, glancing from me to Reginald, a strange look crossing his face. His usual bright hazel eyes hold something dark, like the light within them has been snuffed out.

"Sam, you scared me," I say, stepping away from him to get a better look. He's dirty, his dress clothes wrinkled and the face plate of his watch broken. "Are you okay?"

He bobs his head, turning his gaze toward the hallway. "Couldn't sleep."

"You look like you've been running in the forest," I say.

"The forest clears my head. Nikolai says I've been too distracted lately."

An inkling of fear blossoms in my heart. The last time I saw Sam, which feels like forever ago, he was bleeding on the floor after I broke into his mind, trying to get him to block everything out.

I reach out and cup his face, forcing him to look into my eyes. "Why don't you go rest in my room? No one will bother you. We can talk later, okay?" Nikolai had me so concerned about myself, about Luka, about everything, it took my thoughts off of Sam. Another one of Nikolai's games. Games I'm sick of playing.

Sam leans into my hand and then raises his own to cover mine. It's not a romantic gesture, more like he's seeking comfort from me. Just needing to feel that he's not alone. That I'm here for him. Something families do.

The Knezha Family might not be my own family, but deep down, buried somewhere in my mind, I can feel the familial bond I created with Sam. The last thing I want from this life is to see him suffer, though I know I'm the reason for his suffering.

Sam sighs. "Maybe later. I have to find Nik. He's preparing me for tomorrow."

"Tomorrow?"

"My initiation. Don't you remember? You know Luka's guardianship is being made official, too."

I blink a few times. "Oh, yes. It slipped my mind." I didn't realize Luka's was happening so soon. And now Sam? Oh, no.

"You sure he's okay?" Reginald thinks to me, surprising me.

"You're still going to be my guide, right?" Sam asks, forcing me to ignore Reginald.

"Right."

Sam flicks his gaze to Reginald. "Is this a newcomer?" Sam's sudden change of subject, the way his eyes keep averting from mine, his rigid posture—everything about his behavior screams wrong. So, utterly wrong. But I can't even do anything. I hate this.

I nod. "Yeah, this is Reginald. I'm giving him the grand tour, hoping he might choose to stay. He has a lot to offer our family."

"Call me Reggie," Reginald says. "And I think I will stay. At least for a while."

Sam's eyes grow hard. "You won't ever leave."

Reggie glances at me. "I'm sure you're right. Who would ever want to?"

Sam nods once and disappears down the hallway. I stand awkwardly, looking after him, wishing I could follow him. He's not okay. Nikolai got into his head and rewired him despite my efforts to protect him. Doubt doesn't just vanish. Nikolai turned him into a believer and not by providing proof or giving him a miracle. And by tomorrow, Sam will touch death. I'll be forced to guide him into the galaxy and bring him back to be added to Nikolai's collection. Nikolai's acquired ones.

A hand touches my shoulder, drawing my attention from the empty hallway. "Seems like a real devoted kid."

I shrug. "Sure."

"Also sounds like tomorrow's a big day," Reggie says, standing in front of me so I can't turn my attention elsewhere.

"Ceremonies are huge around here. Anything to celebrate together," I say, faking excitement in my voice.

Reggie wags his eyebrows. *"I must've arrived at just the right time."*

I motion him to walk next to me, something about his words digging into my mind. *"Must have,"* I think back to him.

I wish I could tell him it's the worst time ever, but I don't.

If he's not one of Nikolai's tests, he'll realize it soon enough.

He'll regret ever stepping onto the Knezha Estate like I do.

But that seems to be my life. So full of regret.

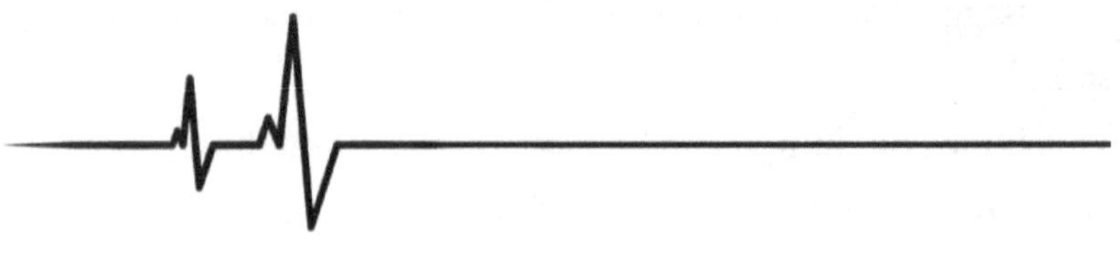

Chapter 17

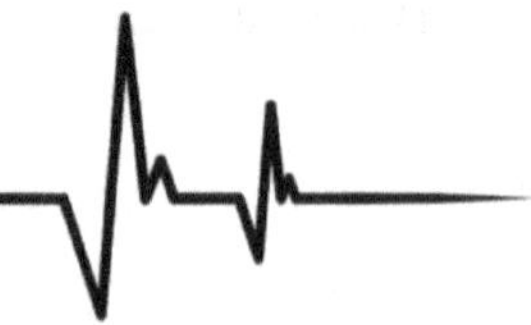

PLAYING GAMES

"WELL, THIS IS your room if you plan to stay the night. The bathroom is down the hall on the left, which you'll share with one other person. The phone on the nightstand will connect you to any room in the house, but you have to use the library phone to call out. You can go online there, too. The TV remote is on your dresser, and help yourself in the kitchen if you get hungry. The staff makes lunch at one, and dinner is at six." I motion to the closet. "I don't know if you brought any belongings with you, but if you did, they should already be there."

Reggie peers around the small room with the twin bed, a

flat screen TV stationed on the wall above the dresser, and a walk-in closet. There isn't much more. Newcomers get the basics. "Do I get maid service, too?"

I raise an eyebrow at him.

He chuckles. "It was a joke—lighten up. You should see my current—previous?" He shrugs. "This is better than my last shithole apartment."

I don't laugh—don't even try to fake it. This would be the perfect chance to ask about the girl at the beach, but something stops me—like I'm afraid that all the memories I have of her could be ruined and end up lost if I say anything out loud.

Thinking about the girl, trying to figure out who she is, who Reggie is, reminds me that I haven't heard her butt into my thoughts in a while. What if I imagined her all along? I can't rule that out. But what if Nikolai... I shake my head. I can't go there. I'm confused enough already. "If you need anything, take this hallway all the way across the house and past the foyer. I'm up the stairs. You can't miss me. My room is the only one in that wing."

"No wonder you don't leave," he says.

I frown. "Of course I won't leave. This is my home."

"I didn't mean you, specifically," he says. *But you know, home is wherever you make it or whatever that bullshit is."*

I twist my lips. *"Welcome home, I guess."*

"Feels like it already. You remind me of my girlfriend, Cora, so charming and sarcastic—hates dealing with my shit all the time. You'd get along. She can throw a helluva punch, too."

Stepping back, I put space between us, startled by his

words. It was like he knew I was thinking about the girl from the beach.

He laughs out loud, tipping his head back. *"You're right. I did know you were thinking about her. And since you're wondering, she's pissed off I came here."*

"Why—I—" Squeezing my eyes closed, I force him out of my mind.

Reggie winces, wobbling back. Shaking his head, he laughs again. I'm pretty sure that's all he's capable of doing—getting under my skin, playing games with me, and being a real jerk.

"Whoa, shit, Skye," he says, still grinning.

I poke my finger into his shoulder. "Do that again, and you'll feel like you have an everlasting hangover. I don't know who you think you are, but you can't do that without my permission. Only those who I've allowed in have that right, and you're not one of them."

He steps back, raising his hands. "Now, that's what I'm talking about. That's what I expected from you."

"Expected from me?" This really is one of Nikolai's games, and Reggie just blew it.

He shrugs, stepping into his room while blocking my way. "That's right. Now, see you later, Skye. I think I need a nap."

I step forward to try to stop him from shutting the door. "Wait, you can't—"

The door slams in my face with a bang. I clench my hands into fists, ready to break the door open, but murmuring voices sound from down the hall. Luka and Nikolai appear from around the corner, forcing me to rein in my annoyance and anger.

Luka raises his hand, motioning for me to come closer.

I hesitate for a second.

"Go to your boyfriend, Skye. Act normal," Reggie thinks to me. *"Nikolai's always watching. He's expecting a full report. Go on and tell him you know his plan."*

"I said get out of my head," I think back, fear jumpstarting my legs so I stroll away from Reggie's closed door.

"See what happens when you confront him," Reggie adds.

I beam a smile at Nikolai and slide my arms around Luka. "Everything's great, Nik. I think Reginald is a perfect fit." For whatever reason, Reggie gave me the warning I needed. He's right. If I tell Nikolai I know what he's trying to do, things will turn from worse to unbearable.

Nikolai studies me. A pinch burns behind my eyes as he tries to get into my head. I don't let him. I block everyone out.

Nikolai narrows his eyes for a split second, noticing that even after last night, I still manage to fight to keep my mind closed. But he doesn't call me out on it. He wouldn't. Because asking about it could risk what he did if he thought it worked. He'll wait until I slip up again. As long as I stay in line and do what I'm told, he won't try to force me otherwise. I know him.

"You make this too fun," Reggie thinks to me.

Impossible. I've pushed everyone out.

"What do you want from me?" I ask.

"Nothing," Reggie says.

"Then stay out of my head!"

His soft laughter sounds through the door, drawing my attention away from Nikolai's hard gaze. Luka only stands there silently.

"Well, maybe you should have never let me in."

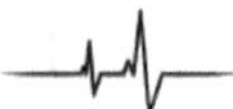

"Calm down, Skye," Luka says, sitting on the edge of my bed.

I pace back and forth, my fingers gripped together on my head. "Don't tell me to calm down. You didn't feel Reggie in your head. I couldn't keep him out. He's messing with me, and I don't know why he doesn't tell Nik. He told me *I* let him in." I huff and drop my hands. "Why is he telling me any of this?"

"You said you had a memory of him before. Maybe it's not what you thought," Luka says.

"I think I shot him, though. He's retaliating. I don't know. I just—" I groan. "I was so stupid for wiping my memories. What was I thinking? It's only left me vulnerable, and I'm still with Nikolai. You're with him, too."

A knock sounds on my door, drawing my attention away from Luka. He gets up from my bed, crossing his arms, like standing tall and puffing his chest out will somehow make me feel safer. But I'll never feel safe. Not as long as I'm within the walls of the Knezha Estate. I doubt I'd feel safe out of them, either. The only place I actually feel safe is among the stars. And it's only going to get worse tomorrow with Sam's induction ceremony. He must die by my hands, something I know he doesn't want. He wanted to leave. Now, he'll be forever a Knezha. Forever one of Nikolai's pawns from this life to wherever our journey leads.

"Skye, it's me." Sam's muffled voice hums through the

thick wood. A shiver trickles down my back, like my spirit almost knew he'd be the one at the door. "Can I come in?"

I turn to Luka. *"Nik got to him."*

Luka's jaw tightens, and instead of commenting on my revelation, he strolls past me to the door and says, "Not now, Sam. Skye's had a long day."

Something hits the door, maybe Sam's palms. "Please, Skye. I need to talk to you. You said I could come here and talk. I need guidance and support. I need to tell you something. It's about Gemma."

I tense, shuffling across the room to press my hands to the door. I hang my head between my arms. Everything's so confusing that I don't even know what to do. There are too many conflicting memories, stories, and more keep unraveling—it's like the universe exploded around me, sending every piece of my life flying in a different direction, in a different life and time even. Now, I must piece things together haphazardly, hoping they make sense and stick.

This afternoon, Sam was changed. He was the perfect Knezha candidate looking forward to joining our family—or he was faking. Of course he was faking. I wasn't alone. He must know about Reggie's games, too. It's the only explanation I have. Nikolai might not have gotten to him after all. Nikolai did say he was strong-willed, and I tried my best to prepare Sam.

Luka touches my shoulder, but I shrug away and open my door. "Thank God you're o—"

My feet fly out from under me, and I hit the ground hard.

My hope snuffs out with the lights in my room. Luka yells my name, lacing his fingers around my wrist. And then he yells out again in pain. Instead of helping me to my feet, he yanks me up and holds me against him, squeezing me harder, still groaning and shaking his head. Avery waltzes into view, her hands on her hips. The lights flicker in the hallway next, and a bulb pops and goes out.

"Let me go!" I scream, jerking my head back to slam it into Luka. Something's wrong.

He drops me to the floor, but Avery flicks her wrist and sends me flying up the wall, pinning me in place. Luka cups his nose, his dark eyes watering in pain, but a different look sweeps across his face—surprise and betrayal. I should know. It's the same look I'm giving him.

"Luka," I whisper, struggling against Avery's telekinetic hold. "I didn't mean to hurt you." I turn to Sam next. "What's happening? What's going on? This isn't about Gemma."

"Shhh. Speaking her name is against the rules," Avery says, stepping in front of Sam.

"But Sam, he—"

"Was testing you. Nikolai's concerned. He thinks you're at risk."

I try to move my arms, do anything, to break free. "Release me!"

Avery's hold disappears, her eyes widening at my command. She raises her hand. "It's going to be okay, Skye."

I hold up my hands. "Nobody touch me. Get back."

All three of them yell and cover their ears like my words

"My doing? I'm just a new guy needing somewhere to belong."

"Well, maybe you don't belong here. Get out while you still can, Reggie."

He doesn't respond to my warning. All he does is click his door closed before I can give him another heated look. What a coward.

Avery waltzes ahead of us, a strange new demeanor about her. She's more confident than the last time I saw her with how she smirks at me from over her shoulder, like she's happy I'm in the position I'm in.

Flicking her hand out, she opens a side door leading outside without touching it, flaunting her ability, which is usually against the rules. We head toward the main entrance, Avery leading the way into the fading evening light. The wintery clouds reflect the reddening sun, igniting the sky in rubies and pinks. I was right. Nikolai's making an example of me. He's trying to shame me and remind me of where my place is supposed to be.

"Where are we going?" I ask. "Where's Nikolai?"

No one answers me.

"Answer me!" Like someone flicks the switch on the sun, night falls upon me, shadowing the world in darkness. Nails dig into the skin of my wrist, and I yank back from Luka, falling to the ground. But it's not Luka who stands over me. It's Nikolai.

The memory drops me into the middle of the sugar pine forest in the dead of night. The whistling of the wind in the winter branches rings in my ears. Goosebumps prickle over my skin, and breath fogs the air in front of me as I heave a gasp.

"Don't fight me, Skye. I'm not going to hurt you," Nikolai says, bending down to pull me back to my feet.

"Don't touch me! Just let me go." My voice echoes through the air, panic lining my words. I realize the exact moment this memory took place. It feels like a time so long ago, though it was only weeks.

"Relax. I'm your friend. I'm here to help you. You're just confused. Come on, look at me, Skye."

I tilt my head to look up, catching sight of Nikolai's vibrant blue eyes in the moonlight peeking in through the trees. I shudder, my teeth chattering. "I—just leave me alone. I don't know you."

"You're wandering in the middle of the forest. It's snowing. Where are you even heading?" he asks, standing over me. He shrugs out of his jacket, holding it over me. "Here, put this on before I have to carry your frozen dead body home to thaw out."

I don't take the jacket, but I do push to my feet and glance around. For what, I'm not sure. "I'm fine. I just need to keep walking."

"Skye, there is nothing out here. Please, be reasonable."

"I am and there is. Just shut up so I can concentrate." Without knowing what's happening in my mind, I have no idea what is unfolding in this memory. This one feels different. Cloudy. But I'm not afraid.

"Concentrate on what?" Nikolai asks, closing the distance between us and draping his jacket over my shoulders without asking me. The gesture, the concern lighting his eyes, sparks something within me. He's not the cold-hearted, self-centered manipulator I've come to know. He's as lost as I feel.

But it doesn't change things.

I shrug his coat off, dropping it to the ground. "My instincts."

Nikolai rushes to stand in front of me. "And what are they telling you?"

I glance behind me again. "To run."

The tree next to me cracks, and snow falls from the branches, dusting over my thin dress. My eyes draw toward the hole in the bark, a starburst from a bullet, but it wasn't directed at me. It's a foot from Nikolai.

His eyes widen with fear, and I race away from him, the world flying past me as I head deeper into the familiar forest. Branches snap, and Nikolai yells my name, but I don't stop. I can't stop. Something pulls at my very soul, keeping me running through the winter forest.

I'm not fast enough.

Something hard hits the back of my head, knocking me off my feet. I skid through the snow on my stomach, only stopping when I crash into thorny vegetation hidden under the glittering snow.

My chest hurts, the air escaping my lungs in a painful whoosh. I blink the haze from my vision, my head throbbing. Blood splatters in the snow next to me.

I'm not on the frozen ground long.

Nikolai hoists me to my feet, wrapping his arm around my waist to keep me from falling. He charges forward, nearly dragging me. His voice hums in my ear, but I can't hear anything over the throbbing in my head.

"Skye, you have to listen to me. We're in danger." His words poke into my mind. It's strange to think about how comforting his voice used to be in my mind.

Everything turns black.

A yell yanks me from the blank spot in my memory. I awake flat on my back, staring up at the glittering stars shining through the bare winter branches of the trees. A dark figure hovers over me, but I can't make out their face through the haze in my vision.

Groaning, I prop up on my elbows. Nikolai lies in the snow next to me, his face pressed into the ground. He puffs a breath, blood staining his blond hair and dripping down his cheek to tint the snow next to us. He's injured. But by who?

A boot crunches the frozen ground, drawing my attention away from Nikolai, who groans. I blink, seeing the familiar girl from the beach, holding onto a branch large enough to be a baseball bat. She frowns, shaking her head at me, tears shining in her eyes.

I always thought Nikolai was the figure in the forest, the one who hit me hard enough to send my soul to the stars, but it wasn't. I know that now. It was the girl—Reggie's girlfriend.

What does that say about Reggie?

"I wish you didn't make me do this," the girl says.

Voices sound through the quiet night. They're calling Nikolai's name.

I open and close my mouth, my tongue tasting metallic.

"Who are you?"

She sucks back a quiet sob, shaking her head. "Until our journeys meet again," she says without answering my question. She raises the branch up again, aiming it at me.

"Skye, come back to me. Please. Please, you have to open your eyes." Luka's voice rips me from my memory, stealing me away from the forest, away from Nikolai and the girl, Cora. I remember Reggie calling her Cora.

Without having to collect every piece of detail from that moment, I know it was the same night I died and woke up in the basement. I knew Nikolai was there, and I knew he was responsible, but there is still so much more I'm missing.

I snap my eyes open, jerking myself back, but strong arms hold me. Luka's heartbeat races against my back, thudding so hard that it might be trying to get to mine. Nikolai stands in front of me, his lips twisted, his ice blue eyes searching my face.

Glaring light illuminates the room behind him. Exposed pipes, vents, concrete walls. I'm in the basement. I know it.

"Gemma!" I can't stop myself from screaming her name. If she's here, I want her to know that I haven't forgotten her, that no matter what Nikolai does, I won't stop fighting. I'll figure out how to win.

Nikolai slaps his hand over my mouth, glaring at me. Pain erupts in my head, and I scream. Something warm drips from my face and onto the floor.

Reaching out, Nikolai touches a tissue to my nose. I cringe at the sight of the blot of blood staining the tissue as he pulls it away. He's not going to lock me away. He doesn't need to. Not like before. I'm not an empty shell of a girl. I'm no use locked away if he can now use me. It's why Avery and Luka are free and why Gemma isn't. Whatever I did to her left him unable to use her. Maybe I broke her to save her. I don't know.

I cry again, pain expanding in my skull, feeling like my brain will explode at any second.

"Good girl, that's right. Just take a breath and let me get a look at you," Nikolai says, his thoughts stabbing into my head.

Pressure rings in my ears, my head throbbing the longer Nikolai locks me with his eyes.

As much as the pain leaves me convulsing in Luka's arms, I resist. And I'll keep resisting.

"Not much longer, my girl. The pain will stop soon enough."

I wail, struggling, sobbing. I can't escape Luka's hold no matter what I do, not with Nikolai cupping my face. Warmth trickles from my ears. My vision blurs, blood replacing my tears. I'm in so much pain I'm not sure how much longer I can last. Nikolai might not only break me, he'll kill me. I almost hope for it.

"Nik, you're hurting her. Please, just stop," Luka says, squeezing me tighter, not to hold me in place but like he's doing everything to keep me together when I'm about to fall apart.

Nikolai blots my face again with another tissue, smearing blood across the white paper. "This must be done, Luka. She's dangerous, and you know it. She must be controlled."

Luka sucks in a deep breath. *"Skye, I can't do this. I can't let him do this."*

A memory breaks free. Luka's holding me from behind,

but he's hugging me. His lips brush my neck, and his warm breath tickles my ear. The sun lights the entire valley as we stand alone on a hillside.

"That's it, my girl. Let's find all those missing pieces." Nikolai's thoughts push Luka's out, leaving me in complete agony.

I scream again, and another memory surfaces, pulling me from my despair. Nikolai hugs me in front of the fountain, laughing and smiling. He pulls out a box from his jacket pocket, showing off a diamond-encrusted brooch with the KF initials. Avery and Sam clap their hands, and Luka hugs me from behind. We're all so happp—

"No!" My voice cuts through the air, pushing the thought away. It wasn't a memory at all. It was Nikolai clawing into my mind. He's getting to me. I can't hold on much longer.

The world begins to shake, and fire burns through my head, devouring everything it touches. I jerk, convulsing, and Luka drops me on the floor, unable to hold onto me.

The room spins again, and I find myself outside. I'm holding hands with Luka and Nikolai, listening to Nikolai recite the morning vows for our family. I sigh, wanting to soak up every second of such a perfect moment, a perfect memory with people I love so much—more than the stars and universe. More than anything.

"My beautiful girl," Nikolai says. *"We're so happy to have you in our lives. You're the best thing that has ever happened to us."*

"I love you, Nik," I whisper, the edges of my vision darkening. "I couldn't have asked for a better journey than with you."

Nikolai takes me from Luka's arms, the pain in my head

nothing but a faint memory. Why I put up such a fight, I have no idea. This is how life is supposed to be. I don't know why I couldn't see how much Nikolai has helped me, how Luka's adapted so well to our family. It's like the emotions from the galaxy world have come to my life without even opening a door.

"Don't ever forget it, okay?" Nikolai says.

"Skye." It's Luka.

I twist to gaze at Luka. "You're the best, Luka. I'm so happy we're here. I can't wait for tomorrow." Tomorrow? My mouth speaks, but my brain can't keep up.

"Skye, focus," Luka says.

But I can't. There are too many emotions rushing through me. I'm floating on the wind of everything good in the world, this life, the galaxy manifesting around me through the people I feel most connected to. I could ride the breeze to wherever my journey is supposed to lead.

A blip of pain in my head causes me to wince, but I still smile.

"Skye, you better fucking remember how to resist." I frown at the masculine foreign voice in my head. It's neither Nikolai nor Luka. But it's familiar.

My ears pop, the room fading in and out. Too many voices crowd my head. I can't concentrate. I can't think.

"Reggie, you better not mess up." Another familiar voice drifts through my mind. Cora? I think so.

The happiness I felt seconds ago washes away. When I meet Nikolai's blue eyes, I freeze. He reaches out and touches my cheek, running his fingers through my hair to push the loose strands behind my ears.

"I'm tired, Nik," I say, sinking to the floor. "What's happening?"

Nikolai kneels next to me. "You're going to be okay, my girl."

"She's going to be okay," Reggie says. The world fades and drops me back into the forest in the minutes before my death that took me to the basement and then back to Nikolai.

"She shouldn't do this alone," Cora says, her concern pulling at my very soul.

"She's not alone," he says.

I blink again, the dark forest suddenly lighting.

I'm back in Nikolai's arms. "Nik." It's all I can manage to say.

"Deep breaths. You'll feel better soon."

Without even having to look at him, I know he's lying.

I'm about to feel a lot worse.

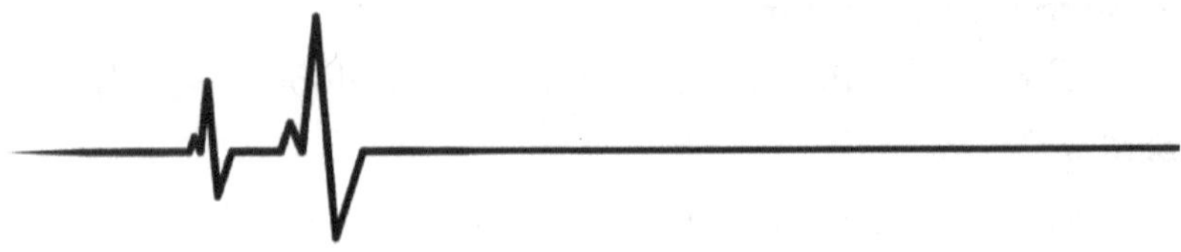

Chapter 18

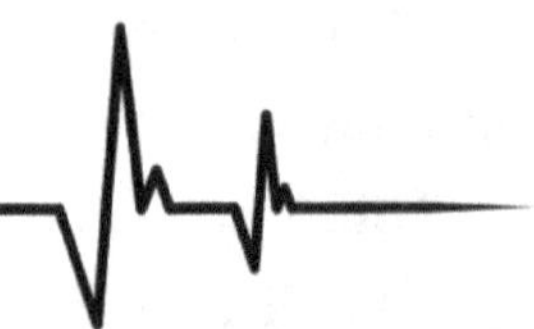

REALIGNMENT

"*PLEASE, NOT AGAIN. Don't kill me again.*"

I bolt upright and scream, my heart racing so hard I think it might give out at any second and send me to the galaxy world. Thrashing, I jerk around, throwing my arms out, the familiar voice echoing in my mind.

"*Gemma?*"

"Skye, stop. You have to stop. You're going to hurt yourself."

I inhale a huge breath, fluttering open my heavy eyelids. Pain throbs in my head, and it takes me a moment to regain my vision. I run my hand over my face, flakes of something brown rubbing off to fall onto the white sheet covering my legs. I try not to gag at the sight of the dried blood.

"Where's Gemma?" I ask, my voice quivering with a sob. "I heard Gemma."

A warm hand slides around my back, lifting me from the mattress. Luka hugs me on his lap, resting his forehead on my shoulder.

"Gemma ran away, Skye? Don't you remember?" he asks. Another pulse of pain pinches from behind my eyes. I think he's trying to get into my head, but something's happened. I'm subconsciously blocking him. But why? What's happening? Where am I?

My breath catches, tears lining my eyes. Everything hurts. "No," I whisper. "I heard her."

"You were having a nightmare, my beautiful girl. It's a side effect of your realignment." Nikolai's voice hums softly in my ear, like he knows he must whisper to stop me from panicking.

I shake my head, more tears escaping to roll down my cheeks. "That can't be right. I heard her." Gemma wouldn't leave. She loved it here. We were her family. And the voice I heard? It was full of fear and agony. "She needs help, Nik."

Nikolai takes my hand in his. "I'm so sorry. It's hard for me to accept she abandoned us, too. Gemma meant the world to all of us, and I hate that she chose to embark on a different journey."

A trickle of fear runs from my mind and into my heart. "Oh, stars. We have to fi—"

"You know the rules, Skye. There can't be any exceptions.

It's not good for our family to have someone question and ultimately leave us and then to allow them back into our lives. That's not what our family's about," Nikolai says. "Now, I know you're hurting because of your realignment, but I must ask that you not mention her name again. We're about walking forward and not looking behind us."

I blink. My realignment? He's mentioned it twice now, and the ideas finally settle in. "Wait, what's going on? My realignment, Nik? *My* realignment? How can this be?"

Luka breathes his warm breath on my neck. If he wasn't holding me, I might fall apart. How could *I* have ever needed a realignment? People who doubt the Knezha Family and our journeys have the option of getting help from Nik, but me? That's unbelievable. I'd never turn my back on those who promise to stand with me from this life and beyond.

Nikolai frowns, leaning forward to embrace both me and Luka, sandwiching me between them. "There is nothing to be embarrassed about, my beautiful girl. Things happen. But you made the right decision, and now you're better. Don't you feel better? The doubt you were carrying was tormenting your soul. I fixed you."

I sniffle. "I'm so sorry, Nik. I didn't mean to cause any trouble. What led me to such a dark place? I must know so I never return there."

Nikolai doesn't respond. He sits quietly, letting my question hang in the air. Was it something so terrible that he's afraid to tell me? We talk about everything. We've never kept any secrets between each other.

"Nik," I say, reaching out to grab his hand.

"You lied to me, Skye. I don't even know how to handle this. I thought you trusted me. I thought we were in this together. How could you keep such a secret?" The sharpness of Nikolai's voice cuts through the air, startling me.

I wince, pulling my arms to my chest to hug myself. "You wouldn't understand."

"You didn't even let me try!" Nikolai turns his back on me, spinning to face the window of his office. The world changes so fast, taking me from Nikolai's silence to his yells from a different time. Fear grips me, tightening every muscle in my body.

Oh, shit.

As the memory unfolds, I realize the emotions I felt weren't real. There's no way I'd be happy waking up, covered in dried blood, falling into Nikolai Knezha's arms for comfort. My feelings, my emotions, those arose because Nikolai used his ability against me, trying to revert me back into the naïve girl he took into his home so long ago.

"Because he's *my* soul mate. My soul and his collided. We awakened together, and I love him, Nik." My words ring through the air, causing Nikolai to freeze in place. His eyes narrow, and he turns to face me. The way he looks at me with betrayal in his eyes, with something else indiscernible crossing his face, I want to shove this memory back into the dark recesses of my mind. I don't want to experience it again just like I didn't want to live through it the first time.

Nikolai steps closer, towering over me. "Then he belongs here with us."

Tears blur my vision, my heart pounding in my ears. "But you'll ruin him." The words don't come out more than a whisper.

I don't even get a chance to react before Nikolai brings his hand up and slaps me across the face. The sting of his open palm buzzes through me, and I raise my hand to press the warming patch of skin.

Nikolai throws his arms up, and then covers his face. "He's already ruined you, so what does that matter, Skye?" he asks, bringing his cold blue eyes back to me.

I'm stunned silent.

"You will bring him to us. Do you understand? And if you don't, his journey with you will end. I've invested too much into you to have you throw everything away for a boy."

"But Nik—"

"Go to your room. I need to meditate about all this," he says, cutting me off. "Tomorrow, you'll go to him. You'll convince him to join us."

"I'll need time," I say. "He has family."

"I'll give you a month. Treat it like you would any newcomer."

"What if I can't do it?" I ask.

"That is not an option."

The world shifts, my vision darkening with a rage so intense it threatens to implode my entire world. I suck in a breath to tell Nikolai that he can't control me, but something wet drips on my face, drawing my attention away from him.

"Come on, my girl. You have to stay awake a bit longer."

The memory vanishes, throwing me back in the present. Nikolai holds my chin in his fingers, running a wet washcloth across my face. "You'll feel much better when you're cleaned up."

I swallow, bringing strength back into my head so I don't tip it forward from exhaustion. Confusion grips me. How much time has passed? I've been moved from the basement and back into my bedroom.

"I hurt," I whisper, turning my face away from him and the wet washcloth.

Luka stands by my door, leaning on the wall with his arms crossed. His sad eyes stare at the carpet, not meeting mine, and I can't help mirroring the despair marring his face with my own. I know something's wrong. So utterly wrong. I just need to remember.

"My name is Skye Stone. I'm seventeen years old and from Los Angeles, California. I have blond hair, gray eyes, and..." My thought trails off.

"And you're not a fucking Knezha nor will you ever be."

I blink, startled. It wasn't Nikolai's or Luka's thoughts in my mind.

Nikolai pokes my nose. "There, all done."

He moves the bowl of red water from his lap and onto my night table. He could've left me to bathe on my own, but he's hovering. For good reason. The torture he inflicted on my mind did nothing but put a temporary bandage on his problem.

Because I remember as much as I did before he tried to rewrite my very soul. I remember more.

I force myself to smile. I can't give myself away again. He

can't know I've resisted him. "You take such good care of me, Nik, but you're hovering. I'm fine. Just tired and hungry."

He chuckles. "Let me hover a little longer. We can have Friday night dinner together as planned."

I bob my head. "I'd like that very much."

Nikolai turns to Luka. "Gather our family. Tonight, we'll celebrate such a blessed moment and continue with our plans in our journey. I knew the stars would see to it."

I'm missing a day. An entire day just gone.

Luka flicks his gaze to me, and I pout my bottom lip at him.

"Just do as he says," I think to him.

He touches his finger to his temple, and I realize he's silently asking for me to let him into my head. He can't hear me in his thoughts, either. And for some reason, I can't hear him in mine. I don't know if it's him or me, but one of us is blocking the other.

Nikolai's eyes bore into the side of my face, his gaze so intense, my cheeks flush under his scrutiny. Something warm trickles onto my top lip again, and I dab the blood on my sleeve. It's like my own body responds, reminding me of the treacherous territory I'm wandering in. Next time, I might not be so lucky. My mind can only take so much, go through so much, before it decides to give out. The thought of being a little puppet, even if I'm blissfully unaware, freaks me the hell out.

Luka leaves the room, and I want nothing more than to jump to my feet to follow him, but Nikolai waiting for me to make a mistake snuffs out the need within me.

"I think I'm okay, Nik, really. You don't have to stay," I say. "I can manage."

"I suppose I'm just worried about you, my girl." He sighs. "I want to make sure you're okay."

Instead of arguing, I put my arms around him and rest my head on his shoulder. I can't shake the love a part of me has for him, which has been yanked to the surface. He wasn't always a bad guy. He took care of me after Angelica left this life. The day everything changed.

Nikolai sniffles and then laughs. He pulls away, his blue eyes shining with tears. "Now look what you did."

"Such a softy," I say.

He blinks the sheen from his eyes. "Can't help it. You're my family. I'm relieved you'll be okay."

"I was never not going to be okay." My voice cracks. I don't even believe the words myself. I just can't stop thinking about the forest, the girl, the figure. And now, after experiencing a moment in time where none of that happened in my mind, I'm scared. Terrified. "But I'm better. Well, maybe after I change from these clothes."

Nikolai hugs me once more and helps me to my feet. Without asking for my permission, he strolls to my wardrobe, as big as some of the guest rooms, and peers around. There's something about him running his fingers across my clothing that ignites alarm bells within me.

What if none of this is real? It wouldn't be the first time for me to question my reality. Things keep shifting so quickly, I can't recount everything from today. It's all the missing pieces leaving huge holes in my mind, making me want to give in. It'd be so easy to...

"*Snap out of it, Skye,*" a familiar voice says, drawing me away from Nikolai as he pulls out one of the many gowns hanging in my closet.

"*Snap out of what?*" I think back. Why is it I can hear Reggie and not Luka?

"*Now's not the time to forget who you are.*"

"*I'm Skye Knez—*" My words falter. Taking a deep breath, I gather everything I know to be true. Everything I know about me. "*I'm Skye Stone. I'm seventeen years old. I have blond hair and gray eyes. My birthday is January first. I have a soul mate named Luka Landon. I'm the guide—*"

"*You're not a fucking guide. You're a fucking disaster is what you are.*"

My mouth falls agape. "Excuse me?"

"I asked if you wanted to wear the necklace or the brooch," Nikolai says. I had no idea he was talking to me.

I tilt my head, focusing on him. "The brooch."

"*You hate those damn brooches.*" The voice mocks me, making me want to change my decision. I should be scared. I should worry that some stranger is in my head, speaking to me. Someone I didn't allow in. But there's something about Reggie's presence that makes me more confident staring at Nikolai.

"I should've guessed," Nikolai says.

I smirk. "You know me."

The voice in my head releases a laugh, startling me.

I try to push it away. "*Get out of my head.*"

"That's not how this works."

"What works?"

"Me and you," the voice says.

"Who are you? There isn't a me and anybody."

"Not even a you and Luka?"

I press my lips together, nodding as Nikolai tries and fails to talk over the voice now consuming all my attention. *"He has nothing to do with this."*

"He has everything to do with this."

Annoyance sneaks into me. *"Just stop. Leave me alone. You're not welcome in my head."*

"I'm always welcome."

My muscles stiffen.

"Don't you remember, Skye Stone of Los Angeles? You invited me here," he says.

"I'll wait in the hallway." Nikolai's voice yanks me from my silent conversation.

"Reggie," I think. *"Please, leave me alone."* He should've listened to my warning and left.

"Like you listened to my *warning?"* he thinks to me, getting more from my mind than I allowed. He's deeper in my head than I thought.

"Your warning?"

"About going after Luka."

My bedroom door shuts, and I stare around my empty room, half expecting Nikolai to change his mind and return to me, forcing me to get dressed in my bathroom.

I purse my lips. *"Of course I'd go after Luka. Gemma and*

Avery, too."

"*Obviously a huge mistake.*"

A small pinch in the back of my mind sends tears to my eyes. "*Shut up. He's never a mistake.*"

"*Whatever.*"

"*Just leave me alone, Reggie. I don't know who you are, but I don't want you here.*"

"*Too bad. You're why I'm here,*" he says.

"*What?*"

Silence.

"Skye, are you ready yet?" Nikolai asks through the door.

I spin around in a circle, like I'll somehow be able to pinpoint Reggie through the wall. "Almost." I cross my room to the clothes Nikolai set out for me. "*Answer me, Reggie,*" I think, broadcasting my thoughts.

More silence.

A pinprick of fear blossoms in my chest, stealing my breath. I have enough to deal with already. Why in the stars would the universe send another complication into my life? I don't know who Reggie is, but I do know that we've met at some point in my past.

But how does he affect my future?

I'm afraid to find out.

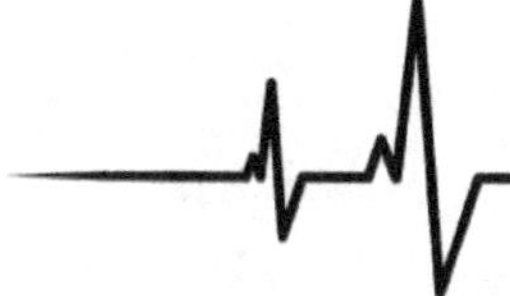

Chapter 19

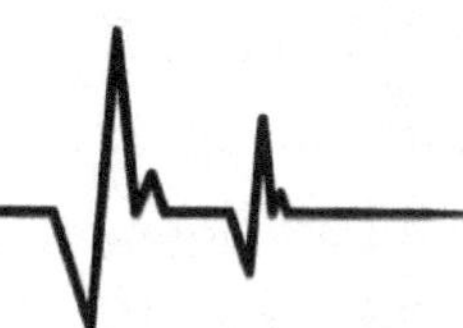

THE KNEZHA FAMILY WAYS

THE BALLROOM HUMS with excitement and life. Tonight, Luka will be officially marked as my guardian while Sam will enter the door to return as a Knezha. But not until later.

Now, I must act the part of the perfect Knezha Family representative and speak to all those outside our family who have come to join us to share a meal. It's Nikolai's way of showing the outside world we're not some crazy cult or whatever. It's the first thing people assume. But they don't know or understand.

"Why are you defending Nikolai and the Knezha Family's ways?" The thought overpowers mine, and I stiffen, straighten-

ing my shoulders.

I don't have an answer to Reggie's question. There are few things I know about myself, and one of them is I hate being told what to do or how to feel. Before Angelica took me in, I was an outcast in society, living on my own after my real dad disappeared. It's all I know about the me before Angelica. I know I was the only one looking out for myself until I let Angelica in. And then Nikolai. Things would be okay if Angelica were still here. If Nikolai would've just let me forge my own journey alongside his instead of forcing me to stand behind him and follow along.

"Exactly." Reggie stands next to me, bumping his arm with mine. I hadn't heard him approach me, and as much as I want to give him the cold shoulder, too many eyes are on me. He wears the newcomer's nametag, and the last thing I need is to be caught treating someone supposedly interested in our family poorly.

I clench my teeth, faking a smile. "You don't work for Nikolai, do you?"

"Would you prefer if I did or didn't?" he asks, talking through his teeth, grinning right back at me.

"I remember you, you know. You shot at me," I say. "You chased me through the forest."

His smile falters. "Out of all the fucking things in the world, that's what you remember?"

Someone waves, and I lift my hand and acknowledge them. "Maybe because I shot you."

Reggie raises an eyebrow, amusement crossing his face.

"Damn, your mind really is messed up now. I thought you were bad before, but this? Shit, Skye."

A scream burns in my throat, but I swallow it back. I want to yell that of course my mind is messed up. I can't seem to remember things I should, and I'm at a point where I don't know if I'll ever be okay or normal. And I'm sick and tired of people popping in and out of my memory. I'm tired of reliving things over and over again. The universe twisted my stone, sending me back to my past, and because of that, I'm afraid I don't have a future. That my existence is pointless. I'm not some key to the galaxy or some guide to the stars. I'm not some powerful telepath or beyond this life.

I'm Skye Stone, a confused seventeen year old, who misses feeling like she belonged. Who misses sharing moments with Luka unblemished by Nikolai Knezha. And I'm damn tired of this stranger poking into my head like he owns my mind or something.

"Relax, Skye." Reggie reaches out and touches my hand.

I open my mouth to tell him off, but a figure creeps up in the edge of my vision. Luka's shadow casts over me, and he stands close enough to make Reggie pull his hand away and step back. The heat of the whole room's scrutiny flourishes in my neck, and I inhale a breath through my teeth, wishing this night would be over with.

"Are you having a good time?" Luka asks, a sharp edge to the tone of his voice. "I feel like I haven't had a chance to be with you at all tonight."

I side glance Reggie. "Dance with me?"

"You hate dancing," Reggie comments.

I glare at him. *"You don't know me."*

Luka smiles and nods. "I'd like that." He turns to Reggie. "Enjoy yourself."

"You better enjoy yourself, *Skye."* Reggie's words sound like a threat in my mind. It's hard to get past the fact that he can still get into my head when I'm pretty sure I've locked the whole universe out after what Nikolai did to me. I wish I knew how. I haven't met anyone as powerful as Nikolai, and it leaves me questioning everything. Because Nikolai wouldn't knowingly allow someone who can threaten our family into our lives without reason—I still can't be sure if he actually works with Nikolai or not. But even if he doesn't, what is he doing here? Why bother and torment me? Was I such an awful person in my life before willingly following Nikolai?

Luka spins me around, pulling me from my thoughts, but I can't stop my gaze from darting around to track Reggie. He's staring right at me, watching my every move with Luka in a way that leaves me unnerved. The way he spoke to me like he knew me ignites something deep within me, and a memory breaks free.

Reggie laughs, tilting his head back. "Like this." With a flick of his hand, he lifts me off my feet and spins me around.

"Knock it off before I knock you out," I say. "You know I hate dancing."

A feminine laugh sounds through the air, and I turn my attention away from Reggie to a girl. Not just any girl, but Cora. I can't stop thinking about her in the forest, how she knocked

Nikolai out. How she...I think she's the one who killed me. But I wasn't afraid of her. Relieved almost.

"But I *love* dancing, Skye. Do it for me, okay?" Cora says.

"You owe me," I say, fake grimacing.

Cora sticks out her tongue at me, crossing her eyes. *"Anything you want, bestie."*

"Anything?" I ask.

We peer at each other, having a silent conversation without saying anything out loud or in our minds.

"Anything but that," she says.

"I think we can sneak out of here for a few minutes," Luka whispers into my ear, pulling me from the memory of Reggie and the mysterious girl from my past, one that was only a few weeks ago, I think. I suck in a breath, shooting a look toward Reggie, but he's no longer in the same spot. I want so desperately to return to that specific memory where I felt as happy as I do among the stars, even though I have no idea who they are or why I was with them. Why Reggie is with me now. It reminds me of my first memory of Luka, and I'm afraid of what it means.

I nod and smile, standing on my tiptoes to kiss Luka's cheek. "I'd like that." Peering around once, I spot Nikolai speaking to a woman in a business suit, studded with glittering jewels on her fingers. Another couple patiently waits for his attention, and I know it's why Luka suggested we sneak away. Nikolai will be too busy entertaining to come after us.

Lacing our fingers together, we head toward the double doors leading to the brightly lit hallway. Cedric stands outside the door, his arms crossed over his chest. He greets me with a smile, and I expect him to stop us to tell us to turn around to head inside. He's probably the only guardian to really pay attention to me, as the others have always let me do what I want. Cedric's the most loyal family member I know.

Before he can say anything, I lift the skirt of my dress a few inches to show off the too tall stilettos. "If Nikolai asks, I'm changing shoes. I can't stand in these a moment longer."

Cedric bobs his head, waving us out, and Luka tugs me down the hallway in the direction of my wing of the estate. The second we turn the corner, he pushes me against the wall, pressing my back to it, and leans in to kiss me softly on the lips.

My body reacts to the feathery light touch of his lips, sending tingles rushing from my lips to my toes, and I smile against his mouth as I pull him closer with my hands around his neck.

"I wanted to do that all night," Luka whispers, brushing his lips across mine again. He sucks my bottom lip between his teeth before slipping his tongue into my mouth to deepen his kiss, a kiss so full of desire, I'm not sure I ever want him to stop. The desperation in his every movement, every kiss, even the way he squeezes my hips reminds me of how much I want to run away with him, to get out of here and never look back.

The fact that we can't sends a wave of anger through me strong enough that Luka pulls away. His dark eyes lock mine in his intense gaze, and I press my lips into a line, my wave of desire now dissipating by the second.

"Let's go back to my room," I say, pulling myself together before I fall apart at the carelessly stitched seams of my existence.

Luka stares at me without saying anything.

I frown. "Everything okay?"

A grimace sweeps across his face, and he puffs his lips. "You can't hear me, can you?"

I blink a few times. *"Something is wrong with me."*

"I can't hear you, either," he whispers. "Are you blocking me?"

"I don't know. I don't think so. I wouldn't. Something happened—" I snap my mouth closed and shake my head. "Come on. Not here. I think even the walls listen."

Strutting forward, I tug Luka along the empty hallway to my living quarters. It's a relief everyone in the entire estate is in the ballroom, socializing and getting amped up for the private ceremonies soon to follow. We have at least an hour until Nikolai makes the final toast. I don't mind spending the entire time in my room with Luka, where I don't feel the walls closing in around me, hearing my name whispered through the air, feeling the heat of everyone's scrutiny boring so hot through my skin that it touches my soul.

Luka clicks the door shut behind us and wraps me in his arms again like he can't stand even a foot of space between us. "I wanted to ki—"

I lift my fingers to his lips. "I hope you're about to say kiss, because it's the only thing I want to hear from your mouth right now."

He smiles, his shoulders relaxing, and then he hugs me, brushing his lips against my ear. "Are you okay?"

I blink oncoming tears from my eyes, but he can't see the hurt hovering below the surface of my stone façade.

"Yeah," I manage to say, though he sees right through my quivering voice.

Nothing about this situation is okay, and I'm not sure it'll ever be. Nikolai invaded my mind. Instead of uplifting me and protecting me like he promised when I arrived at the Knezha Estate, he tore away everything Angelica had built up. He broke my trust. And more importantly, he broke my heart with his betrayal, one he can't even see because in his mind, it was I who betrayed him. Betrayed everyone.

And for what? For this boy holding me close, petting my hair, wiping my tears away? I can't accept that everything has fallen back to Luka and how our souls collided and connected us to the universe. A deep, dark part of me begs to surface, to show me that it was more. If everything that has led to this moment had occurred because of Luka, then I'd have never given up the thing that was me, all my memories, my identity, everything. I'd have stayed in that forest after I had accidentally shot him. I'd have waited for whatever lurked around the corner.

As much as I hate to think it now, I'm not so sure all of this is about me and Luka. It's about this journey, about every single person that makes up this world, this time, this way of living and how it pieces together.

Luka might be my soul mate, and we share a soul, but it's the rest of the world we were living in that was important. How could it not be? Because the universe doesn't revolve around

Luka and me. It's more. It's why my mind fights so hard to remember. If it were about Luka, I'd just forget. I'd live in ignorant bliss.

I straighten my shoulders, pulling my weight from Luka to stand on my own feet without his help. "I really am okay. I don't want to make tonight about me. You should be excited about the ceremony. Nik trusts you enough to be my guardian. And then there's Sam. He'll finally be our family."

Luka's eyebrows knit together at my words, yet something stops him from questioning them. "It's almost unbelievable—me being you're guardian." Because we both know I don't need one. From my memories before, I have always been the one to do the guarding and protecting.

"I expect the best protecting," I say.

It'd be too easy to reveal to Luka that Nikolai almost succeeded and how my spirit fought hard against him to keep my mind present and in reality, to spell it out and let him know I have yet to break. To say out loud I'm aware that everything I know hangs in the balance. But I'm afraid to utter the words, even if it means Luka will momentarily think we've lost.

No matter how much I want to run onto my balcony, hoist myself down, and run as fast as I can to escape, I can't. Luka's vulnerable and in need of believing I'm no longer the girl he knew before. I saw it when Nikolai sent Avery and Sam after me and how Nikolai overtook his mind, turning him into his puppet. Who's to say Nikolai won't continue to try to get to Luka or me for that matter? Outside of these walls is a world I have no idea how to survive and live in. If I had, I wouldn't have ended up right back where I started.

Luka grins. "You can have the best of everything."

Something shifts in my room, the lights flickering for a second, a strange buzz exploding through the air. My hair flies around my head, drifting in static that sets a spark off between mine and Luka's lips. Reaching up, I touch my fingers to my lips, gazing into Luka's eyes so closely that the whole world around us blurs.

I smile. Not the forced ones that seem to constantly leave an ache in my cheeks, but an actual real smile so full of happiness it's easier to hold onto a semblance of hope. It carries the hope I need to know that even in the end, as long as I fought as hard as I could, I'd find peace. It captures the faith I need to remember that as long as Luka and I are together, wherever our journey leads, no matter if it's a place full of darkness like under the Knezha Family's roof or a place full of light and love and joy like the galaxy, we'll both make it out okay wherever we end.

I don't know if he's responding to the sudden shift of my body language, but the moment Luka gazes at me smiling at him, his worry melts away, leaving the boy my soul recognizes not only in this life but everywhere.

He reaches up, tucking strands of my blond hair behind my ear. Sunlight halos him in a hazy glow, reflecting off the streaks of caramel in his hair. Leaning forward, he kisses me again, sliding his hands around my lower back so there isn't even an inch of space allowed between our bodies.

Pulling back ever so slightly, Luka tickles my lips with his warm breath, begging to meet Luka's again. "Are you sure about this? I will go with you wherever you want me to."

I don't let the space between our mouths last more than his last word. *"Only if you want to. But there's something about them—I can't even describe it. They remind me of..."* My thoughts to Luka fade, and an image of Angelica erupts in my head. But he can't see her. There's something fiercely protective within me over the woman who saved me, even if she brought me into Nikolai's world, because she wouldn't have let him get away with whatever he's doing. I'm afraid even thinking her name to Luka will sully who she was to him because of the Knezha Family association.

Her memory will thrive through me and only me.

The memory...

The realization hits me hard, winding me, nearly knocking me away from Luka's arms in the present. He's no longer smiling at me—and maybe he never was—not now at least. His smile stayed in some other lifetime, a lifetime I miss full of smiles and hope and true belonging.

"Angelica." I can't stop her name from escaping my lips despite my best efforts to grab at the very sound of my voice in the air to mute it out of existence.

The buzzing in the air suddenly vanishes, and the lights blink a few more times before they hum back on without interference.

I suck in a gasp, bringing my hand up to my heart. "Oh, no."

Luka tenses, peering around the room. "What is it?"

"The end. There's no way I'll ever survive this."

A loud bang erupts on my door, startling me so much that I nearly topple over in my stilettos. I thought I'd have more time before Nikolai realized I'm not made of glass to be broken. I'm built of steel and stone and bulletproof glass. Break down one of my walls, and there are ten more behind it.

"Skye!" a voice yells through the door. "Open up."

Fear clenches my heart, threatening to steal the rhythmic beating away. I spin around, looking for something, anything, I could use to stop everyone on the other side of the door from invading my room to steal me away to destroy the person I'm trying to be.

But there's no point.

Strong arms slide around me, hugging me from behind. Luka rests his head on my shoulder, but it's not in the comforting touch I yearn for so much every time I'm near him. This one is new, different, dangerous. He's not protecting me. He's locking me in place.

More banging sounds on the door. "Skye!"

The door flies open, smashing into the wall. Luka spins me around and away from the door, fighting with himself against whatever hold Nikolai maintains on him. He releases me, and I fall to my knees, hitting them hard enough on the wood floor to cause me to cry out. I push through the pain and get back to my feet to face the intruder.

I don't have a moment to even blink as I watch in utter surprise as Reggie charges Luka and knocks him back, sending them both skidding across the floor. Arms flail, both of them swinging to punch, to fight, to hurt each other.

"Stop it!" I scream. Rushing forward, I fist my fingers to knock Reggie away. I don't even get within a foot of him before I fly across the room and land on the cushion of my bed. Scrambling back to my feet, I head toward Reggie and Luka again. "Don't hurt Luka. I'll go with you. I'll do whatever Nikolai wants."

Reggie punches Luka in the face, sending his head jerking sideways. "You sure about that?"

"Please," I beg.

Reggie hops to his feet, holding out his hand to mine. With a throbbing, breaking heart, I let him take my fingers into his. Luka heaves on the floor, his breath ragged, but then something shifts in his face. His lips twist, and he props up on his elbows.

"Don't go with him, Skye," Luka says.

I scrunch my nose. "I don't have a choice. Nikolai knows he failed. It's over. I can't keep fighting him."

Reggie tugs my hand. "Come on. Nik's waiting." Yanking my arm, he nearly drags me a few feet, but not in the direction I expect. Instead of taking me to the door for my walk of shame through the house, he heads in the direction of my balcony.

I resist, pulling my arm away. "Who are you?"

"Just listen to me. We're short on time," Reggie says.

"You really don't work for Nikolai," I say.

"Skye, get away from him," Luka says from behind me.

I glance at Luka over my shoulder. "It's okay, Luka. I think I know him."

"Skye, get away!" Luka yells, rushing forward. I don't even

have time to react before Reggie raises his hand and flings it out, sending Luka crashing into my wall. The lights flicker and pop, leaving us in darkness except for the outside lighting shining in through my window.

Reggie tries to grab my elbow, but I spin on my heels and race toward Luka. "You didn't have to hurt him. I could've explained everything." A strange sensation crawls across my entire body, and I realize Reggie lifted me a few inches into the air, preventing me from getting near Luka.

"It doesn't work like that, Skye. Come the fuck on. Knezha is in his head. He's lost to us," Reggie says.

"They're all lost to us." I push the memory of Cora's voice away.

A spike of fear stabs through my soul. "What?"

The air whooshes around me, and Reggie squeezes me against his chest, yanking me along toward the balcony and away from Luka. This can't be happening. I didn't give up all my memories trying to return to Luka to be ripped away again by some stranger who knows more than I do.

"We're leaving," he says. "Time's up. You've failed."

I struggle in his embrace, trying to break free. Jerking my arm back, I manage to strike him with enough force in the ribs to get him to let me go.

"Damn it! You don't get to choose what to do. I didn't come into this hellhole, put my life in danger, to leave empty-handed. You better get it in your head that you don't belong here and fast. I will drag your ass out by your hair." Reggie steps forward again, but I step back.

"I'm not leaving Luka. If that means I stay here, then I stay here. I don't even know you that well. I shot you. I ran from you. There's a reason I'm here," I say.

"You don't belong to the Knezha Family, Skye, but Luka does," he says.

"Who even sent you here?"

A loud yell sounds in the hallway, sending Reggie rushing forward to grab me. Panic seizes my chest at the thought that I might not get the choice to face Nikolai after all and that everything I've been through is about to be wasted because I'm getting taken from Luka. That this guy is forcing me away. Ruining my world.

Reggie jerks out his hand, slamming the door shut with his mind. The whole house shakes, furniture shuddering and shifting. My bed flies across the room and collides in the door, stopping anyone from entering on the other side.

Pain erupts through my arm as Reggie yanks me from my feet and drags me across the room. He shakes me, anger sweeping across his face. "Don't make me kill you, Skye, but if you keep fighting I don't mind carrying your body."

I stop fighting.

I stop moving altogether.

And then, I do something I never expected I'd do in my entire life. "Nikolai! Help me!" I scream, my voice booming through the open window.

Pain bursts in my head, the walls of my mind crumbling to pieces. I let Nikolai in.

"Where are you, Skye?"

"My room. Hurry. Reggie is kidnapping me."

"Don't worry, my beautiful girl. I'm always here for you. Always."

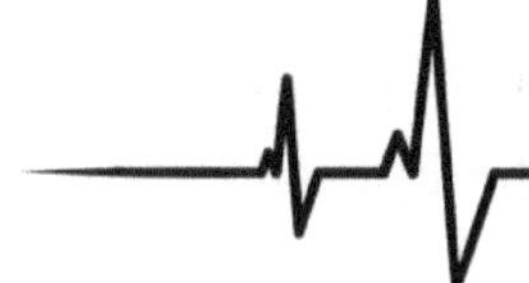

Chapter 20

A DANGEROUS WORLD

"NO!" I SCREAM, hitting the ground and tumbling away from Reggie. My stilettos spike the soft grass, stopping me from bolting away.

Reggie reaches down and grabs my wrists, yanking me from the ground.

I expect him to toss me over his shoulder to move faster, but all he does is drag me alongside him. Every few feet, I stumble in the grass, tugging from his hands, using my inability to keep up in heels to my advantage. After the third time of losing his grip, Reggie tugs a pocket knife from his pocket and flicks it open.

I cringe. "You don't have to do this."

"Hell yeah, I do. Those shoes are going to get me caught." Grabbing my leg, he takes the knife to the intricately wound straps and cuts them off.

"You could've unbuckled them," I say, nearly spitting the words out.

He chuckles, shaking his head. "Didn't think heels were your thing. Plus, I know you. You'd kick that heel right into my forehead."

He might be right.

My shoes fall from my feet, and I scramble back, trying to get back up. If I can put enough space between us, I can evade him and run for it.

Grabbing me by the back of my gown, he hoists me up and breaks out into a jog. I only move my legs because I know if I don't I'd end up face first on the ground, and now that we're on the cement drive, I'd rather wait until I get my chance. There's no possible way he's getting off the property with me.

Headlights flash from the line of cars in the circular drive, and my stomach twists, making me sick enough that I'm afraid I'll throw up dinner. He's not alone. Of course he's not alone. I was stupid to think otherwise.

"You better pick up the pace. I can feel the ground shaking, and I can only block us for so long," Reggie says.

"I'm not helping you get away," I say.

He swings out his arm, moving a car out of our way. Metal crashes behind us, sending a screeching noise through the air, making me wince. He's not messing around. He's barricading any kind of path the others could easily follow us by.

"I swear if you make me pick you up I—"

"Pick me up, and you'll get an elbow to the spine," I say.

"Same damn Skye." Reggie yanks me along faster, and the only reason I'm not putting up a fight is because I know this is a losing battle. The Knezha Family will never let me go. I've tried.

"You could've left whenever you wanted," Reggie thinks to me. *"But you didn't because of Luka."*

Hearing Luka's name in my mind, especially coming from Reggie's thoughts, sends an ache through my chest strong enough that I gasp before I groan.

"Shut up," I say out loud instead of thinking it to him.

Reggie presses his lips together, and surprise washes over me. I can't believe he listened, and it wasn't because I made him. A horn honks, drawing my attention to the car idling nearby.

Another man stands by the driver's door. He's quite a bit older than Reggie, and fear crashes over me in a sizzling wave. I know him. I recognize his startling eyes, one brown and one blue from a memory I had of Gemma in the forest.

He's the man who took her away from me. He kidnapped her and did something to her, but what? She came back. This whole time, I thought it was Nikolai who was responsible. I thought he had someone kidnap her as a part of his game. Maybe take her to the basement. But it wasn't him. It was this man with Reggie, both connected to my past, involved with the girl who killed me. And now, they're kidnapping me. These people are part of the dangerous world Nikolai warned me about, the world he was protecting me from, and somehow, I was involved with them. But what is my part?

"Stop!" I scream, sending the command hot and fast from both my mouth and mind. "You're not taking me."

Reggie yells out, covering his ears with his hands, and I jerk my hand out, slapping him across the face. Spinning on my feet, I charge back to the house. I'll never get into a car with people who might tear Luka from my life.

"Skye!" Reggie yells from behind me.

I don't stop. I can't. Everyone in the universe is against me. I don't know who or what to believe as my memory continues to evade me, mislead me, blind me from everything that's in front of me.

"Where are you, Skye?" Nikolai's thoughts travel through my mind. The ballroom was across the estate from my room. If Nikolai made his way there, then it means he's not here.

"We jumped from the balcony. We're down the driveway. What's taking you so long? I need help," I think back.

"You need to fight until I get there. I'm sorry. I couldn't make a scene. Tonight is important, and your careless behavior is putting our entire family at risk."

Shock rolls over me. I don't believe what he's saying. *"You're blaming me?"*

"I should let them take you," he says. *"Maybe you'll appreciate what you have here. Maybe that's what you need to remember who you are and where your place is on this journey."*

"Nik, no! Please. Don't do this. I'll do whatever. I don't want to go with them. I don't want to leave Lu—you." I regret thinking

the last part, and I'm not so sure I was fast enough changing my thought.

"Skye!" Reggie yells again from behind me.

The world spins around me, my feet falling out from under me. There's nothing I can do as Reggie uses his mind to yank me back toward him. I skid across the cement, my gown tearing at the quick movement.

"Release my girl." Nikolai's voice booms through the air, startling me. He stands so far away, right under the balcony of my bedroom, but the command he holds extends far past the space closest to him. It's like his words bend and move through the world without him having to raise his voice.

Reggie yells out, his pull on me loosening.

I've never been so relieved to see Nikolai stroll in our direction, arms extended, his blue eyes so cold I swear they're glowing in the silvery moonlight overhead. Not far behind him stands Luka, his face shadowed in bruises caused by his fight with Reggie.

"Skye, this is your chance," Luka thinks to me. *"Run. You have to run. You can escape when everyone's distracted."*

Like a breath of precious air in a moment of drowning desperation, Luka's thought travels to me, stirring such love inside me that I hop to my feet and use the strength of his presence in my head to push me forward.

"You need to run, too," I say. *"I'll find you."*

Voices yell through the air, pulling my attention away from Luka. Reggie flicks his hand out, knocking Nikolai off his feet. Nikolai yells out, and his voice sends Reggie back to his knees.

It's a battle of who wants me more, and I refuse to take any part of it.

"Run now! The front gate is your best hope. I'll take the back," Luka says.

I spin again away from Nikolai, turning my back on the fight. My chest heaves with every breath. I refuse to take my eyes off the opened gate without any guardians watching over it because they're in the ballroom. We haven't had any trouble with people in so long that Nikolai never thought it was necessary to keep someone posted when we're all together, because together, the Knezha Family is strong, powerful, dangerous even.

More voices sound through the air.

Gunfire rings out, the sudden pops sending me to my knees. Complete chaos overtakes the quiet night intended for celebration. Tires squeal, and burning rubber wafts through the air, contaminating my heavy breathing and sending me into a coughing fit.

"Thanks for making it easier on us, Skye," a voice says, the rumble of an engine humming from the driveway feet away. "Now, get in."

I shake my head, pushing myself faster. The gate leading out is still a mile away. Nikolai keeps the perimeters far enough from the mansion to not feel gated in.

"No," I say, pushing my feet harder.

"Come on. Stop being a stubborn ass and get in. You're already leaving Luka so might as well—"

I raise my hand. "I'm not leaving Luka. He's meeting me."

Reggie lets out a loud laugh. "Nik will never let him go. I saw it for myself. Luka was already on his knees with everyone else, probably with a killer headache. Good thing for us, we know Knezha well enough to be prepared."

Fear trickles through me. No. This can't be. This was our chance.

I swivel to head in the other direction, but a strong arm hooks around my waist, yanking me off my feet. Fear explodes in my chest, sending a wave of panic over me. I flail, swinging my arms out, and pain radiates through my elbow as I connect with Reggie's knee. I crash to the pavement, skidding over the ground, unable to do anything but brace myself as I plow into the side of a black car idling in wait for me.

The lights lining the driveway flicker and the bulbs pop. Glass sprays out over my head, forcing me to close my eyes. The world rattles with life, and pain pinches behind my eyes. I clench my fingers into fists, trying to push to my feet.

"Help!" I scream. I don't know why I do it. Why I keep begging for help from people hell-bent on dooming me, I wish I knew. But I'm afraid of Reggie. I'm afraid of the memories I have of him. I'm terrified of the strangely familiar man in the driver's seat yelling at me. How can all my options be so terrible that I have to decide which of my enemies I prefer to be with? Nikolai's predictability is the only reason apart from Luka I'd rather submit under his leadership and rules. I've had enough uncertainty with my memory loss to last me for eternity.

Rocks fly from the picturesque landscape pelting me so hard in the chest I lose my breath. My back hits the tire as I crabwalk sideways, using the car to help me to my feet, but another wave of agony rushes through me. My knees hit the grass next to the driveway, and my fingers dig into the soil of a sleeping flowerbed.

Footsteps thud closer, but I don't get the chance to look up. Reggie throws a blanket over my head, blocking my vision of the world around me. Cold hands grab my arms, yanking them behind me to knock me flat on my stomach. He's no longer playing games. He's no longer giving me a chance to agree to go with him. He's snuffing out all my chances of a fair fight, stealing my senses away. I cough and spit, my mouth pressed into the dirt, leaving me unable to scream again without inhaling a mouthful of soil.

Tears burn down my cheeks, turning into mud. My heart pounds in my head, and I give up struggling. All I can hear are more footsteps, the crunching of glass under shoes, and the heavy breathing of Reggie and the strange man as they hoist me up from the ground.

Reggie slings me upside down over his shoulder, sending the blood pumping hard through my heart and into my head, adding more pressure to the sting behind my eyes. His muscular shoulder digs into my stomach, hurting me with every step.

"Luka?" I call out, pushing my voice to him, hoping to get into his head. If I can talk to him, tell him what's happening, maybe he'll fight against whatever Nikolai is doing or he'll tell me that Reggie is lying about what's happening to him.

He doesn't respond.

"Skye, hold tight. I cannot act until the newcomers and visitors

calm down and return inside. Those men have everyone in a panic to leave. They knew I'd have to deal with them before I could retrieve you." Nikolai's sharp voice swirls in my mind, sending a wave of pain through my head. He speaks of me like a piece of property, like everything else in the world is more important to him. Maybe that's true. I'm not useful if I can't be used.

Squeezing my eyes shut, I concentrate on listening in on the thoughts around me while pushing Nikolai's away. A masculine voice erupts in my head, but they're not Reggie's thoughts. He's purposefully singing a song, repeating the chorus over and over again. He knows what he's doing. He knows how to fight Nikolai, and he's not taking any chances.

Sucking in a breath, the fabric of the blanket over my head sticks to my lips. "Stop," I say, my voice barely audible.

"And risk Nikolai sending you somewhere I can't get to like before? Allow him to have your journey with his family realigned to his liking or whatever damn excuse he gives for messing with your mind? Hell no. That's some messed up bullshit and you know it. There's no magical journey or special place for those who take on the Knezha name."

The world continues to bounce around as I'm relocated. "Shut up." His words stab my heart. He's belittling what I know to be true—not about Nikolai, but about where I'm supposed to be in life and where my journey leads. Reggie must've never seen the stars. Anger rushes through me, and I twist and wriggle my torso, throwing him off balance. "Stop!"

My stomach drops, and I land on the pavement, pain reverberating through my shoulder. I flip, my legs splaying over my head, and my stomach presses into the cold ground. Bindings keep my hands behind my back, making it hard to get up.

I yell out, grinding my teeth, thrashing against my restraints. I manage to throw the blanket from my head, and I peer around the property, catching sight of Reggie and the man a few feet away, standing there frozen, wide eyes peering at me. Both their familiarities press against me, but I can't place them from what I know. All I see in them are people who attempted to ruin things for me before and again now.

"Release me!" I yell, my voice traveling through the air. The air itself shudders, the wind picking up to blow strands of blond hair from my face.

Like a robot, Reggie moves one foot in front of the other, each step forced and heavy. "Stop it, Skye," he says.

A new wave of panic grips me, because I remind myself of Nikolai. I possess the same abilities he does, but it hasn't been until this moment that I can feel the world around me, touching my very soul. It's like I'm extending from my skin and bones, filling up every molecule of existence. I'm everything and nothing. It reminds me of the galaxy world come to earth, but without all the love and relief that flows through it.

Everything feels utterly wrong.

Reggie continues to stroll toward me until he bends down and loosens the binding on my wrists. Hopping to my feet, I get up and face him, ignoring the darkness traveling over my skin, raising my hair and giving me goosebumps. I slam my hands into his chest, knocking him away from me.

Reggie reaches into his jacket. "I don't want to hurt you,

but I will. You're messing with my ability to block Nikolai, and I didn't come here to negotiate with you. I have a job to do, and we're running out of time."

His green eyes shine in the light of the moon, glowing with warmth instead of the iciness Nikolai's always seem to carry. It makes me calm down enough to release him from my command.

"A job?" I ask. "This is a job?"

His lips press in a line, and he takes a step closer, his hand still in his jacket. He looks ready to launch at me to try to restrain me again. "It's not how it sounds. I'll explain it in the car, but we have to move."

I hold my hands up. "Why can't you get it into your head I'm not leaving without Luka."

Reggie narrows his eyes. "He'll be okay here. Nikolai is anything but wasteful when it comes to useful people."

My vision darkens around the edges. "That's why I can't leave him."

"And that's why you can't stay anymore, Skye! Damn it! I can't do this. I can't talk to you like this." He eases closer, pulling out a taser, surprising me. I expected a deadlier weapon. "You have two seconds to get in the car or I'll use this on you, and I know how much you love it." He nearly drenches me with sarcasm, his heated gaze flicking behind me.

I suck in another deep breath, my chest heaving as I try to calm myself. Where's Nikolai? Where are the guardians? Why am I afraid of the taser? I've been hurt worse, but I cringe when he aims it at me.

"Please, I can't leave without Luka," I say.

"Just tase her already," the strangely familiar man yells from the car a few dozen feet away. "Knezha's breaking through."

I want to ask through what, but I don't have a chance. Reggie nudges me forward, gripping onto me with one hand. A glimpse into his thoughts proves he's contemplating listening to the man and tasering me so he can get me out of here. He struggles to keep his thoughts on the repetitive song, but other thoughts seep through.

"I swear if you hurt me, you'll regret it," I say, hoping he'll reconsider. He's not affected by my pleas so maybe I need to try to get to him another way.

"You think so?" Reggie asks. "I think I'll regret it if I don't. You know you deserve it."

I frown. "What? I deserve it?"

He sighs. "Of course you wouldn't remember."

I pry into his head, making him wince, hoping to listen in on his thoughts to better piece together what I mean to him. Reggie knows me. He's treating me in a certain way based on what he knows about me. And I never knew I wanted to know someone so badly until this moment because I could use the information to my benefit. I can use it to go back to retrieve Luka. Reggie keeps saying Luka can't come, but I refuse to think of leaving him behind. I can fix this. I can steel Luka from Nikolai. What I can't do is steel myself from Reggie.

We glance at each other, assessing and trying to determine what we're both going to do next. Because I'm not leaving with him, and I'm pretty sure he's certain about not leaving without me.

Before I can make a move, he rushes me, wrapping his arms around me instead of using his taser. I elbow him in the face, and blood spurts from his nose and splatters across my pale blue gown like eerie abstract roses. The injury doesn't stop him, though. All he does is drop me and latch his strong fingers around my ankles to drag me toward the car.

"Damn it, Skye. I think you broke my nose," he mutters.

I reach out to grab onto something, anything, but come up empty-handed. I wish he'd stop talking to me like he knew me and would just explain what's going on. "You have to let me go. I can't go with you until you explain things."

He glances at me over his shoulder, the air buzzing with static. "Shit."

The echo of a gunshot rings through the air, and the man at the car fires his weapon, aiming toward the estate. I spin, struggling against Reggie, and I realize what he meant by blocking Nikolai. It's like the air itself is alive and moving, creating an actual barrier around us impenetrable by any of the Knezha Family members who stand gathered, trying their best to get to me.

Another gunshot rings out.

The sounds drag me into my memory, ricocheting through my head, my very first death rushing back to me, taking over all my thoughts. This isn't the first time an outsider like Reggie intent on interrupting our lives has gotten onto our estate. Nikolai keeps things pretty open to not draw attention to us.

And because of that, because Reggie knew, he chose the perfect time like the last intruder—a man who accidentally shot me, trying to save me from Nikolai. There are a ton of people out there who can't fathom the Knezha Family way of life, brushing us off as freaks of a society we don't want any involvement in, but one we still have to deal with, laws we still have to abide by. And Reggie, his presence screams that he abides by another set of rules, ones outside of the Knezha Family and society's. People outside our family can't see the galaxy. Reggie obviously doesn't believe in it or the journey.

"You're not a Knezha. Stop thinking like you are." It's the girl's voice—Cora's. Her thoughts ignite confusion in me, battling the fear caused by Reggie.

A dozen thoughts cross my mind. Reggie knows too much. It's like he's studied our family, studied Nikolai. But why isn't Nikolai his target? Why me?

I stop fighting. "Please stop. I'll go as long as you don't hurt anyone."

"Don't talk to me like I'm the one who's the monster. You have no room to talk." Reggie's thoughts come to me, riddled with pieces of the same song he was thinking about earlier. He's trying to keep his head clear, but shutting off one's thoughts is nearly impossible. A person can't just clear their head, and something like trying to think of something else doesn't last long.

The roar of a car engine draws my attention from my thoughts and to the familiar stranger sitting behind the wheel of the sleek, black Dodge Challenger. The fact that it has a silver

KF emblem attached to the rear side panel freaks me out. These guys went through a lot of trouble to get to this spot.

The man in the car glances up, sending another wave of uncertainty through me. Smiling, he revs the engine, motioning for us to hurry. My instincts scream for me to not get in the car. To do everything I can to get away.

Taking a small step forward, I meet the driver's mismatched eyes. My expression must give away my next move, because he yells out, reaching into the glove compartment. A hand locks onto my shoulder, shoving me forward. I was too slow.

"Get in, now!" Reggie yells from behind me. "I lost control." His fingers lock into my hair, and he shoves me into the backseat.

My ears ring with the sudden gunfire as the driver shoots his gun out the window. He hits the gas pedal, launching the car forward. The putrid smell of burning rubber clouds the air, and I catch sight of the man's wild eyes in the rearview mirror.

I can't believe this is happening. I can't believe I was wrong about Nikolai being the biggest monster and how he might've been right all along about me needing the Knezha protection with what feels like the world out to get me, to keep me and Luka apart.

I turn in my seat and glance out the back window. A figure emerges from the dust. It's Nikolai.

"Put your seatbelt on, Skye," he thinks to me.

I click my seatbelt into place.

"Now hold on."

Chapter 21

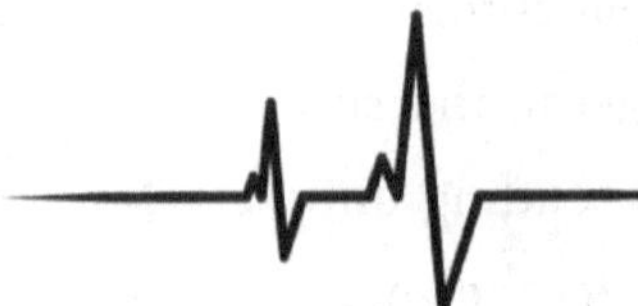

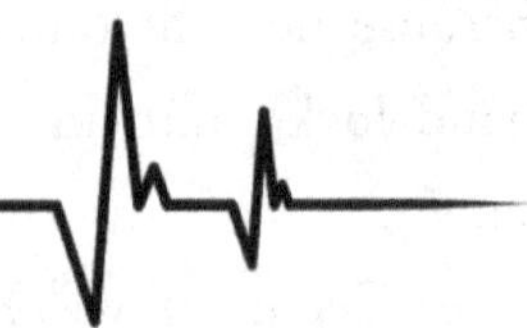

KNOW MY ENEMY

GLASS EXPLODES, METAL crunches, and my entire world spins. I flail in my seat, unable to brace against anything, jerking around with the car. It flips, and both guys in the front seat yell out. My stomach twists and knots, threatening to make me sick.

"Get ready to unbuckle your seatbelt. Get out through the back window," Nikolai says. I still can't believe I'm following his orders. Part of me wants to find out if I can escape these guys on my own, but another part of me, the one that's in control of my instincts, tells me to stay where I know my enemy.

The car jerks to a stop, my head still spinning with dizziness. Reggie waves his hand, flipping the car back onto its wheels, but the engine doesn't start when the other man turns the key. He smacks the wheel with his hands and swivels in his seat to glare at me—no—behind me.

Reggie groans, but he doesn't pause to assess the situation. He jams his finger into the seatbelt latch and unfastens it. The car rattles, the windshield exploding. His partner releases a long wail, clutching his head. He passes out, hitting his forehead to the wheel and sags in his seat.

"Fucking hell," Reggie says, turning to me. "Look what happens when you let your guard down."

I smash my fingers into the seatbelt, trying to force it to unlatch while Reggie is preoccupied touching the strangely familiar man's throat. The buckle doesn't unclasp, locking me in place. *"Nik! Nik I'm trapped! I can't get out."*

Nikolai doesn't respond.

"I hear you calling for Nik. It won't work. He's probably knocked out like Zane after that power burst." Reggie shifts in his seat, kneeling on his knees. The glint of a knife sparkles in the solar light trickling in through the shattered back window. He reaches back, and I twist and jerk, punching out my arms. He grunts through my hits but doesn't back down. Grabbing the front of my ripped dress, he swings the knife at me. I flinch, expecting hot pain to course over my chest.

My seatbelt snaps free, and I scramble to get it off my lap, but Reggie doesn't let go of me. I kick my feet into the back of his seat, pushing myself up to try to squeeze through the back window. He reaches for me again, and I slap him, fighting him the best I can in the small space.

Nothing stops him. The moment he finds an opening in my attempt to hurt him, he takes it, locking his fingers onto my dress again, this time yanking me forward. He locks his free hand into my hair and pulls me between the front seats and then pushes me out through the broken windshield. I land on the hood and flip over, falling onto the soft grass.

He launches to his feet and jumps from the hood, rushing me. Hooking his arm around my waist, he lifts me up like a bratty child, holding me under his arm, abandoning his partner in the wreckage.

I scream, clawing at his side, trying to pull his dress shirt up to rake my nails over his skin.

He ignores me, running right toward the front gate of the property. And it's open, not a single guardian around to intervene.

"I have her," Reggie says, his voice echoing through the air.

It's then that I realize he's wearing an earpiece, talking to someone on the other line. But who?

Skye, I'm right behind you. Keep fighting. Nikolai's thoughts enter my mind, and for the first time in a long time, I'm not afraid of them. They're a welcomed sound in my head.

"Nik!" I scream, my voice ripping through the air. "Nik!"

Reggie swears, yelling something I can't understand through the pounding in my head. Gunshots pop through the air again, and I flinch, afraid I'll get hit in the crossfire. But they're not coming from the estate behind us. A figure appears near the gate ahead of us, and a girl my age stands there, waiting for us.

I recognize her. It's Cora, Reggie's girlfriend, the one who killed me in the forest. The one tied to my time after I shot Luka and ended up in the basement. As much as I should be terrified, I'm not. Because something about her presence calls to me. Memories of her laugh swirl through my mind.

"What the hell happened?" she asks, raising her gun again, pulling me from my head. She doesn't shoot, though.

"Skye's a feisty little shit like fucking always is what happened. She left the damn dinner a little too early, and I had to go with Plan B," Reggie says.

Plan B? What was the original plan?

"Please," I say. "Don't do this. You can't take me from my family. Don't make me leave Luka."

"Nik? Nik, where are you?" I ask.

"I've been shot, Skye. I can't get to you."

Fear laces around my heart, squeezing it. *"Where are the guardians?"*

"They're not coming for you. I can't put everyone in danger. We must protect the many over one, remember? You've already caused too much chaos. I'm sorry. Just keep your mind open, and I'll find you soon enough."

"Nik, please. Please."

Silence.

"Come on, Skye. The car's waiting." Cora grabs my arm, pulling me forward to push me in front of her. "Easy now. I don't want to have to kill you for easy transportation."

I shift to look over my shoulder. "That's not necessary."

"Just thought I'd put it out there. I know how much you hate dying, Skye."

"You know nothing about me."

"What did I tell you? Fucking pain as always," Reggie says.

"Reggie, quit it," she says, glaring at him.

A sleek, silver Acura ILX idles in the middle of the road leading away from the estate. Cora nudges me to the open door. I stand frozen outside the car, ready to fight all over again. I thought I was worth the fight to Nikolai. I thought he'd do everything he could to protect me. But, here I am, facing an unknown threat with two people who know things about me they shouldn't.

"Nikolai will find me," I say, turning to look at the gate to the Knezha Estate.

"I hope he does," Reggie says. "I've been dying to see the Almighty Nikolai Knezha in action."

"He'll kill you," I threaten.

He leans forward and slaps his knee like what I've said was the most hilarious thing in the world. *I'd be more worried about you. You used to do all the murdering for Nik, remember?*

I try to push him from my head.

Cora sighs. "We'd be dead already if that were true. Now, get in the car."

"No," I say.

She shoves me forward, not giving me a choice. "Just get in and stop being difficult. You know you wanted to leave that place. Stop fighting to stay."

Tears burn in my eyes. "That's my family."

"You're not a Knezha."

"But my boy—"

"This wouldn't be the first time you've left Luka behind," she says, cutting me off.

"Who are you people?" I ask.

"Your rescue team. You can thank us later," she says. Reggie slides into the seat in front of me, and Cora climbs behind the wheel, hits the gas, and peels out, leaving smoke in our wake.

Pain pinches behind my eyes. None of this makes sense. "I'm so confused."

Cora glances at me in the mirror. "Just hold tight, okay? And close your mind off, will you? Knezha has already had enough fun playing in your head."

"What?"

"Just do it or we'll knock you out."

Reggie shows me a syringe, which I'm pretty sure is filled with a sedative of some sort. The last thing I want to be is unconscious, so I do as Cora says and concentrate on pushing everything out except for Luka.

"Skye?"

Like he knew I was thinking of him, Luka says my name in my head. Hope rushes through me, sending the panic away. Maybe Reggie was wrong about Nikolai getting to him. Maybe he did escape and I can find him.

"Luka, I've bee—"

"Luka, too," the girl says, interrupting my thoughts. "Especially him."

"What?"

"Those are the orders," she says.

"I—"

"She warned us," Reggie says.

Cora glances in the rearview mirror at me again. "You're right. Sedate her."

"No!"

But it's too late. Reggie jabs the syringe right into my thigh through my dress before I have a chance to fight.

"Skye, what's happening?" Luka thinks to me.

My brain's too foggy to answer.

"Skye?"

I fall into darkness.

⎯⌁⎯

"Don't do this. Not again. Please." The sound of Avery's voice in my mind tugs at my consciousness. Bright sunshine trickles in through the windshield, causing me to squint my eyes.

I sit up, staring at Reggie in the rearview mirror as he shifts lanes. "I hear her again," I say. "She's in so much torment."

A hand touches my knee. "Avery's strong, Skye. She'll recover."

I swivel in the seat and face the familiar girl sitting next to me. "I knew I should've made her wait, Cora. She was just so desperate to get out of there with Cooper. If only I told her what was going on, none of this would've happened. She'd still be free."

Cora shakes her head. "She wasn't strong enough. Nik would've gotten right into her head and then what? We'd be in trouble. You know how important it is that we stay off the radar."

Reggie slaps the wheel. "Of course she knows, Cora. She's not scrambling her damn head for fun."

Cora groans. "And I'm still trying to convince her not to."

I sigh. "I have to, Cora. Luka needs me."

"And we need you," she says.

I rub the palms of my hands into my eyes. "What if it was Reggie he had?"

She twists her lips to the side, flicking her gaze to the mirror to meet Reggie's eyes. "Nikolai can have him. The universe played a joke on me colliding my soul with this guy's. Out of all the people in the world—"

"I fucking love you, too, Cora," Reggie says, chuckling from the front seat.

I smile at them, basking in the nearly palpable emotions that flow between the two of them. While it stirs happiness within me, it reminds me of how much I miss Luka. How hard it was for me to abandon him after I underestimated Nikolai, thinking I'd finally outsmarted him. But Nikolai was already in Luka's head long before I realized it. And running didn't help. I never had a chance. We never had a chance.

My body jerks, and I smack my head on the window. Pain radiates from every part of me, stealing me away from a memory I had no idea I was reliving. The only thing stopping me from screaming out is that Cora's name keeps sounding through my mind as I replay the memory over and over again in my head.

"Cora," I say, tilting my head back, blinking the haze from my eyes.

"I'm right here, Skye. Everything's going to be fine."

"Luka," I say next.

A warm hand grips mine. "Don't do it, Skye."

"Luka."

"Sedate her again, Reggie."

"No," I whisper.

A pinch burns in my leg. "Sorry, Skye. We'll be safe soon enough."

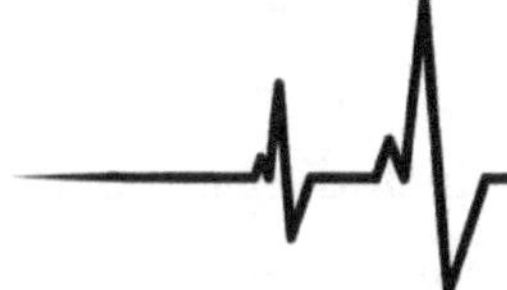

Chapter 22

GAME OVER

"**C**OME ON, SKYE. *Wake up. You've been asleep long enough.*" The foreign voice intrudes my mind, pulling me from the dark recesses of my consciousness. "*We don't have all day.*"

Someone shakes me, and it takes everything in me to open my eyes. Staring up, I blink the haze from the light fixture overhead away. I half expected to wake up on the cold floor of some basement, wearing a hospital gown, with a deranged doctor all over again, but I'm in a bed, wearing the same gown Nikolai picked out for the ceremony at the Knezha Estate. Surprisingly, I'm not restrained.

I jerk upright and find Reggie leaning on the frame of the open door. Unlike at the Knezha Estate, he freely uses his acquired ability to do whatever it is he pleases, including annoying me. I'm pretty sure he might be doing it from a distance so I don't launch from the bed to attack him again, to scream at him for kidnapping me and forcing me to leave Luka behind, but I'm just so tired. I can't keep up anymore. I wish he'd go away. I could fall back asleep and finish my dream of spending time with Luka in the cabin.

"Afternoon, Sunshine. I bet you feel like shit," he says, not moving from his position.

I get to my feet, trying to decide what to do. "You have three seconds to explain everything to me before I scramble your brain. Who sent you for me?"

He presses his lips into a line, tightening his jaw. "You."

Confusion knits my brows. "Me? I don't understand."

"Of course you don't. That's what happens when you come up with crazy ass plans that involve inflicting amnesia on yourself. And what did you even accomplish?" Reggie folds his arms across his chest. "I'm just fucking glad to have you back, even if you broke my damn nose and wrecked my favorite car."

"Back?"

"Oh, Jesus Christ." He leans out the door. "Cora! I can't deal with this bullshit anymore. Get in here. I think she has brain damage now."

I glare at Reggie. I'd like nothing more than to cuss him out for everything he put me through, since it seems that maybe it's the only way for him to understand considering half his vocabulary is made of swear words.

The girl from earlier, the one from my memory, the same one who demanded I push even Luka from my head, peeks her head in. Rage burns through me, and I rush forward toward her and Reggie.

"Fucking shit! Skye, knock it off." Reggie waves his arm, and my feet fly out from under me. I land on the carpet hard enough to freeze me in place. Reggie places his hands on his head. "Damn it! You don't attack family."

I stare at him, stunned, my thoughts racing. "You attacked me first!"

"You f—"

Cora elbows him in his side, cutting him off from unleashing a tornado of curse words upon me. "Chill out. You're scaring her."

"Skye doesn't get scared," he says.

Cora lifts her hand and points. "Well, this version of Skye obviously does. So, either relax or get out. I don't care if she's the one who asked you to be here for her when we brought her back." She glances at me. "Yeah, that's right. You chose this dumbass for the job. He almost didn't even make it out of the Knezha Estate with you. He *left* Zane behind."

"And Luka," I say, my voice barely coming out a whisper. "Why, why would you do that?"

Cora grimaces. "Those were your orders. Luka isn't the priority."

"He is to me," I say.

"He's dangerous to you, that's what. You knew this. It's

why you instructed me not to try to get him out. You messed things up, though. I wasn't going to act like a crazed lunatic, but you obviously weren't ever leaving his damn side. And when you weren't with him, you were with Nikolai," Reggie says. "Didn't even give me a chance to earn your trust and then Nikolai tried to break you. I'm just glad I was there to help out."

I squeeze my eyes shut and scream. I don't know what else to do. "You helped me? You're lying! You stood there and shut the door in my face. Now, you're messing with my head just like Nikolai. I'd have never told you to leave Luka. I know me."

"Do you, though?" he asks.

Cora stares at me without answering any of my questions, just letting Reggie take charge. This feels like the moment I woke up in the basement with Luka, and he knew everything about me, and I knew nothing about him or myself or anything. I was a blank slate. But now, I've already recreated myself, my life, my entire world, and these two people have crashed into it, trying to implode everything I know all over again.

I heave a breath, covering my eyes. "I want to be alone. I can't think."

"All right, I'll go pick up something to eat," Cora says. "Reggie will be down the hall."

I don't respond.

"And Skye?"

I force myself to look up.

Cora offers a small smile. "I hope you remember we're not the bad guys, because I'm so happy to have you back. If you can't tell, this was—is your room, and everything is exactly how you left it. You might find something to help you remember if you look." She points to the closet. "There's a safe in there. Maybe you'll remember the combination."

Reggie and Cora both leave, closing the door behind them. I expect to hear a lock click, but they don't lock me in. I'm not a prisoner, though I'm not sure they'd let me walk out the front door.

I wait a few seconds to make sure they're not going to barge back into the room and then cross over to the closet to push it open. I'm surprised by all the T-shirts and hoodies, the built-ins on one side with tons of pants and jeans. Not a single pleated skirt or silk blouse in sight. No gowns. No stilettos. Just tennis shoes, flip-flops, and boots. This really feels like my closet and not something of Nikolai's doing.

Bolted to the floor is a small, black metal safe—nothing fancy. Just big enough to hold a few treasured items. I kneel down and glance at the keypad. What combination could I have possibly used? I try my birthday, which seems too easy. I try my first time of death. I even try the address of the Knezha Estate. Nothing opens the lock.

Then it hits me. I'm the key. *7-5-9-3*—I spell out my name numerically, and the safe beeps. I don't know what I was expecting, personal documents, pictures, weapons even, but not a cell phone with nothing else. And its battery is dead. I thought past me would be better prepared.

Pulling it out, I glance around the room. I head to the nightstand, and sure enough, a phone charger hides in the top drawer. I'm more predictable than I realized, and maybe that's what I was counting on. Couldn't make it too hard for the girl who has no idea what's happening.

I plug in the phone and cup it in my hands like it might explode at any second, waiting for it to have enough battery power to turn on. The phone lights up, and a digital keypad flashes on the screen. I've pass code protected the phone, too. I enter my name again, but it doesn't work. Of course I would use two different codes. I might be predictable, but I'm not going to make it too easy.

I try the same codes as before and nothing works.

Sighing, I stare at the numbers. Okay, I *am* super predictable. Or I just know myself. *5-8-5-2.* I used Luka's name numerically. The phone unlocks, and I suck in a breath at the photo displayed as the background. It's of me and the girl, Cora, with our faces squished together, taking up the entire screen.

Instead of looking at my call log or contacts, I click open the photos. There are thousands of them. But what catches my eyes is the last thing taken was a video, which looks like it's of me talking to the camera in the tiny thumbnail display.

I press play.

My image pops up, and I watch a video I have no memory of recording light up the small screen. In the video, I look at the camera before sitting back in a chair.

"This video is for me, so I swear if you're watching this Reggie, I'm going to kick your ass and brainwash you to think you're a damn guard dog or something for a week."

I grip the phone tighter, my heart racing at the familiarity of the stranger—of me—talking to the screen.

I lean forward in the video, resting my elbows on my knees. "All right now. I don't know how to start this, so I'm just going to say it. If you're watching this, Skye, it means one of two things—you either succeeded in your mission or you failed."

"My mission?" I ask myself out loud, half hoping my video self will have the ability to answer.

Video Skye laughs. "Damn it, I know I'd only watch this if I fail."

I sigh. I swear I better not have just created a video to remind myself that I suck.

"Okay, Failure Skye. Here's the deal. I need you to forget everything you think you know about your life, about your journey, the Knezha Family, about Nikolai, and—"

"Just spit it out," I say to the screen.

Video Skye takes a breath. "And about Luka." I watch myself swipe a tear from my cheek. "Especially Luka."

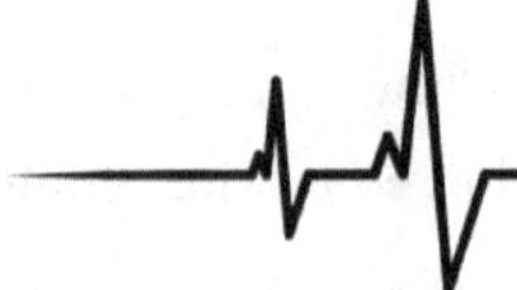

Chapter 23

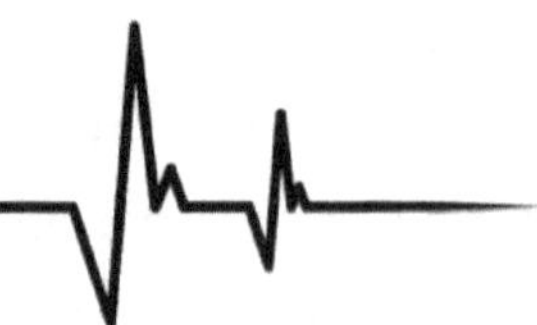

ONE OVER THE MANY

"**I** KNOW THIS is hard, believe me."

It takes everything in me not to turn off the stupid video.

"But you are strong, and you will get through this whether or not you remember everything. I know the risk I'm about to take, but I know it is for the best. Having no memory is better than having Nik warp your head, right? He's done enough damage." Video Skye puffs out her bottom lip. "I want you to know that you're lucky. This room you're in. Those people who are probably still pissed off at you, are your people. You might not all be soul mates like you and Luka are, but you're pretty

320

close. Closer than Nikolai ever tried to be. So try to play nice with them, and they'll remind you exactly of how awesome they are. You're in the spot you are now solely by my doing. They all disagreed with you but supported you anyway. Because that's this life. The choices you make from now on are yours and yours alone. But don't forget how it affects everyone else."

Video Skye takes a breath, looking at her hands, a thousand thoughts seemingly crossing her mind.

She clears her throat. "Like with Luka. Since you're watching this video, you must be wondering why I ordered Reggie to leave Luka behind. What the hell am I doing, leaving behind one of the most important people, right? You probably think we're crazy."

She stops talking again, another tear splashing on her cheek. She rubs her hands over her face. Watching myself cry on camera, seeing the emotions softening my face, it goes against what people have been telling me about my old self. About the Skye who was brave or fearless. The Skye I remember who did things because she thought she had to. Maybe I'm still that Skye and she is me.

She groans and then laughs. "I hope I get my act together. I'll never hear the end of it if Reggie catches me crying. Please, tell me, it's not so hard, future Skye."

"It's harder," I whisper.

She sucks in a breath. "Luka's going to be fine, all right?" It sounds like I'm talking to myself, trying to convince myself. Video Skye looks at the camera again. "He will be okay, but right now, Luka's dangerous. Nikolai got to him, understand?

He outsmarted you and took advantage of the opportunities your dumbass handed right to him with a pretty bow. Nikolai messed up Luka. He messed up Gemma and Avery. I'm sure he'll either kill Sam or mess him up, too." Video me sniffles. "Gemma will never forgive you if he does. Cooper will never forgive you if something happens to Avery, either. You made the mistake of putting one over the many, and now you lost some of the most important people in your life. Angelica would be ashamed."

Tears burn my eyes, and I blink them away, hearing me mention Angelica. I want so badly to know everything about her. Know why I put her in such high regards despite her bringing me into the Knezha Family.

Video Skye rolls her shoulders and then pushes her hair behind her ears. "But I've learned now. I hate to admit it, but Nikolai is right in a way. If only he practiced his own teachings. And because everyone in my life is important, hard decisions have to be made. Luka got tied up in the fray of it all. But don't blame yourself. There's nothing you could've done at the time. I fully believe that even if I fail to bring Luka home, it's not over. This is one battle, and we know that we can't win them all."

"Luka would be here if you'd have given me more time," I say to the phone, wishing I could reach in and shake myself by the front of my shirt.

"Now, I know what you're thinking."

"No, you don't," I snap.

"You just needed a little more time. Luka was better. You

just know it. But you're wrong."

I sigh. I guess I do know myself better than anyone.

"Luka might sound and act like the Luka you know—or not. Damn it. What am I getting myself into?" I watch myself look at the ceiling and blink. "Whatever. Just know that Nik's too far into Luka's mind and can use him against you unless you manage to fix him. Did you? If you did, that changes things. Please, tell me you did."

"But how do I know?" I ask.

"If you're questioning whether or not you did, then you didn't. You have to go deep into Luka's mind and rip Nikolai free. You have to give him nothing else to hold on to. You have to break him no matter how hard it hurts. You can't fix something that isn't broken. I'm not strong enough at the time of this recording. My emotions cloud too much of me. I'm hoping that changes, and I remember what Angelica taught me about my instincts. Don't listen to them. They're tied to your heart, and what you need is a clear thought process. Got it?"

I nod like I understand.

"I've lived by the motto of not hurting people I love, but that must change. It's sick and twisted, and I'm not strong enough. But you are. Because now you know what's at stake."

My entire existence with Luka, the most important person in the world. Deep down, I know it's more. It's bigger than me and him.

"Also, part of the agreement to get Cora's support in this matter is I'm to instruct you to not take out your frustration on Reggie or Cora, okay? If things have changed with Luka, they'll know. You will learn a lot from them." Video Skye smirks. "But don't tell that to Reggie. He'll hold that over you."

It's so strange hearing myself talk about these people I know I know, but I can't quite remember. At least it helps lessen the fear coursing through me.

"Until then, Luka must stay with Nik. I know it's going to be tough, but you've been without him before. Too many times, really. But the universe always brings you back together. Leaving Luka with Nik will guarantee that Nik won't suspect you arranged any of this. It's important Nikolai doesn't know where you are or who you're with. If he does, this will have all been for nothing. You have your own family to protect now."

"My own family?"

"We're at war," Video Skye says. "And we're losing. Nikolai's power is growing, his charm is taking over the area, people are begging to join him. He's threatening not only your whole world, he's threatening your universe. He wants endless access to the stars. He wants his key to open the door back. He wants you."

I glare at the phone. "He can't have me."

"He can't have me," Video Skye says. "He can't keep Luka and Avery. He can't continue to torment Gemma. Bring in Sam. He can't. This ends now. I'm done playing his mind games. You're done playing his mind games. It's time for you to break him, Skye. It's the only way. Angelica knew it. He murdered her because of it. Don't let him take anything more away from you."

"I won't." I watch the screen freeze as the video ends. "I

won't," I repeat.

Sucking in a few deep breaths, I settle my nerves the best I can. It's so much to take in. I'm not even sure where to start. Video Skye was right. I know nothing. I've spent these last few weeks struggling with my Knezha Family identity and beliefs, thinking Nikolai got to Luka because of me, but he had him all along. I struggled with the idea of family. But I don't even know what that is right now. The Knezhas are only a group of people under Nikolai's influence needing to be set free from this. They need to be shown that we lead our own journeys, make our own choices, believe in whatever the heck we want to say this life is what we wanted—and as for the next? Who knows.

I have my galaxy, my soul mate, and apparently people who know me and love me well enough to make my own mistakes. It's those things that count to me. Those things that push me to move forward despite all the obstacles Nikolai has set to interrupt my journey.

Video Skye was right.

It all ends now.

And in the end, there is a new beginning for me. New mistakes to make. A new life to embrace. Nikolai might have shut the door on my journey to try to lock me away. He might have changed the locks, sealed off the door, trapped my friends, my soul mate in his twisted house of mind games, but the thing about closed doors is that they can be busted down. They can be ripped from the hinges. His games can be beaten.

I'm changing the rules.

A soft knock sounds on the door, and Cora peeks her head in to look at me. "I hope you still like pizza. I can bring it in here if you want."

I grip the phone in my hand. "I'd like to eat with you if that's okay."

A smile pulls at the corner of her lips. "You're not going to try to take me out or anything, right?"

Holding up the phone, I run my fingers over the screen, scrolling through the thousands of pictures. "I don't think so. You're my friend, right?"

She swings the door open wider and rushes into the room, throwing her arms around me. "I thought that damn phone was lost forever."

"I have a lot of catching up to do, huh?" I ask. "Would you mind helping me?"

"Of course I wouldn't mind. I'm your BFF, which is some serious business, you know."

I smile, basking in the warm, pure, perfect emotions nearly shining from her as bright as one of my galaxy stars. I didn't know it until this moment, but this girl—Cora—and this place feels exactly like home, like the shining stars. Like the light I need to see.

"That's what I hear." I wave the phone around. "Past me had a lot to say, but I think I still need some explanations."

Cora nods. "I think I can manage that with one condition."

I grimace. "What's that?"

"Don't ever put me through this again. It's been so sucky

without you. I've had to rely on Reggie for my sole form of entertainment, and you know how he gets about that."

I shrug.

She groans. "He loves thinking he's my everything because our souls collided."

"He's not?" I ask.

Lacing her fingers around my elbow, she pulls me to the door. "Definitely not. I can't stand him half the time. Such a damn pain."

My chest clenches, and I release a small gasp, her words digging into me, reminding of something Luka has said to me time and time again. Tears burn in my eyes, and I squeeze them shut to keep the tears away.

Cora stops to look at me. "What did I say wrong?"

I compose myself, breathing slowly through my nose. "You sound like Luka."

Her bottom lip pouts. "We'll get him back, Skye. It's just going to be a lot more complicated than we expected."

"More complicated than this?"

She laughs. "Right? What the hell was the universe thinking?"

I've been asking myself the same question—not just about the universe but about me. What the hell was I thinking?

"Come on, the others are waiting," Cora says.

"The others?"

"Just wait. You'll see."

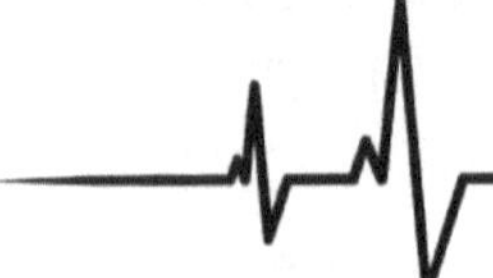

EPILOGUE

BEAT THE GAME

"**M**Y NAME IS *Skye Stone. Today is my birthday, and I'm officially eighteen years old. I have blond hair, gray eyes Cora says sometimes change to cornflower blue when I'm about to pop a blood vessel. I'm from Los Angeles, California living in the Sonora Desert far enough away from the Knezha Family that Nikolai can never find me. I have a soul mate named Luka Landon, who I wish could blow out my birthday candles with me, but a short birthday wish will have to do.*"

"*You forgot to mention you have an awesome bodyguard making this all possible.*" Reggie's thought trickles into my mind, pulling me away from my own.

Reminding myself about who I am makes each day away from Luka and everything I thought I knew easier. It helps that Cora makes it easy to remember why she's in my life. Reggie, though? *"Bodyguard? You wish."*

He chuckles in my head. *"Hey, I was the chosen one."*

"I chose you because you deserved the beating I gave you, and you know I'd never have put Cora in a position to fight me."

"And because I'm a rock star."

I turn to glare, but a buzzing sensation slides over my skin. It's been weeks since I've seen Luka in real life and not from photos Reggie has come accustomed to taking for me. Luka pauses, glancing around the sidewalk, feeling the same sensation I do.

"I hate that you weren't lying about being a rock star, Reggie. I can't believe it worked."

"Happy birthday, Skye," Reggie says with a smile.

My lip quivers as I watch Luka rub his hand over his hair, pushing it from his face. He searches the area, probably wondering where the sensation is coming from, and he's about to soon find out.

"Hurry up. You have thirty seconds until Nikolai knows something's up."

I frown, wishing so much with everything in me that I could run to Luka, throw my arms around him, and shower him with dozens of birthday kisses.

A doorbell chimes, and I watch Avery exit a nearby store, holding a gift bag in her fingers. She freezes and looks at Luka.

"Happy birthday, Luka," I say, sending my thoughts to him.

"I miss you so, so much."

Luka touches his fingers to his temple. *"Skye, is that you? Where are you? Are you okay?"*

"I'm fine. Everything's fine."

"You vanished. Nikolai couldn't track you."

I swipe a tear from my eye. *"I know, and I'm sorry."*

"It's okay. You've come back for me. You found me like you said you would," he says.

My heart nearly explodes from my chest to splatter across the cement. *"I just wanted to wish you a happy birthday."*

"What?"

Reggie nudges me with his elbow. "Finish up."

"I have to go, but I will be back for you."

"Skye, don't leave me. Please. Don't—"

"Trust me, okay? Can you do that?" I think, cutting him off.

Luka nods without responding.

"I love you, Luka."

Reggie grabs my hand and nearly drags me away from Luka and Avery on the sidewalk. Cora waves her hand from her silver car, motioning for us to hurry. We both buckle up, me in the front and Reggie in the back. Cora presses her fingers into my knee.

"Time to really celebrate now," she says, driving from the curb. "We can all use a little fun."

"Only if it involves explosions," I say, though my heart isn't really into it.

"Sure thing," she says.

Reggie meets my gaze in the mirror of my sun visor.

"You're going to be okay, Skye. So is Luka," Reggie thinks to me.

I can only hope he's right.

The static in the air dissipates the farther we drive from Luka. It takes everything in me not to look back. I can't. I can't keep focusing on a past I did everything to escape from. A past that my mind refuses to let me remember.

And it's because my journey isn't about the past.

It's the future unfolding in front of me with Luka waiting behind a dozen walls Nikolai's tried to build to stop me from moving forward. What he doesn't know is I'm going to blow up his world. I'll blow up his universe if I have to.

I'm going to destroy his journey and rebuild my life for a better future.

I'm going to beat his games.

This time, I won't fail.

To be continued...

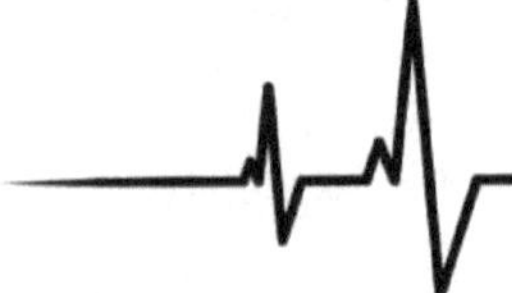

OTHER YOUNG ADULT SERIES

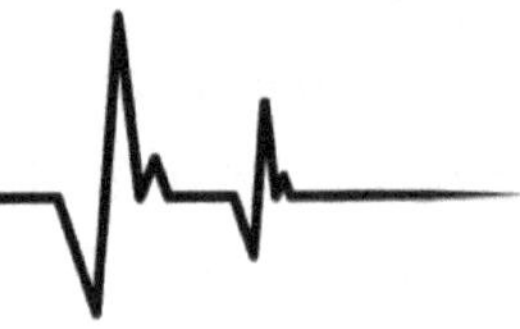

PARANORMAL

Destined for Dreams Series
Demon Within Series
Finding Nate Series
Going Ghostly Series
Spark of Life Series
When Souls Collide Series
Demon Watcher Series
Call of the Ocean Series

CONTEMPORARY

Falling into Fame Series

STANDALONES

Life After Lila

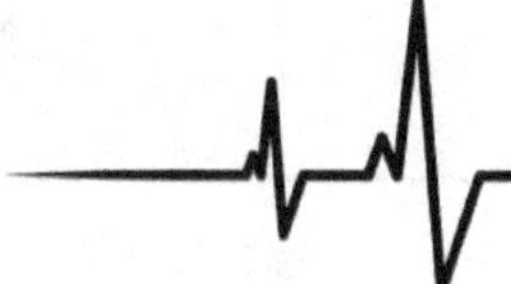

ACKNOWLEDGEMENTS

THANK YOU TO the amazing women who suffered through my drafts and helped me polish and bring this series of mind games to life. Sarah and Katie, your hard work and enthusiasm for each of my novels is invaluable, and I'm so thankful to have had you work on so many of my books. Here's to many, many more!

Thank you to my mother-in-law for helping me flesh out the story and for being a sounding board as I write. Your encouragement is the best.

As always, thank you to my family and friends, who are far too many to name. I appreciate how you pretend not to be a little afraid of my imagination. Much love to you!

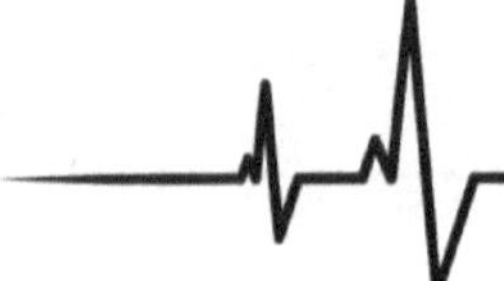

ABOUT GINNA MORAN

GINNA MORAN IS a writer from sunny Southern California. She started writing poetry as a teenager in a spiral notebook that she still has tucked away on her desk today. Her love of writing grew after she graduated high school, and she completed her first unpublished manuscript at age eighteen.

When she realized her love of writing was her life's passion, she studied literature at Mira Costa College in Northern San Diego. Besides writing novels, she was senior editor, content manager, and image coordinator for Crescent House Publishing Inc. for four years.

Aside from Ginna's professional life, she enjoys binge

watching television shows, playing pretend with her daughter, and cuddling with her dogs. Some of her favorite things include chocolate, anything that glitters, cheesy jokes, and organizing her bookshelf.

Ginna Moran loves to hear from her readers so visit her online at www.GinnaMoran.com. You can also find her on Facebook, Twitter, Instagram, and Snapchat. To stay up-to-date on new releases, sign up to her newsletter. You'll not only get a FREE story, but you'll be able to participate in monthly giveaways!

Ginna Moran is currently hard at work on her next novel.

www.ingramcontent.com/pod-product-compliance
Lightning Source LLC
Chambersburg PA
CBHW051634180726
48284CB00006B/1727